DCS MACCORMAC OXFORD

SANCTUM SANCTORUM

GERRY CULLEN

Copyright © 2024 GERRY CULLEN

All rights reserved

The characters and events portrayed in this book are fictitious. Any similarity to real persons, living or dead, is coincidental and not intended by the author.

No part of this book may be reproduced, or stored in a retrieval system, or transmitted in any form or by any means, electronic, mechanical, photocopying, recording, or otherwise, without express written permission of the publisher.

ISBN-13: 9798338072646
ISBN-10: 1477123456

Cover design by: Art Painter
Library of Congress Control Number: 2018675309
Printed in the United States of America

THIS BOOK IS DEDICATED TO MY MUM AND DAD

CONTENTS

Title Page
Copyright
Dedication
aBOUT THE AUTHOR GERRY CULLEN
THE VATICAN MONSIGNOR   340
SKY HIGH: 344
BOOKS BY THIS AUTHOR   348
MY NEXT PRESENTATION   360
DCS MACCORMAC SANCTUM SANCTORUM   362
About The Author   368
Praise For Author   370

ABOUT THE AUTHOR
GERRY CULLEN

My first book, BETWEEN WORLDS: MY TRUE COMA STORY, is a true adaptation of what happened to me, before and after, having major open heart surgery at Leeds General Infirmary in March 2018.

It is a very real and true account of the "gift" I received after being in an induced coma.

All of my books to date, SKY HIGH! COTE D'AZUR, ANGEL'S EYES/CHRISTMAS ANGELS, THE VATICAN MONSIGNOR, and IT'S A KIND OF LOVE are adapted from my series of stories, written for television.
I had never written books or for television prior to being in a coma.

My very real and true story continues today!

FOLLOW MY STORY ON TWITTER - @GerryCullen15

ALSO BY GERRY CULLEN

BETWEEN WORLDS:

MY TRUE COMA STORY

SKY HIGH: COTE D'AZUR

ANGEL'S EYES:

CHRISTMAS ANGELS

THE VATICAN MONSIGNOR

THE SAVIOUR'S COMING

IT'S A KIND OF LOVE

DCS MACCORMAC OXFORD

Detective Chief Inspector Daniel MacCormac, now Chief Superintendent of Thames Valley Police, reports directly to the Chief Constable.

Sergeant Paddy Sheridan, is an Inspector based in Oxford, and still an endorsement of his old mentor, the Chief Super!

The dreaming spires of Oxford are the perfect backdrop to this series of stories. A sartorial splendour of everything quintessentially English!

Oxford boasts fine University buildings clustered between other beautifully refined compact colleges and ecclesiastical structures. Oxford is also well known for it's elegance ... the Radcliffe Camera and the Bodleian library to mention just two of them.

Oxford is definitely one of England's most beautiful cities.

When the sudden retirement of Chief Superintendent Alex Samson takes place in Oxford, Detective Chief Inspector Daniel MacCormac, is asked to take on the mantle of Chief Superintendent, by the Chief Constable of Thames Valley, Ben Gardiner.

MacCormac is reunited with his loyal colleague, Paddy Sheridan, who is successful in his own right, and is now an Inspector in Oxford.

Both undertake several investigations to find the

truth, along with Pathologist, Mike Mortimer who assists them.

MacCormac and Sheridan investigate into sharp malpractice, ancient Egyptian codes and puzzles, Atropa Belladonna, Parasympathetic Rebound and a situation linking the Chief Superintendent to a murder at the Opera in Oxford!

THE LEADING CHARACTERS

CHIEF SUPERINTENDENT DANIEL MACCORMAC is in his late 40s, 5 feet 10, has dark hair and brown eyes. MacCormac is a strict disciplinarian. Very methodical in his ways of Policing and detection. A Widower with no children. He loves architecture and the Italian way of life. He is an old Etonian and lives on the outskirts of Oxford.

CHIEF CONSTABLE BEN GARDINER is 6ft tall, has greying brown hair, brown eyes, and very knowledgeable with regards to all Police matters in the Thames Valley area. He is responsible for influencing the development of regional and national policing. Ben Gardiner is very much his own man but he takes orders from the Home Office. He is married and has three children.

INSPECTOR PADDY SHERIDAN is 6 feet tall, in his late 30s, has blue eyes and brown hair. Paddy is a graduate of Dublin University. His character is best described as a rough diamond. Former Detective Sergeant to Detective Chief Inspector Daniel MacCormac. Paddy is married to Jill and has 2 children.

CHIEF PATHOLOGIST, MIKE MORTIMER is also 6 feet tall, has brown hair and green eyes. His case work includes Thames Valley and Oxford Police area. He deals with various fields of pathology and DNA.
ASSISTANT PATHOLOGIST, ANN DRAPER is in her

mid twenties. She has brown shoulder length hair, green eyes and of average good looks.

EMILY PEARSON, an associate who also likes Opera.

Emily is blonde, has green eyes, tall and a former student at Oxford University. She and Daniel MacCormac have become best of friends.

ASSISTANT CHIEF CONSTABLE, JAMES MANNERING, 45, six feet tall, has blue eyes and brown hair. He eventually takes over as CHIEF CONSTABLE when Ben Gardiner, the previous Chief Constable, retires.

He is responsible for Justice and Counter Terrorism Policing in the South East and Regional Crime unit.

The newly promoted Chief Constable is a stickler for the rules. He keeps Chief Superintendent Daniel MacCormac in check but works with him in making justice prevail. James is engaged to be married to Ruth. They both live together on the outskirts of Oxford. They have no children.

DCS MACCORMAC OXFORD

CODED MESSAGES ... DIVIDED LOYALTIES

OLD HABITS, DIE HARD!   5

A LESSON LEARNED   15

THE WOLVERCOTE CONNECTION   25

BREAKING THE CODE   33

SANCTUM SANCTORUM

DEADLY FIND   42

DEADLY PURSUIT   50

DEADLY GAME   57

DEADLY ILLUSION   66

DEADLY NIGHTSHADE

RECITAL 75

SUSPICIONS 81

BREAKTHROUGH 92

STAND OFF 101

THE PLETHRON CONNECTION

CONNECTION 110

A BRILLIANT DEDUCTION 118

SMOKE SCREEN 127

TRAGEDY 136

SUBTERFUGE

EVASION 145

ENCOUNTERS 153

CHICANERY AND SHARP PRACTICE 160

CUNNING DECEIT 168

PARASYMPATHETIC REBOUND

HALLOWEEN PARADE 179

FRIGHTENED TO DEATH 187

THE NEXT VICTIM 195

ENTRAPMENT 203

EQUILIBRIUM

A STATE OF PHYSICAL BALANCE

INFLUENCES 212

PATHOLOGY REPORT 219

STATE OF ILLUSION 227

GERRYCULLEN

*INTELLECTUAL AND
EMOTIONAL BALANCE 234*

CODED MESSAGES ...
DIVIDED LOYALTIES

Detective Chief Inspector Daniel MacCormac, now Chief Superintendent of Thames Valley Police, reports directly to the Chief Constable.
Sergeant Paddy Sheridan, is now an Inspector based in Oxford, and still an endorsement of his old mentor, the Chief Super!
The backdrop to the investigation are the dreaming spires of Oxford. A sartorial splendour of everything quintessentially English! Oxford boasts fine University buildings clustered between other beautifully refined structures. They are also well known for their elegance ... the Radcliffe Camera and the Bodleian library to mention just two of them.
Oxford is definitely one of England's most beautiful cities.

When cryptic Egyptian messages are found after several murders, MacCormac is reunited with Paddy Sheridan, at the Chief Constable's request.
Both have to crack the codes, after a series of murders in Oxford, by someone known as the Sphinx!
In this complex investigation, MacCormac and Sheridan have to use all their ingenuity, and passion to succeed, which may well break them!
Does the key to the murders have anything to do

with the Institute of Criminology?
Is a distinguished Oxford Don behind it all?

The new Chief Superintendent will have to be at his best to outwit the murderer, to bring them to justice!

CODED MESSAGES ...
DIVIDED LOYALTIES

OLD HABITS, DIE HARD!

When the sudden retirement, of Chief Superintendent Alex Samson takes place in Oxford, Detective Chief Inspector Daniel MacCormac, is asked to take on the mantle of Chief Superintendent, by the Chief Constable of Thames Valley, Ben Gardiner.

After a murder takes place in Oxford the Police fail to catch a suspect. The Chief Constable asks the new Chief Superintendent to take on the investigation.

MacCormac is reunited with his loyal colleague, Paddy Sheridan, who is successful in his own right, and is now an Inspector in Oxford.

Late evening, the Bodleian Library in the centre of Oxford ...

The Bodleian Library is one of the oldest libraries in Europe. It is connected to the Radcliffe Camera via the Gladstone Link. It was founded over 400 years ago and is now a World renowned Institution. It's buildings are impressive and majestic.

"I'm just about to lock up, Mr. Vincent" advises an assistant (Smiles)

"OK, Sarah, make sure all the alarms are set" replies Mr. Vincent

"See you tomorrow, Sarah" adds Mr. Vincent (Smiling)
"See you" answers Sarah (Waves goodbye)

As Mr Vincent leaves, a shadowy figure, moves in the background ...

Sarah is suddenly startled and frightened ... (Turns round)
"Who's there?" asks Sarah (Looks startled)

" ... Is someone there?" pleads Sarah (Looks afraid)
It is met with no response ... only the cool still of the evening is all that greets her and the chill of what could happen.
Sarah leaves the Bodleian and makes her way towards a door, but she is suddenly grabbed from behind ...
Sarah screams, but no one hears her pleas for help ...
Sarah struggles but she has been strangled!
Next morning, the body is found by a member of the public ... the Police are called and are quick to arrive at the scene.
Police Crime officers tape off the area, and the crime scene ...

Detective Inspector Paddy Sheridan is now at the scene with Chief Pathologist, Mike Mortimer ...
Detective Inspector Paddy Sheridan is 6 feet tall, has blue eyes and brown hair. Paddy is a graduate of Dublin University. His character is best described as a rough diamond. Former Detective Sergeant to

Detective Chief Inspector Daniel MacCormac. Chief Pathologist, Mike Mortimer, is also 6 feet tall. His case work includes Thames Valley and Oxford Police area. He deals with various fields of pathology and DNA.

Assistant Pathologist, Ann Draper, is in her mid twenties. She has brown shoulder length hair, green eyes and of average good looks.

Ann is checking over the body ...

"OK, what happened, Mike?" asks Sheridan (Looks serious)

"It looks like she was strangled, Paddy" advises Mortimer (Looks concerned)

"Yes, I'll confirm that" adds Ann (Nods in agreement)

"Time of death, Mike?" asks Paddy

"I'd say early evening, last night ... I'll tell you more, later, Paddy" explains Mortimer (Looks serious)

"We did find something else, though" advises Ann (Hands over plastic wallet)

Ann passes over a note, in a sealed clear plastic wallet, to Mike Mortimer ...

"See, if you can decipher this, Paddy" explains Mortimer

"By the way, where's MacCormac?" asks Mortimer (Looks around)

"He's now the Chief Superintendent, Mike" advises Paddy (Looks serious)

"Well, the actual hand over is, today" explains

Paddy (Smiles)
"Oh, he'll love that, Paddy" replies Mortimer (Laughs)
"I doubt it, Mike" explains Paddy (Looks serious)
Sheridan reads the note, handed to him by the Chief Pathologist ...
It reads as follows ...
THOSE WHO LIVE TODAY, WILL DIE TOMORROW ... THOSE WHO DIE TOMORROW WILL BE BORN AGAIN ...
"What does it mean, Mike?" asks Paddy (Looks serious)
Suddenly, another unexpected voice, enters the scene of the crime ...
"It means, Paddy, we've got a problem" advises the voice
Both turn round to see a very familiar figure ...

Detective Chief Superintendent Daniel MacCormac is now on the scene ... He is 5 feet 10, has dark hair and brown eyes. MacCormac is a strict disciplinarian. Very methodical in his ways of Policing and detection ...

"Sir?" asks Paddy (Looks stunned)
"That, Paddy, is a quote from the Book of the dead and Egyptian proverbs" explains MacCormac (Smiles)
"I don't understand, Sir?" replies Sheridan (Looks surprised)
"Enlighten him, Daniel" advises

Doctor Mortimer
"The note is also signed, Paddy" explains MacCormac

"Oh?" replies Paddy (Looks stunned)

"Look at the name" advises MacCormac

Paddy looks at the note in the plastic wallet ...

"The name is signed, by someone called, the SPHINX, Sir" advises Paddy

"Now I know, that is Egyptian, Sir" explains Paddy (Looks pleased)

"Quite right, Paddy ... but the riddle is in the name" explains MacCormac

The new Chief Superintendent continues to enlighten his sidekick ...

"As you know, the Sphinx is a large statue that stands near the pyramids in Egypt" advises MacCormac

"That, I do know, Sir" replies Paddy

The Great Sphinx of Giza, is a statue of a reclining mythical creature, with the head of a human, and the body of a lion. It stands on the West Bank of the Nile in Giza, Egypt.

"In my theology, sphinxes, gave people puzzles to solve ... so a person who is mysterious or puzzling is sometimes referred to as a sphinx" explains MacCormac (Looks serious)

"Is that what this is all about, Sir?" asks Sheridan

"Someone who calls themselves the sphinx is trying to puzzle us, Paddy" replies MacCormac

"Us?" asks Sheridan (Looks puzzled)

"I'm here at the Chief Constable's request … he wants you and I to take on the case" advises MacCormac (Looks serious)

"It'll just be like old times, Paddy" explains MacCormac (Smiling)

"What about your inauguration, Sir?" asks Paddy (Looks puzzled)

"That takes place, later today, Paddy" advises MacCormac

"Come on, Paddy, we're needed back at the nick" explains MacCormac

"See you later, Mike" advises MacCormac

Oxford Central Police Station … Daniel MacCormac is in retiring Chief Superintendent Alex Samson's office …

"I thought this day would never come" advises Samson (Looks sad)

"Enjoy it while you can, Daniel" explains Samson (Laughs)

"Yes, Sir" replies MacCormac (Looks glum)

Alex Samson is an over weight man in his late fifties, has a bald head and is a sarcastic so and so …

"Think of it, as a step up, to the big time" laughs Samson

"I will, Sir … thank you, Sir" replies MacCormac (Smiles)

"Your now the Chief Constable's right hand

man, Daniel" explains Samson (Smiles)
A sudden knock on the door …
"Come in" advises Samson (Shouts)

In walks, Paddy Sheridan …

"Sorry, Sir" advises Paddy (Looks serious)

"But there's been a development" explains Sheridan

"Don't forget to be here later, for the inauguration, Sheridan" advises Samson

"Wouldn't miss it for the World, Sir" replies Sheridan (Smiles)
Paddy Sheridan leaves the Chief Superintendent's office …

"Bright lad, Sheridan … I always knew he'd make Inspector" advises Samson (Looks serious)

"I taught him well, Sir" explains MacCormac (Smiles)
"You'd better get on top of it, with Sheridan, then?" asks Samson
"Yes, Sir" replies MacCormac
The new DCS leaves Alex Samson's office, and walks down the corridor, to his old office …
MacCormac enters and asks Sheridan for an update …

"OK, Paddy, what have we got?" asks MacCormac (Looks serious)

"We've been summoned to the Institute of Criminology" explains Sheridan

"Why?" asks MacCormac (Looks puzzled)

"An informant wishes to meet us, Sir" advises

Sheridan (Looks serious)
"OK, let's go, Paddy, it might be important" replies MacCormac

Sheridan and MacCormac leave Oxford Police Station, and jump into a gleaming white A4 Audi 2, 2 litre Quattro, and head to the Institute ...

A sudden call on Paddy's mobile from Doctor Mike Mortimer ...

"Hello, Mike" answers Paddy

"It's about the postmortem, Sir" explains Paddy"

OK, tell Mike, we'll meet him in an hour" advises MacCormac

"Will do, Sir" replies Paddy (Nods)

Sheridan and MacCormac arrive outside the Centre of Criminology, at the University of Oxford.

They are met at the entrance by Oxford Don, Matthew Reynolds ...

"Daniel MacCormac, long time no see" greets Reynolds (Both shake hands)

"Likewise, Matthew" replies MacCormac (Smiles)

"What, you both know each other?" asks Sheridan (Looks surprised)

"You could say that" advises MacCormac (Laughs)

"We are both old college graduates" explains Reynolds (Smiling)

"This is Detective Inspector, Paddy Sheridan" advises MacCormac

Sheridan and Matthew Reynolds both

shake hands ...

"Nice to meet you, Sir" replies Paddy (Smiles)

"I hear, your up for a role alongside the Chief Constable, Daniel?" asks Reynolds

"That's right, Matthew, in fact the inauguration is later today" explains MacCormac (Smiling)

"What about Alex Samson?" asks Reynolds (Looks serious)

"Oh, he's retiring today, Sir" explains Paddy (Smiles)

"So, how can I help you, Daniel?" asks Reynolds (Looks serious)

"There have been several murders in Oxford recently ... and we've been left several cryptic Egyptian clues ... I was wondering if you could help us, Matthew?" asks MacCormac (Looks serious)

"Help?" replies Reynolds (Looks intrigued)

"Oh, you mean decipher their meaning?" adds Reynolds

"While you look into the investigation, Dan?" replies Reynolds (Smiles)

"Yes, exactly ... while we deduce the matter, Matthew" explains MacCormac

"Glad to see your still loyal to your roots, Daniel" replies Reynolds

"Can I get you both some tea?" asks Reynolds (Smiling)

"That would be nice, Sir" answers Paddy (Smiles)

"Sorry, Matthew, we'll have to hold on that ... we have an appointment to see Mike in Pathology" explains MacCormac (Looks serious)

"Remember, Paddy?" asks MacCormac (Looks daggers)

"Oh, yes, Sir ... sorry, Sir" replies Paddy (Looks embarrassed)

"Fear doesn't prevent death ... it prevents life" explains the Don (Looks serious)

"Another Egyptian proverb?" asks Sheridan (Looks surprised)

"Precisely, Paddy, precisely" explains MacCormac

Sheridan and MacCormac leave the Centre of Criminology to meet Mike in Pathology ...

"Any more news for us, Mike?" asks MacCormac

"Sarah Townend ... the name of the dead girl" advises Mike

"What about it, Mike?" asks MacCormac (Looks concerned)

"I was just about to get to that, Daniel" explains Mike

"Paddy, I hope your not picking up any bad habits from Dan" adds Mike

"Not yet, Mike" replies Paddy (Smiles)

"Go on, Mike ... we haven't got all day" advises MacCormac (Laughs)

Mike asks both detectives to view the body ...

"You see those markings on the body" asks Mike (Points)

"Yes, I see them" replies MacCormac (Looks serious)

"They confirm that she was

strangled" advises Mike

"We know that, Mike ... anything else?" asks MacCormac (Looks serious)

"Tiny fragments, of what seems to be, Egyptian cotton" explains Mike

"What about DNA?" asks MacCormac

"I was just coming to that, Dan" explains Mike

"We've analysed the tissues ... it could be one of several people" adds Mike

It's now early evening at the Institute of Criminology. Oxford Don, Matthew Reynolds is leaving a meeting and begins to walk through the University grounds.

Suddenly, he is grabbed from behind ... by the Sphinx ... who leaves yet another note and another puzzle.

Chief Pathologist, Mike Mortimer, Daniel MacCormac and Paddy Sheridan are now at the scene ...

The Doctor checks over the body ...

MacCormac and Sheridan are shocked to see who the victim is ...

"Why it's Matthew Reynolds" advises Sheridan (Looks shocked)

"Yes, Paddy ... looks like Matthew was in the wrong place at the wrong time" replies MacCormac (Looks equally shocked)

"Well, Doctor, what have we got this time, Mike?" asks MacCormac

"Same as last time, Daniel ... a brutal

strangulation" advises Mike "... and another message" explains Mortimer

The Doctor hands MacCormac a sealed plastic bag containing the note ...

"What does it say, Sir?" asks Paddy
(Looks intrigued)

"I'm just about to find out, Paddy" advises MacCormac

DCS MacCormac looks at the note, then reads it out loud ...

"PEOPLE BRING ABOUT THEIR OWN UNDOING THROUGH THEIR TONGUES"

advises MacCormac (Looks puzzled)

"Another cryptic message, Sir?" asks Paddy (Looks stunned)

"Or is it, that they want us to find them?" adds Paddy

"Maybe, Paddy ... maybe" replies MacCormac

"OK, get it analysed, Paddy" advises MacCormac

"Right away, Sir" replies Sheridan (Looks official)

"Old habits, die hard, Paddy" explains MacCormac

"Mike ... anything else?" asks MacCormac

"Time of death?" asks MacCormac (Looks serious)

"I'd say early evening" replies

Mike (Looks cautious)
"That's two bodies in two days, Dan" explains Mike (Looks stunned)
"Who on Earth would want to kill an Oxford Don?" ponders MacCormac
A Don is a fellow or tutor of a college or University, particularly so in Oxford.
"Possibly, someone with a grudge, Sir?" replies Paddy
"OK, we need to check over Matthew Reynold's quarters, here at the University" advises MacCormac
"Did he live on the campus?" asks Sheridan

"Yes, maybe we can pick up some clues, from there, Paddy" explains MacCormac (Looks serious)
"What about your inauguration, Sir?" asks Paddy

"We've still got time to make that ... we've got another three hours, Paddy" advises MacCormac
"Don't worry, Paddy ... I'll contact Alex Samson" explains MacCormac
Daniel MacCormac makes a call on his mobile to retiring to Detective Chief Superintendent, Alex Samson ...
"What's that you say, Dan?" asks Samson (Sounds angry)
"We're just tying up loose ends, Sir" explains MacCormac
"Loose ends?" asks Samson (Sounds concerned)
"Get yourselves over here now ... that's an order ...

I'm still in charge ... and don't you forget it" bellows Samson (Looks serious)
"Not that I would, Sir" replies MacCormac
"What's that, MacCormac?" asks Samson
"I said ... as if I could, Sir" replies MacCormac (Smiles)
"OK, you and Sheridan, here now" bellows Samson
"You'll have to continue your investigation, tomorrow" advises Samson
"Yes, Sir" replies MacCormac (Grumbles)
"Don't keep the Chief Constable waiting" bellows Samson
"No, Sir" replies MacCormac

A LESSON LEARNED

It's Chief Inspector Daniel MacCormac's official inauguration!

The Chief Constable and retiring Chief Superintendent Alex Samson clash!

Paddy Sheridan averts a rather hostile situation by getting MacCormac off the hook!
Somewhere in Oxford ... The Chief Constable asks for an update ...

"Tell me, Daniel, how's the investigation progressing?" asks the Chief Constable

Ben Gardiner is 6ft tall, has greying brown hair, brown eyes, and very knowledgeable in all Police matters in the Thames Valley area. He is responsible for influencing the development of regional and national policing. Ben Gardiner is very much his own man but he takes orders from the Home Office.

"It appears to be shrouded in ... ancient Egyptian cryptic clues, Sir" replies MacCormac (Looks serious)

"Cryptic clues?" replies the Chief Constable (Looks stunned)

"Whenever we find a dead corpse, a note is left behind by someone claiming to be called the Sphinx" explains MacCormac

"What about Oxford Don, Matthew Reynolds?"

asks the Chief Constable

"Just like, the other victim, Sir ... death by strangulation" advises MacCormac

"Forensics have however, found tiny fragments of Egyptian cloth on the body, Sir" adds MacCormac

"We're testing for DNA now, Sir" explains MacCormac

"Excellent, Daniel ... I know you and Sheridan will handle the case with dignity" replies the Chief Constable

"Sir" replies MacCormac

Enter outgoing Chief Superintendent Alex Samson ...

"Good evening, Alex" greets the Chief Constable (Smiling)

"Evening, Chief Constable" replies Samson (Smiles)

"Well, are you ready for your retirement?" asks the Chief Constable

"As ready as I'll ever be, Sir" replies Samson (Looks sad)

The main hall starts to fill with Police officials, Civil dignity, members of the Press and specially invited guests.

The Chief Constable begins his speech ...

Suddenly, Sheridan enters and whispers to MacCormac ...

"There's been another one, Sir" advises Sheridan (Looks serious)

MacCormac indicates to the Chief Constable ...

"I'm sorry, Sir, but I'll have to leave ... another body has been found" advises MacCormac (Looks serious) Everyone in the hall is startled at the new Chief Superintendent's news ...
"I'll get back to you in an hour, Sir" advises MacCormac
"See that you do, Daniel" replies Samson (Looks daggers)

"Don't keep the Chief Constable waiting" explains Samson (Looks annoyed)

"Even for a murder, Sir?" asks MacCormac (Looks serious)
"I'll smooth things over, but be back here in an hour" bellows Samson
"I will, Sir" advises MacCormac
"See that he does, Sheridan"
replies Samson
"Yes, Sir" replies Sheridan
MacCormac and Sheridan head off in the white, gleaming Audi Quattro arriving at the Ashmolean Museum on Beaumont Street, which is close to the Institute of Archaeology ...
Daniel MacCormac receives a call on the Police radio, inside his car ...
"Base to Chief Superintendent MacCormac" advises the voice
"MacCormac" replies the Chief Superintendent

"Ask for Professor Bewick on arrival in Ancient Artefacts" explains the voice

"Roger ... over and out" ends MacCormac
Sheridan and MacCormac arrive and head into the magnificent Ashmolean Museum.
It's the World's second University Museum and it was erected in 1678-1683, housing a wealth of curiosities. Elias Ashmole gave his name to the University of Oxford in 1677.
It's architecture is typically ornate, impressive and magnificent.
MacCormac and Sheridan arrive on foot,
at the gate house ...
Both flash their Police identity cards ...
"We're here to see Professor Bewick" advises MacCormac

An elderly gentleman in a black bowler hat, known as the Gate Keeper, begins to point MacCormac and Sheridan in the right direction.
"Detective Chief Superintendent MacCormac and Inspector Sheridan" advises MacCormac
"OK, through the gardens, second floor ... east wing" replies the Gate Keeper
"Thank you, Sir" replies MacCormac (Smiles)
The Museum houses the World famous collection from Egyptian Mummies to contemporary art ... telling stories across time ...
"This is it" advises Sheridan
(Points the way)
"So I see, Paddy" replies
McCormac
"Well, go on man, ring the bell"

advises MacCormac
Paddy rings the bell, and a lady of distintion answers …
"How may I help you?" asks a voice
MacCormac and Sheridan flash their Police identity to the camera …

"Detective Chief Superintendent MacCormac and Detective Inspector Sheridan, Thames Valley Police" advises MacCormac
"Yes, how can I help you?" replies the voice
"We're looking for Professor Bewick"
asks MacCormac
"You've just found her" replies the voice
The Professor opens the door ...

"A woman" adds MacCormac (Looks stunned)

"How very perceptive of you, Chief Superintendent" replies the Professor (Smiles)
"Please, call me Sophie" advises the Professor

Professor Bewick is an elegant looking brunette, has brown eyes and is obviously very well groomed ...
"Call me Daniel or MacCormac ... everyone calls me MacCormac" explains the newly promoted Detective Chief Superintendent
"Now can I get you both something?" asks the Professor

"Tea perhaps ... or maybe something stronger?" adds the Professor

"Tea, for me" replies Paddy (Smiles)
"Maybe, a small scotch for me"
replies MacCormac
"Coming up" replies the Professor
"Your name is quite familiar to me" advises the Professor (Looks serious)
"MacCormac you say?" asks the Professor (Ponders)

"Sorry I can't remember why ... it'll come back to me" explains the Professor

"So, gentlemen, how can I help you?" asks the Professor (Smiles)

"We're investigating a murder" advises MacCormac

"A murder?" replies the Professor (Looks stunned)

"No murder has been committed here ... or been reported" replies the Professor (Looks cautious)

"I'm sorry, but you've had a wasted journey" adds the Professor

"Not entirely" replies MacCormac

Suddenly, a loud scream can be heard from the grounds of the University ...

MacCormac and Sheridan rush to the scene ...

Both are astonished to find yet another body, face down ...

"Don't touch him" advises Sheridan

"How do you know that it's male, Paddy?" asks MacCormac

"Sorry, Sir ... I don't at this stage" explains Paddy (Looks surprised)

"OK, get Mike on the scene, fast" asks MacCormac

"On to it, Sir" replies Sheridan (Phones Mike on Mobile)

The area of the University is cordoned off by a swarm of Police officers.

Chief Pathologist, Mike Mortimer arrives on the

scene ...

MacCormac and Sheridan are at the scene already ...

"Not another one, Daniel" asks Mortimer
(Looks up to the sky)

"I'm afraid so, Mike" replies MacCormac
"This is getting to be a habit" replies Mike (Looks serious)

"OK, Mike ... let me know the fine details later" advises MacCormac

"As soon as, Daniel" explains Mike
"Thanks, Mike" replies MacCormac

Sheridan is left at the scene, while MacCormac goes to reinterview Professor Bewick ...
"Lost none of his usual charm has he, Paddy?" advises Mortimer (Smiles)
"No, Mike ... he's just the same" advises Paddy
"What do you make of him becoming the new Detective Chief Superintendent?" asks Mortimer
"Not before time, if you ask me ... mind you he's more at ease doing what we do now" explains Paddy
"See that it doesn't go to his head, Paddy" replies Mike (Looks serious)
"I'll try, Mike ... I'll try" replies Sheridan (Laughs)
MacCormac rejoins Professor Sophie Bewick in her chambers ...
"What happened?" asks the Professor (Looks concerned)
"We've found another body, in the grounds of the

University" explains MacCormac (Looks serious)
"My God ... have they been identified?" asks the Professor

"Not yet ... forensics and pathology are on to it" explains MacCormac

Suddenly, a call from Sheridan ...
"Sorry, I'll have to get this" advises MacCormac

Paddy Sheridan begins to put MacCormac in the picture ...

"Mike has checked ... the time of death occurred between 6pm and 8pm ... and the name of the dead man is ... Alfred Donaldson" advises Sheridan
"Alfred Donaldson?" replies MacCormac (Looks serious)

"Alfred ... not Alfred" answers Professor Bewick (Looks stunned)

The Professor is in shock. MacCormac asks her to sit down ...

Alfred Donaldson was in his late fifties, brown hair, green eyes ...

"Did you know him well, Mrs Bewick?" asks MacCormac
"It's Miss, actually" replies the Professor

"Alfred is, was a Professor of Ancient Egyptian artefacts, here at the University" responds the Professor (Looks sad)
Suddenly, Chief Superintendent, Alex Samson appears on the scene ...
"Where the hell is, MacCormac?" asks Samson

(Looks angry)

"Here, Sir ... interviewing Professor Bewick" explains MacCormac

"Well, have there been any developments?" asks Samson

"The deceased in question is one Alfred Donaldson, Sir" advises MacCormac

"He was a Professor of Ancient Egyptian artefacts, here at Oxford University, Sir" explains MacCormac
Suddenly, Paddy Sheridan
enters the room ...
"Sir" asks Sheridan
"Yes, Sheridan" replies MacCormac

"An update from the Pathologist" advises Paddy

"What does he say?" asks Samson
(Looks annoyed)
"Same as before ... strangulation and another note, Sir" explains Sheridan
"Not in Egyptian, I hope?" asks MacCormac
"No, Sir ... this time it's in English" advises Sheridan
"Well, what does it say, Sheridan?" asks Samson
"The message reads ... beware of Wolvercote" explains Paddy
"Is that it?" asks MacCormac
"Sorry, Sir ... it is" replies Paddy

"OK, Paddy ... have it checked for DNA" advises MacCormac

"I'll see to it straight away, Sir" advises Sheridan

"I've asked for a portfolio of staff here at the University ... Professor Bewick is arranging it" explains MacCormac (Looks serious)

"Is that all, MacCormac?" asks Samson (Looks puzzled)

"Remember, the Chief Constable is waiting" bellows Samson

"Yes, I'm aware of that, Sir" replies MacCormac (Looks anxious)

"It's always duty before protocol with you, MacCormac" advises Samson

"You'll have to change" explains Samson (Looks serious)

"Yes, Sir" replies MacCormac

"OK, Paddy ... I'll have to attend the inaugural meeting ... let me know anything when you have it" advises MacCormac

"See you later, Sir" replies Sheridan

"See you later?" asks Samson (Looks puzzled)

"I've been invited, wouldn't miss it for the World, Sir" replies MacCormac

Chief Superintendent Alex Samson and Daniel MacCormac head back to the inauguration.
Paddy Sheridan looks in on Chief Pathologist, Mike Mortimer, and is given the verdict on Alfred Donaldson ...

"Well, what's the story, Mike?" asks Sheridan (Looks serious)

"Strangulation ... just like all the others" advises Mortimer

"Anything else, Mike?" asks Paddy (Looks stunned)

"Well, there was another thing that was noticeable with the note" explains Mortimer (Looks cautious)

"What is it, Mike?" asks Paddy (Looks surprised)

"It would appear that this man had an aneurysm in the brain" advises Mortimer

"An aneurysm?" asks Paddy (Looks serious)

"Is it relevant to his death, Mike?" asks Sheridan

"It may be beneficial, Paddy" advises Mortimer (Looks serious)

"I think MacCormac will think so, too" explains Mortimer

"Is that all, Mike?" asks Paddy

"Apart from the note about Wolverton?" asks Paddy

"I've detected some hairs on the back of the corpse" explains Mortimer

"Do you think they belong to the victim?" asks Paddy (Looks surprised)

"Hard to say, Paddy ... we'll get DNA on to it" advises Mortimer

"Where's MacCormac?" asks Mortimer (Looks around)

"At his inauguration, Mike" advises Sheridan

"Detective Chief Superintendent Alex Samson insisted he attended, at the Chief Constable's request" explains Paddy (Looks serious)

"Poor sod" replies Mortimer (Laughs)

"MacCormac always was gullible to top ranking" adds Mortimer (Looks serious)

"If you ask me, Mike ... he'll probably have his work cut out ... it's all technology now" explains Paddy
"The essence of a new World ... time moves on, Paddy" quips Mortimer
"Where's the booze up?" asks Mortimer (Looks facetious)
"It's in the Randolph, later, Mike" advises Paddy

"Tell, MacCormac, I'll be there, Paddy" replies Mortimer (Smiles)

"OK, will do, Mike" replies Sheridan

THE WOLVERCOTE CONNECTION

Daniel MacCormac is finally made the Chief Constable's right hand man, taking over from retiring Detective Chief Superintendent, Alex Samson.

As Paddy Sheridan digs deeper into Professor Alfred Donaldson's death ... Chief Pathologist, Mike Mortimer has some startling news!

Is the Sphinx about to be revealed?

Why has Wolvercote acquired a mysterious status?

At the Randolph Hotel, central Oxford ...

"Glad you could come, Mike" advises MacCormac (Both shake hands)

"Paddy, get Mike a drink" asks MacCormac (Looks serious)

"Yes, Sir" replies Sheridan (Smiles)

"I'll have a scotch on the rocks, Paddy" advises Mortimer (Smiles)

"Coming right up" replies Paddy (Walks over to Bar)

"So, now it's official, Dan" asks Mortimer (Looks serious)

"Yes, it's official, Mike" replies MacCormac (Smiles)

"You sound pretty keen" adds Mortimer

"I'm overwhelmed ... if you really must know" explains MacCormac

Sheridan returns with Mike's drink ...

Another young copper enters and whispers into Sheridan's ear ...

"There's been another one, Sir" advises Paddy (Looks shocked)

"My God, where is it this time?" asks MacCormac (Looks equally shocked)

"Down by the river bank, Sir" explains Sheridan

"I'll get my bag" replies Mortimer (Looks serious)

"I'm coming with you" advises MacCormac (Looks equally serious)

"Don't worry ... I'll make my excuses to the Chief Constable" adds MacCormac

Sheridan, MacCormac and Mike Mortimer arrive at the scene of the crime, alongside a river boat ...

Mike checks over the body ...

"What have you got, Mike?" asks MacCormac (Looks serious)

"Female, early fifties" replies Mortimer (Points to body)

"Take a look, Dan" advises Mortimer

MacCormac is reluctant, but does so ...

"Why ... it's Professor Sophie Bewick" advises

MacCormac (Looks shocked)

"My God" replies Sheridan (Looks equally shocked)

"Another link in the chain, Dan?" asks Mortimer (Looks concerned)

"Quite possible" replies MacCormac

"What do you think, Mike?" asks MacCormac (Looks serious)

"Between you and me, Dan … there's a link to all of this … I'll perform an autopsy and let you know, when I know" explains Mortimer (Looks cautious)

"Thanks, Mike" replies MacCormac

MacCormac ponders the unfolding situation …

"Paddy, get to the Institute of Criminology … I don't like this … something is not right" explains MacCormac (Looks cautious)

"Will do, Sir" replies Sheridan

"Any Egyptian cryptic clues with the body, Sir?" asks Sheridan

"Something's been written in Egyptian writing" adds Sheridan

"Do you mean hieroglyphics, Paddy?" asks MacCormac (Looks puzzled)

"Yes, that's it, Sir" replies Sheridan

"We'll need that analysed, too" explains MacCormac (Looks serious)

"OK, next stop … the University of Oxford" replies MacCormac

Sheridan and MacCormac jump into the gleaming

white Audi and arrive by the gate house into the University.

They are both met at the entrance, by another gate keeper.

"Where's the other gate keeper?" asks MacCormac (Looks serious)

"Day off, Sir … can I help you?" advises a voice

"We're here to see Miles Moorcroft" advises MacCormac (Shows warrant card)

"Sheridan and MacCormac … Thames Valley Police" explains MacCormac (Sounds serious)

"Second floor, across the grounds, Sir" advises the gate keeper

"Paddy, get the details of the other gate keeper" asks MacCormac

"It may be prove to be significant in our investigation" adds MacCormac

"Yes, Sir" replies Sheridan (Starts to make notes)

MacCormac climbs the stairs and knocks on 2A's door …

"Yes?" asks a voice (Sounds stunned)

"Chief Superintendent MacCormac, Thames Valley" advises MacCormac

"Can I have a word with Mr. Moorcroft?" asks MacCormac

"Yes … please come in" greets the voice

Professor Miles Moorcroft is the Vice Chancellor of the University of Oxford. He is 6ft tall, balding, has blue eyes and is a proven scholar and associate ...

"How can I help you, Mr MacCormac?" advises Moorcroft

"Call me MacCormac ... everyone else does" replies the Chief Superintendent

"Are you aware that Professor Sophie Bewick was murdered tonight?" asks MacCormac (Looks serious)

"Murdered?" asks Moorcroft (Looks shocked)

"No, I'm sorry I'm not" replies Moorcroft (Looks stunned) "The body was found, by a river boat" replies MacCormac

"She had connections in Wolvercote" advises Moorcroft (Looks serious)

"Connections?" asks MacCormac (Looks puzzled)

"She didn't want it to be known, but she was having an affair with an ex Don of the University" explains Moorcroft (Looks serious)

"Now I understand, we may need to eliminate them from our inquiries ... so if you could advise his name?" asks MacCormac

"Tobias Carmichael" advises Moorcroft

"Carmichael?" asks MacCormac (Looks stunned)

"Do you know him, Chief Superintendent?" asks Moorcroft (Looks shocked)

"We were at Oxford together, some time ago" explains MacCormac

"An Oxford man?" asks Moorcroft (Looks stunned)

"Yes, it's true, I was … well, I still am, Sir" advises MacCormac

"… but your a Policeman?" replies Moorcroft (Looks surprised)

"Yes, by some strange twist of fate, I am" adds MacCormac (Looks smug)

"A high ranking Policeman?" asks Moorcroft (Looks serious)

"Well, I have just been made Chief Superintendent, actually" explains MacCormac (Smiles)

"Can I offer you a drink, Chief Superintendent?" asks Moorcroft

"A small whiskey would be fine, Sir" replies MacCormac

"Tell me more about, Tobias Carmichael" asks MacCormac (Looks serious)

Paddy Sheridan arrives on the scene and updates MacCormac concerning the missing Gate House keeper …

"Thanks Paddy … run the usual check" advises MacCormac

"OK, Sir … will do" replies Sheridan (Looks serious)

"Mike Mortimer, has asked us to meet him as soon as possible" advises Paddy

"Right" replies MacCormac

"I'm afraid we'll have to leave you, Mr Moorcroft" advises MacCormac

"My Sergeant, sorry Detective Inspector Sheridan, will be in touch" explains MacCormac (Smiles)
"Why, Chief Superintendent?" asks Moorcroft (Looks surprised)
"We may need further information, Sir" advises MacCormac
"Yes, I quite understand, Chief Superintendent" replies Moorcroft
"We would be obliged if you could help with anything, Sir" advises MacCormac
Sheridan and MacCormac leave the confines of the University and head to the autopsy inquest with Chief Pathologist, Mike Mortimer ...
"Well, Mike ... what have you got for us this time?" asks MacCormac (Looks serious)
"Conspiracy theories abound, Dan" advises Mortimer (Looks equally serious)
"But this one's different" adds Mortimer (Looks serious)
"Go on" asks MacCormac (Looks puzzled)

"There's a fifty, fifty chance this woman was shot in the head" explains Mortimer
"Here's the gunshot wound" advises Mortimer (Points to lethal wound)
"Between you and me, Dan ... there's something very sinister about this" advises Mortimer (Looks concerned)
"Sinister?" asks MacCormac (Looks puzzled)

"That's my contribution, Dan ... I'll leave the detective work to you" explains Mortimer (Smiles)

"Thanks, Mike" replies MacCormac

"I'll get the autopsy report over to you in due course" advises Mortimer

"By the way ..." adds Mortimer
"Yes" replies MacCormac (Looks stunned)

"Congratulations again, Dan, on becoming Chief Superintendent" advises Doctor Mortimer (Smiles)
"Thanks, Mike" replies MacCormac (Smiles)
Sheridan and MacCormac leave the inquest. Both jump back into MacCormac's white Audi
... "Where to now, Sir?" asks Paddy
"I think we need to speak to ex-Don, Tobias Carmichael" advises MacCormac
"Do you think he has anything to do with it, Sir?" asks Paddy (Looks concerned)
"What I think, Paddy ... doesn't come into it ... but you may be right he may well have some contribution" explains MacCormac (Looks serious)
Sheridan and MacCormac head to Wolvercote ... a pretty village on the outskirts of Oxford. They pull up outside of the property of ex-Don ... Tobias Carmichael. MacCormac knocks on the door of the pretty cottage.

"How can I help you?" asks a voice

"MacCormac and Sheridan, Thames Valley Police" advises MacCormac

"Did you say MacCormac?" asks Carmichael (Looks stunned)

"Yes" replies the Chief Superintendent

"After all these years" laughs Carmichael (opens the door)

"Good to see you again, Tobias" replies MacCormac (Both shake hands)

"This is Inspector Sheridan" advises MacCormac

"We go way back" replies Carmichael (Laughs)

"Sorry, Tobias … we're here on official business" explains MacCormac

"OK … come in … come in" replies Carmichael (Smiles)

Sheridan and MacCormac enter a well furnished front room …

"Can I offer you both a drink?" asks Carmichael

"Tea, will be fine, Tobias" replies MacCormac

"Not for me, Daniel" replies Carmichael

"I usually take a whiskey at this time of the day … are you sure you won't join me?" asks Carmichael

"OK, I'll have a small one" replies MacCormac (Smiling)

"Mr Sheridan?" asks Carmichael
"Tea for me, Sir" replies Paddy (Smiles)

After several minutes, Tobias returns with the tea and whiskey ...

"Now, how can I help you, Daniel?" asks Carmichael (Looks stunned)

"We understand you had a relationship with Professor Bewick at the University?" asks MacCormac (Looks serious)
"Ah yes, Sophie and I had a mutual understanding" advises Carmichael
"We're sorry to bring you bad news, Tobias" explains MacCormac
"Bad news?" asks Carmichael (Looks stunned)
"Miss Bewick was found murdered, yesterday" advises MacCormac
"My God ... where?" asks Carmichael (Looks shocked)
"Along the towpath in Oxford ... we thought she'd been strangled but we've been advised by pathology that it was a gunshot wound to the head that caused her death" explains MacCormac (Looks serious)
"It's unbelievable, Daniel" replies Carmichael (Shocked)

"A hieroglyphic message was also found on the body circa 1900 BC" advises MacCormac
"Hieroglyphics you say?" replies Carmichael (Looks surprised)

"Yes, an ancient Egyptian papyrus from AD180 was

also found with the body" explains MacCormac

"It also carried an encrypted message no one has ever solved" adds MacCormac

"Maybe, I can help, Daniel" advises Carmichael (Looks serious)

"Are you in Hieroglyphics, Sir?" asks Sheridan

"I was at the University" replies Carmichael (Looks smug)

"Send me the exact words, and I will try to break the code" advises Carmichael

"Thanks, Tobias ... we'll get it over to you later today" replies MacCormac

Paddy Sheridan suddenly receives a message on his mobile phone ...

"What now, Paddy?" asks MacCormac (Looks annoyed)

"A message from Mike Mortimer, with an update, Sir" replies Paddy

Sheridan and MacCormac leave Tobias and Wolvercote and head back towards Oxford.

"There's been another development, Sir" advises Paddy (Looks serious)

"Not another body, Paddy, surely" replies MacCormac (Looks surprised)

"No ... another message, Sir" advises Paddy

"This time it bears an ancient Egyptian curse" explains Paddy

"Messages and curses" replies MacCormac (Looks shocked)

"What's going on, Paddy?" asks MacCormac
(Looks puzzled)

BREAKING THE CODE

Chief Superintendent Daniel MacCormac is summoned before the Chief Constable. The conclusion to the investigation draws near.
Tobias Carmichael is not all he seems to be ... but who is the Sphinx, and when will all the ancient Egyptian curses come to an end?
At the Centre of Criminology, which is based within the University of Oxford, the Centre is

home to various vibrant programmes of research in Criminology. Sheridan and MacCormac are advised the Gate Keeper's name …

A message on Paddy's mobile phone updates him with a break through they have been waiting for …

"It's just come through, Sir" advises Sheridan (Looks at mobile phone)

"What has, Paddy?" asks MacCormac

"The identity of the other Gate Keeper" explains Paddy

"Well, who is it, Paddy?" asks MacCormac (Looks serious)

"One … Samuel Carmichael" advises Paddy

"Samuel Carmichael?" replies MacCormac (Looks stunned)

"I wonder … is he related to Tobias Carmichael, the ex-Don?" asks MacCormac

"I didn't know he had a brother, Paddy … the plot thickens" explains MacCormac (Looks serious)

"That's not all, Sir" replies Paddy (Looks serious)

"Go on" replies MacCormac (Looks equally serious)

"We've found out that Samuel Carmichael worked in History at the Cambridge Institute of Criminology" adds Paddy (Sounds serious)

"Oxford and Cambridge … that's quite rare" answers MacCormac

Suddenly, another call from Police HQ …

Paddy answers the call

… "Sheridan" advises

Paddy

"It's the Chief Constable's Secretary for you, Sir" explains Paddy

"OK, put her on, Paddy" replies MacCormac (Looks serious)

Paddy transfers the call to Daniel MacCormac ...

"Chief Superintendent MacCormac"

"Right, Joyce ... 2pm ... I'll be there" advises MacCormac (Looks serious)

The new Chief Superintendent has been summoned before the Chief Constable, presumably to update him with regards the investigation.

"We need to break this code, Paddy" advises MacCormac (Looks cautious)

"Something is staring me right in the face ... but I just can't put my finger on it" explains MacCormac (Looks puzzled)

"Another puzzle, Sir?" asks Paddy

"Maybe, Paddy ... maybe" replies MacCormac (Looks serious)

"Check with Cambridge and put the two together, Paddy ... then let's see what we come up with" advises MacCormac

"Yes, Sir" replies Sheridan

Meanwhile, back in Pathology, Mike Mortimer has some startling news ...

MacCormac and Sheridan check in with Mike ...

"Well, what have you got for us, Mike?" asks

MacCormac

"That's what I like about you Dan, no hello or good morning ... straight to the point" replies Mike (Looks cynical)
"Well?" asks MacCormac (Looks serious)

"I take it, you know of Samuel Carmichael?" asks Mike

"Yes, Mike ... what's it all about?"
asks Paddy
" ... but did you know that Samuel was Tobias's twin?" asks Mortimer
"Twin brother ... now that's very interesting" advises MacCormac (Looks stunned)
"That could explain it, Sir"
replies Paddy
"Explain what you mean
by that, Paddy?" asks
MacCormac
"Why he can be in two places at the same time" explains Paddy (Looks serious)
"Your a genius, Paddy ... your right" replies MacCormac (Smiles)
"... and the Sphinx?" asks Mike

"We're still working on that, Mike" advises MacCormac

"What if I was to tell you that tests confirm that both Samuel and Tobias Carmichael's DNA was found on the messages, left at the scene of the crime?" asks Mike
"Mike ... your a genius, too ... that's it ... the evidence

we've been looking for" explains MacCormac (Looks pleased)

"At last the code has been broken" advises Mike

"But who is who, Dan ... is Carmichael one in the same?" asks Mike

"I don't follow, Mike?" asks MacCormac (Looks surprised)

"Check records, Paddy" instructs MacCormac

"Has anyone ever seen, Samuel Carmichael?" explains Mike

"Next stop?" asks Mike (Looks serious)

"The Chief Constable at 2pm ... I've been summoned" explains MacCormac

"Not in the bad books already are you, Dan?" asks Mortimer (Laughs)

"You know what, Mike ... I wouldn't be surprised if I was" replies MacCormac

Paddy Sheridan heads back to the Police station. He checks records ... then rechecks and advises Daniel MacCormac.

The new Chief Superintendent returns to the Police station ... Paddy brings him up to speed concerning the investigation ...

"I think we have a break through, Sir" advises Paddy (Looks pleased)

"OK, Paddy ... bring in Samuel and Tobias Carmichael for questioning" instructs MacCormac (Looks serious)

"No ... hold on that" advises MacCormac (Looks startled)

"Sir?" asks Paddy (Looks puzzled)

"We'll confront Tobias ... something tells me to follow our noses on this one" explains MacCormac (Looks curious)

Sheridan and MacCormac head out into the Police car park, and jump into the gleaming white Audi Quattro. They head towards Wolvercote, arriving outside of Tobias's cottage ...

Tobias greets MacCormac and Sheridan, at the front door, almost immediately ...

"Come in Daniel ... welcome Detective Inspector Sheridan" advises Carmichael

MacCormac doesn't beat about the bush ...

"OK, Tobias ... where is he?" asks MacCormac (Looks serious)

"Where's who?" replies Carmichael (Looks surprised)

"Your brother ... Samuel?" advises MacCormac

"I've not seen him in years, Daniel" explains Carmichael (Still shocked)

"If that's the case, why has DNA, matching both of you , been found on clues found at the murder scene?" asks MacCormac (Looks serious)

"My brother, Samuel?" replies Carmichael

Sheridan and MacCormac smell a rat ...

"You can come out now, Samuel" shouts MacCormac (Looks serious)

No response to this request ...

Then, a sudden, appearance of Samuel Carmichael!

"Quite clever, aren't you ... MacCormac" greets Samuel (Smiles)

"Not clever enough, to stop you, Sir" replies MacCormac

Samuel Carmichael produces a weapon

...

"No ... not quite" replies Samuel (Looks serious)

"The Sphinx ... I presume?" asks MacCormac (Looks serious)

"Yes, that's me ... quite a character I'd say" replies Samuel (Smiles)

"An elusive character and murderer, I'd say" advises MacCormac

"You have no proof, MacCormac" replies Samuel

"We have DNA evidence, linking you to all of the victims" explains MacCormac (Looks serious)

Samuel Carmichael offers no response.

"Paddy" asks MacCormac (Looks around)

"It seems Detective Inspector Sheridan has abandoned you MacCormac" replies Samuel

"Yes, so it seems" advises MacCormac

Samuel Carmichael takes hold of Daniel MacCormac and a struggle unfolds ... Paddy Sheridan, enters the room ...

"Are you alright, Sir?" asks Sheridan

"Get him off me, Paddy" replies MacCormac (Shouts)

"Did you get that?" asks MacCormac

"Yes, every word, loud and clear, and it's recorded on my phone, Sir" explains Paddy

Several Police officers enter the cottage ...

The Chief Constable is now also at the scene ...

"Take them away" advises MacCormac

"Them?" asks Paddy (Looks surprised)

"Both Tobias and Samuel Carmichael are partners in crime, Paddy" explains MacCormac

Sheridan and MacCormac head outside to the waiting, Chief Constable ...

"I asked to see you at 2pm, Daniel" advises the Chief Constable

"Sorry, Sir ... but it was crucial to the arrest" explains MacCormac

"So I see, Daniel ... Chief Superintendent Samson warned me about your methods and timing" advises the Chief Constable (Looks serious)

"He also told me ..." explains the Chief Constable

"Yes, Sir?" asks MacCormac (Looks serious)

"Just how brilliant you were" adds the Chief

Constable (Smiling)

"I couldn't have done it without Paddy Sheridan" explains MacCormac

"You've both played your parts well" advises the Chief Constable "What of the hieroglyphic's tie in, Daniel?" asks the Chief Constable
The Centre of Criminology and the University of Oxford were both part of the puzzle, Sir" advises MacCormac (Looks serious)
"Puzzle?" asks the Chief Constable (Looks surprised)

"We managed to decipher some of the words" explains MacCormac

"Go on, Daniel" asks the Chief Constable
"One of the tablets read … intelligence uses the unconscious thoughts and dreams of men, as an address to men unborn" adds MacCormac
"Men unborn?" ponders the Chief Constable (Looks surprised)
"Unborn or reunited, Sir" explains MacCormac
"What does that mean, Dan?" asks the Chief Constable

"Tobias and Samuel Carmichael were reunited to commit murders on a prolonged scale" advises MacCormac
"It's all in the detail, Sir" explains Sheridan
"Thank you, Paddy" advises the Chief Constable

"What about Professor Bewick?" asks the Chief

Constable

"Sophie Bewick had an affair with ex-Don Tobias Carmichael" adds MacCormac

"Samuel Carmichael had suffered a nervous breakdown due to the pressures of what was expected of him by his family. He assumed the role of Gate Keeper at the University" explains MacCormac

"... and Tobias?" asks the Chief Constable (Looks shocked)

"He made out that Samuel was unknown to him ... yet in some twist of fate, he was bound to his brother" advises MacCormac

"Why all the murders?" asks the Chief Constable (Looks serious)

"Infatuation and Egyptian malpractice ... both were insane, Sir" explains MacCormac

"What will happen to them now, Sir?" asks Paddy

"Both will come before the beak, Paddy ... and the justice system" explains MacCormac

"We'll leave that to the powers that be, Daniel" advises the Chief Constable

"Sir?" asks MacCormac (Looks stunned)

"We have more pressing matters to attend to" explains the Chief Constable

"Yes, Sir, I believe we have" replies MacCormac (Smiles)

"What about that beer, Sir?"
asks Sheridan
The Chief Constable

intervenes …

"I'm afraid Chief Superintendent MacCormac will have to leave you, Paddy" explains the Chief Constable

"Maybe, later, Sir?" asks Sheridan

"Later, Paddy" replies MacCormac (Smiles)

"… before you go" advises MacCormac (Looks serious)

"It's been a pleasure working again with you, Paddy" adds MacCormac

"You, too, Sir" replies Paddy

Both men shake hands. MacCormac and the Chief Constable leave the scene of the investigation

Detective Inspector Paddy Sheridan is left to tie up the investigation.

SANCTUM SANCTORUM

Detective Chief Inspector Daniel MacCormac now Detective Chief Superintendent of Thames Valley Police, reports directly to the Chief Constable.

Sergeant Paddy Sheridan is now an Inspector based in Oxford. He is still an endorsement of his old mentor, the Chief Super!
When forensic evidence emerges, it links four unsolved murders in Oxford, from twenty years ago! A young woman, on her way home, is found strangled by a canal.
A cryptic "crossword" has been left at the scene of the crime, with Daniel MacCormac's name on it!

Sheridan and MacCormac are drafted in by the Chief Constable, to solve the riddle and puzzle left by the murderer!

Can MacCormac solve it in time, before more murders are committed?

DEADLY FIND

Wednesday evening, Midnight, by the canal in Oxford.

A young woman notices that she is being followed, and reaches into her handbag for a mobile phone. She begins to dial a number and is put through almost immediately …
"I'm on my way … can you meet me, Jason?" asks the young woman
"Where are you, Molly?" asks Jason (Sounds serious)
"Close to the canal bridge" advises Molly

"OK, I'll be there in a few minutes" replies Jason

Suddenly, Molly is attacked from behind, a struggle takes place followed by a loud scream …
"Molly?" shouts Jason (Shouts)

He runs to find Molly laying on the ground, and phones immediately for the Police. Within minutes, the Police arrive on the scene. They liaise with plain clothes officers …
"I'm on my way" advises Sheridan (Looks serious)

Thursday, early morning, dawn is rising on the Oxford skyline …

Detective Inspector Paddy Sheridan arrives at the scene of the murder, within minutes.
Doctor and Home Office Chief Pathologist, Mike Mortimer, is already at the scene …

"OK, Mike ... what have we got?" asks Sheridan (Looks serious)

"Death by strangulation, Paddy" replies Mortimer

"Time of death?" asks Paddy

"I'd say around Midnight, Paddy" advises Mortimer

"Anything else?" asks Paddy

"Oh, we found this, Paddy" replies Mortimer

Mike hands over a sealed plastic wallet to Paddy ...

"What is it?" asks Sheridan

"A cryptic clue, left at the scene ... with MacCormac's name on it" explains Mortimer

"MacCormac?" replies Sheridan (Looks stunned)

Paddy begins to read the note ...

"Sacred or Holy Place" advises Paddy (Looks puzzled)

" and on the reverse ... ask MacCormac" explains Paddy

"Ask MacCormac what?" wonders Doctor Mortimer

"A crossword puzzle?" asks Mortimer

"Maybe, Daniel MacCormac can help, Paddy" replies Mortimer

Suddenly, another voice arrives on the scene ...

"Yes, maybe I can, Mike" replies the voice

"Sir?" replies Sheridan (Looks shocked)

"I've been drafted in by the Chief Constable to work

on this one" explains MacCormac
"We'll work together on this, Paddy" adds MacCormac
"Let me see the note" asks MacCormac
Sheridan passes the note to MacCormac, and he reads it out loud …
"Sacred or Holy place … ask MacCormac?" advises the Chief Superintendent
"Ask MacCormac, what exactly?" adds the Chief Superintendent (Looks stunned)
"To solve the mystery" replies Doctor Mortimer (Smiles)
"What are your thoughts on it, Mike?" asks MacCormac
"I'll leave the detective work to you, Daniel … I'll be in touch when I know more concerning the young woman" explains Mortimer
"OK, thanks, Mike" replies MacCormac
"Sanctum Sanctorum" advises MacCormac
"Sir?" asks Paddy (Looks puzzled)
"Sacred or Holy place … the Holiest of Holies" explains MacCormac
"If you say so, Sir" replies Paddy (Looks surprised)
"That's what the note means, Paddy" adds MacCormac
"A puzzle?" asks Sheridan

"The riddle of a killer" advises MacCormac (Looks serious)

A sudden phone call to Sheridan's mobile from the Oxford Constabulary ...

"Sheridan" advises the Inspector
"It's for you, Sir" advises Paddy (Passes mobile over)
"MacCormac" answers the Chief Superintendent
"... what now?" asks MacCormac (Sounds serious)

"We'll be with you, in ten minutes, Sir" replies MacCormac

The phone call suddenly ends.
"That was a call from the Chief Constable" explains MacCormac
"What does he want, Sir?" asks Sheridan (Looks shocked)
"He wants an update, Paddy" advises MacCormac

"... but we've only just arrived at the scene" replies Sheridan

"I know, Paddy, but we all have to answer to the Chief Constable" explains MacCormac
"Were there any witnesses, at the scene, Paddy?" asks MacCormac

"Just a young man, called Jason ... I think he is her boyfriend" advises Paddy

"Was, Paddy ... was" replies MacCormac
"Was, Sir" replies Paddy

"Is he alright?" asks MacCormac

(Looks concerned)

"More like shocked, Sir" replies Paddy

"OK, get his statement, Paddy" orders MacCormac

"What, now, Sir?" asks Sheridan
"Now, Paddy ... and do it personally, don't let the plods into it" explains MacCormac
"Yes, Sir" replies Paddy

"Right, I'll leave it to you ... meet me back in the office" advises MacCormac

"Sir?" replies Sheridan
MacCormac leaves the scene of the investigation, and drives away in his white Audi Quattro.
Paddy Sheridan interviews Jason, who is clearly in distress ...
"Sorry, Jason ... I have to ask you a few questions" advises Sheridan
"Did you know Molly, well?" asks Paddy
"We were going to be engaged" advises Jason
"I'm sorry" replies Paddy
(Looks shocked)
"Did you notice anything unusual or see anything?" asks Paddy
"A dark shape ... running away" replies Jason
"Can you remember anything else, a description, Jason?" asks Paddy

"No ... sorry I can't" replies Jason
"OK, Sir, that's all for now. We may need to talk to you again at some stage" explains Paddy
"What about the other officer?"
asks Jason
"Chief Superintendent
MacCormac?" asks Paddy
"Will he need to interrogate me too?" replies Jason
"Possibly, Jason ... but we interview not interrogate" explains Paddy
Inspector Sheridan asks a Police constable to escort Jason back to his home.
"Just one more question, before you go" asks Paddy
"You say your name is Jason Lockwood ... are you any relation to Professor Lockwood, at the University?" asks Paddy
"Yes, I'm his son" replies Jason

"Thanks again ... we'll be in touch" replies Paddy (Looks stunned)

Chief Superintendent Daniel MacCormac arrives back at Oxford Police Station where the Chief Constable is waiting his arrival.
MacCormac is taken into
a side room ...
"Daniel" asks the Chief
Constable
"Sir" replies MacCormac
"Your off the case" informs the Chief Constable

"Off the case ... but I've only just been put on it ... by

you" advises MacCormac

"Well, I'm taking you off it, Dan" explains the Chief Constable

"Why, Sir … may I ask why?" asks MacCormac (Looks stunned)

"Protocol, Daniel" advises the Chief Constable

"Protocol?" replies MacCormac (Looks stunned)

"The newspapers have got hold of the story about the crossword puzzle having your name on it" explains the Chief Constable

"Sanctum Sanctorum?" asks MacCormac

"Indeed" replies the Chief Constable

"It means the Holiest of Holies, Daniel" adds the Chief Constable

"I know what it means, Sir" replies MacCormac

"Officially, your off the case" explains the Chief Constable

"And unofficially, Sir?" asks MacCormac

"Your still on it" advises the Chief Constable (Smiles)

"I don't understand, Sir" replies MacCormac

"As it is so high profile, Sheridan will be your eyes and ears … you can work undercover" explains the Chief Constable

"Undercover?" asks MacCormac (Looks miffed)

"You don't get it do you, Daniel?" replies the Chief Constable

"Get what, Sir?" asks MacCormac (Looks puzzled)

"Your in the line of fire ... the named possible next victim" explains the Chief Constable

"We can't risk it, Daniel" advises the Chief Constable (Looks serious)

"Besides, another cryptic clue has been addressed to you, it arrived at the station, this morning" adds the Chief Constable (Sounds serious)

A sealed plastic wallet, containing the note, is handed to MacCormac by the Chief Constable ...

The note reads as follows ...

UNLAWFUL KILLING ... SIX LETTER WORD

and on the back of the note, it reads ... MacCormac knows!

"It's too easy ... the six letter word is MURDER, Sir" replies MacCormac

"Hardly, the Times crossword, Sir" advises MacCormac (Smiles)

"You don't understand do you, Daniel?" asks the Chief Constable

"They want your attention, only your attention" explains the Chief Constable

A sudden knock at the door ... enter Chief Pathologist, Mike Mortimer with Paddy Sheridan ...

The Chief Constable explains the situation ...

"Mike, what about the link between the canal murder and the four unsolved murders?" asks MacCormac
"There's a connection"
informs MacCormac
"A connection?" asks Mike
(Looks serious)
"Are we talking about the murders, over twenty years ago?" asks Mike
"Yes" replies MacCormac
"Mike?" asks Paddy

"The latest evidence and cryptic messages follow the same pattern" explains MacCormac
"Without doubt"
replies Mike
"DNA?" asks
MacCormac
"We're on to that, there's a lot of cross checking, Daniel" advises Mike
"A Policeman's lot is a happy lot" explains MacCormac
"OK, I'll be in touch, when there's more updates" advises Mike
The Chief Pathologist leaves the Chief Constable's office …
"Daniel, continue with your investigation. Inspector Sheridan, the Chief Superintendent is officially off the case" advises the Chief Constable
"And unofficially?" asks Sheridan

"He is still working alongside you, as the Senior Investigating Officer" explains the Chief Constable
"Understood, Sir" replies Paddy (Nods in agreement)
Sheridan and MacCormac leave the Chief Constable's office ...
"Just like old times, Sir" advises Sheridan
"Old times?" asks MacCormac
"Fancy a beer, Sir?" asks Sheridan
"Yes, but not at one of those awful places, you go to" advises MacCormac
"You can choose, Sir" replies Sheridan (Laughs)
MacCormac and Sheridan head off in the gleaming white Audi to the Black Prince pub in Woodstock ... They both enter the bar ...

"What'll you have, Sir?" asks Paddy

The Barman awaits the order ...
"Do you have any real ale?" asks MacCormac (Looks serious) "We thrive on it, Sir" replies the barman (Laughs)
"Perfect ... a pint of your finest"

advises MacCormac

"Make that two" replies Sheridan

The Barman pulls the pints of ale. MacCormac and Sheridan move to an outside table, away from all the other punters.

"I don't understand why the Chief Constable has taken you off the case, Sir?" asks Sheridan

"I'm still on it, Paddy" replies MacCormac (Looks serious)

"What did he mean, unofficially?" asks Paddy

"I'm a marked man, Paddy" advises MacCormac

"Whoever sent those crosswords is actually serious about involving me some way or another" adds MacCormac

DEADLY PURSUIT

MacCormac and Sheridan track down Professor Lockwood in Oxford.

More cryptic crossword clues are received which throws them off the scent!

Chief Pathologist, Mike Mortimer reveals more evidence linking the unsolved Oxford murders of 20 years ago.

Early evening, music is playing loudly at MacCormac's home ...

Suddenly a knock at the door ...

MacCormac turns down the music, and grumpily goes to the door ...

Detective Chief Superintendent Alex Samson is on the doorstep ...

"Sir?" asks MacCormac (Looks surprised)

"Can you turn that off, MacCormac?" asks Samson (Looks grumpy)

"Yes, sorry, Sir" replies MacCormac

"We're both the same rank now, let's dispense with the formalities" explains Salmon (Looks serious)

"Call me Alex" advises Samson (Smiles)

"Only if you call me Dan" replies MacCormac (Smiling)

"What can I do for you, Alex?" asks MacCormac (Looks serious)

"OK, Dan ... I'll get to the point" explains

Samson

"You can be a bit of a daft sod at times, but your a bloody good detective ... and your held in high esteem with the top brass" advises Samson (Looks serious)

"... but there's one thing your not good at ... moving with the times and dealing with top officials" explains Samson (Looks critical)

"That's two things" replies MacCormac (Laughs)

"There's some news, on the grapevine, about a possible candidate for the murders" advises Samson (Looks pleased)

"Anyone, we know?" asks MacCormac (Looks intrigued)

"Professor Simon Lockwood" explains Samson

"Lockwood?" asks MacCormac (Looks stunned)

"You know him, Dan?" asks Samson (Looks serious)

"Well, we were at University together, here in Oxford" replies MacCormac

"Then you'll have a head start" advises Samson (Smiles)

A file is handed to MacCormac ...

"It's all in here, Dan" advises Samson (Passes file over)

"The laboratory report from Doctor Mortimer, and evidence of a link to unsolved cases ... maybe they are all connected" explains Samson

"Did the Chief Constable ask you to tell me all

this?" asks MacCormac
"Yes, like you I'm unofficially still connected to the force" adds Samson
Another sudden knock at the door ...
MacCormac answers the door ...

Paddy Sheridan has arrived to update the Chief Superintendent ...

"What is it, Paddy?" asks MacCormac (Looks surprised)
"Another body has been found, Sir" replies Paddy
"Oh, my God ... where?" asks MacCormac (Looks stunned)
"At the Randolph Hotel ... looks like a poisoning, Sir" explains Paddy

Alex Samson jumps to his feet ...
"Sorry, Sir I didn't know you were here" adds Paddy (Looks surprised)
"I'm just going, Sheridan" replies Samson
"Thank you, Alex" replies MacCormac

"What about the victim, Paddy?" asks MacCormac

"A young woman, brunette, approx early twenties ... death by ..." replies Paddy

"Strangulation" replies MacCormac
"Yes, ... how did you know, Sir?" asks Sheridan (Looks puzzled)

"I didn't but it follows a pattern, Paddy ... here's the file from Mike ... see if we have any potential leads" explains MacCormac
Alex Samson makes his excuses and leaves for the

Randolph, followed by Sheridan and MacCormac in the gleaming Audi ...
The area has already been cordoned off ...

The Randolph is a quaint but stylish Hotel, in the heart of Oxford. MacCormac and Sheridan pull up outside the hotel. Both run up the staircase where they are met by Chief Pathologist, Mike Mortimer.
"What have we got, Mike?" asks MacCormac (Looks serious)
"Another one, Dan" advises Mortimer
"Same method of death by strangulation" confirms Mortimer
"Time?" asks MacCormac (Looks serious)
"Approx 1am" advises
Mortimer
"Anything else, Mike?"
asks Paddy
"The young woman was clutching something" replies Mortimer
"Not another note?" asks MacCormac
"Yes, with your name on it" explains Mortimer

"This is getting to be a habit, Daniel" advises Mortimer (Looks serious)

Mike passes the note to MacCormac in a plastic wallet.
The note reads ... SECRET
DOCTRINE (7 LETTERS)
"It can only be one word"
advises MacCormac
"Well?" asks Mortimer (Looks

puzzled)

"Mystery" explains MacCormac

"… and on the back?" asks Paddy

"MacCormac knows the answer" replies Mortimer

"Well, do you know the answer, Daniel?" asks Mortimer

"If I did, Mike … I would have caught them by now" explains MacCormac

"OK, Mike … let us know if you find anything in the autopsy" adds MacCormac

"Will do … hopefully later today" replies Mortimer
A sudden call to Paddy Sheridan's
mobile …
"Sheridan" greets the Inspector
"Ask MacCormac to …"
advises the voice
"Will do" ends Paddy
"Well, Paddy?" asks MacCormac

"We've been asked to see Professor Lockwood" explains Sheridan

"You, Paddy … not we" advises MacCormac
"Remember, I'm supposed to be undercover" explains MacCormac
"If Lockwood asks, tell him, I'm on another case" advises MacCormac
"No … tell him I'm on leave" adds MacCormac (Looks serious)
"He may turn out to be the suspect, Sir" replies Sheridan

"Precisely, just remember what's in the file, Paddy" advises MacCormac

"It may be a link … to the past" explains MacCormac

Chief Pathologist, Mike Mortimer provides an update ...

"Oh, and this?" asks Paddy
"Not another note?" replies MacCormac

"No, sorry ... not this time" advises Mike Mortimer (Looks serious)

"The victim managed to pull this off her attacker" adds Mortimer

Mike produces a man's scarf ...
"But it could be unisex, Mike?" asks MacCormac

"I don't know anything about that, Dan ... I'll leave the detective work to you and Paddy" explains Mortimer
"Good night" adds Doctor Mortimer

"Good night, Mike" replies MacCormac

"You'll have the postmortem report tomorrow" adds Mortimer

Assistant Chief Constable, Marc Bullman, suddenly arrives on the scene ...

"Well, Daniel?" asks the Assistant Chief Constable
"It's another strangulation, Sir" advises MacCormac (Looks serious)

"... that I do know" adds the Assistant Chief Constable (Looks concerned)

"You need to be on this one, Dan" explains the Assistant Chief Constable

"I'm supposed to be off the case, by order of the Chief Constable, Sir" replies MacCormac (Looks

serious)

"A mere tactic to deter the attacker, Dan" explains the Assistant Chief Constable

"I've just spoken to the Chief Constable, and he insists that your now officially back on the case, no more need to be behind the scenes" explains the Assistant Chief Constable

"Well, at least that's a relief" replies MacCormac (Smiles)

"Where to next, Sir?" asks Sheridan

"I think it's time we paid Professor Lockwood a call" advises MacCormac

"What at this time, Sir?" asks Sheridan

"It is now 9pm" explains Paddy (Looks at watch)

"I suppose we can set it up for tomorrow morning, Paddy" advises MacCormac

"Night, Paddy" replies MacCormac
"Good night, Sir" responds Sheridan

Next day, MacCormac and Sheridan head for Magdalen College, and are met by the Gate Keeper.

"MacCormac and Sheridan, Thames Valley Police, to see Professor Lockwood" advises the Chief Superintendent (Both flash their warrant cards)

The Gate Keeper instructs them both to walk across the courtyard to the private study Quarters. Sheridan knocks on the door …

"Come in" advises a voice

"Detective Inspector Sheridan and …" advises Paddy (Sounds serious)

"MacCormac?" replies the voice
"Is it really you?" adds the voice

"Well, well ... nice to see you again, MacCormac" explains the voice

"Don't you remember me ... Flinty" adds the voice (Shakes hands)

"Ah, yes I remember you now" advises MacCormac

"We go back a long way, Inspector" advises Flinty (Smiling)

"Can I get you tea or coffee ... or something stronger?" asks Flinty

"Tea for me, Sir" replies Sheridan
"What about you, MacCormac?" asks Flinty
"Make that two" replies MacCormac (Smiles)

"So, why are you here, and how can I help you?" asks Flinty (Looks intrigued)

"We're investigating several murders, Sir" advises Sheridan

"Thank you, Paddy" replies MacCormac

"Your son, Jason, was an acquaintance of the dead girl, Molly Peters?" asks MacCormac (Looks serious)

"Yes, they were going to get engaged ... horrible affair" advises Flinty

"So, why the visit, MacCormac?" asks Flinty (Looks surprised)

"Your not suspecting me, are you?" adds

Flinty (Looks serious)
"Everyone's under suspicion at the moment" advises MacCormac
"Is Jason, a suspect?" asks Flinty
"We can't rule out anything, or anyone, at this time" explains MacCormac
A sudden call to Paddy Sheridan's mobile phone … from the Oxford Press …
"There's been a development, Sir" advises Sheridan

"Another crossword puzzle" asks MacCormac (Looks surprised)

"Crossword puzzle?" asks Flinty (Looks intrigued)
"I've heard they were left with your name on it, MacCormac?" replies Flinty
"You heard right, Flinty … we're trying to piece together a chain of events" explains MacCormac
"Sorry, we'll have to go, Flinty" advises MacCormac

"Well, I'm here if you want to interview me again" adds Flinty

"Thanks for the tea, Flinty" replies MacCormac
"Remember when we used to play rugger, MacCormac?" asks Flinty
"Yes, I remember" replies MacCormac
"He was a good player back then, Inspector" advises Flinty
"Really?" replies Sheridan (Smiles)
"Come on Paddy … we have to go, remember?" asks MacCormac

"Yes, Sir" replies Sheridan
Another note has been sent to the Editor of the Oxford Express.

It may hold significant information in the deadly pursuit of the attacker ...

MacCormac and Sheridan leave the University.

DEADLY GAME

The Editor of the Oxford Express provides MacCormac and Sheridan with significant clues regarding the attacker.
A witness and suspect at Magdalen College causes problems. Will the attacker strike again?
MacCormac and Sheridan arrive at the offices of the Oxford Express ... They are summoned to the Editor's office ...
"Come in gentlemen" greets the Editor (Smiles)
"Jeremiah Proctor" advises the Editor (Shakes hands)
"MacCormac and Sheridan, Thames Valley Police" replies MacCormac
"I suppose your both wondering why I asked you here?" asks the Editor
"Well, the thought did cross our minds, Sir" replies MacCormac (Sounds serious)
"It appears that a cryptic clue has been put in the latest edition of the Express" explains the Editor

(Looks concerned)
"By who?" asks Sheridan

"Whom, Paddy ... whom"
replies MacCormac

"By whom, then" replies
Sheridan
"That we don't know" advises the Editor

"Apparently, it was placed over the phone, and paid there and then" explains the Editor
"Check for Bank details, Paddy"
replies MacCormac
"Sir" replies Paddy (Nods)
The Editor shows MacCormac the
cryptic crossword ...
MUCH PUZZLED (9 Letters)
"Nine Letters?" asks MacCormac (Looks serious
"I've got it" replies MacCormac

"Well, what is it?" asks the Editor (Looks surprised)

"MacCormac ... my name" advises the Chief Superintendent (Looks intrigued)

"Much puzzled?" ponders MacCormac
"It appears, he or she, is having us all running around like scolded cockerels" advises MacCormac (Looks concerned)
Paddy returns to the Editor's office ...

"What have you found out, Paddy?"
asks MacCormac

"I've checked into the Bank account,
Sir" advises Paddy

"Well, go on man, what did you find?" asks MacCormac

"Somehow it all leads to …" replies Paddy
"The Oxford University Press?" advises the Editor (Looks serious)
"How did you know, Sir?" asks MacCormac (Looks puzzled)
"I've had my suspicions, Chief Superintendent" replies the Editor
"… and the murderer?" asks MacCormac
"I think it could be someone linked to the University" adds the Editor

"We are also looking into the possibility of the four unsolved murders in Oxford" advises MacCormac
"A pattern?" asks the Editor (Looks serious)

"Maybe, if we can forensically link it all together" adds MacCormac

"So, Jeremiah … maybe you could help" explains MacCormac

"Help?" asks Jeremiah (Looks stunned)
"This is what I want you to do …" advises MacCormac

Sheridan and MacCormac leave the offices of the Oxford Express.

"You were a bit secretive in there, Sir?" asks Sheridan
"Why?" asks Paddy (Looks concerned)
"Why, Paddy … this may be key to what we're

looking for" advises MacCormac
"Next stop?" asks Paddy (Looks serious)

"Oxford University Press" replies MacCormac (Looks serious)

"What are you hoping to find there, Sir?" asks Paddy

"Answers, Paddy ... answers" explains MacCormac
A sudden phone call to Paddy Sheridan's mobile phone ...
"Tell them, we have a lead, Paddy" advises MacCormac
"Sir?" asks Sheridan (Looks puzzled)
"Well, Paddy ... what did they want?" asks MacCormac

"A witness and suspect at Magdalen College has come forward" advises Paddy

"Come forward?" asks MacCormac (Looks surprised)
"Blast, that'll throw a spanner in the works" adds MacCormac
"A red herring, Sir?" asks Paddy
"Possibly, Paddy ... OK, tell them we're on our way" instructs MacCormac
"We'll visit the Oxford University Press, later" advises MacCormac
Sheridan and MacCormac arrive at Magdalen College, and witness someone running before them.
"Head them off, Paddy" advises MacCormac (Points the way)

"I'll take the stairs" adds MacCormac
After several minutes, Sheridan and MacCormac reach the roof …
MacCormac confronts the runner …
It turns out to be … Jason Lockwood!

"No need to run, Jason … we only want a word" advises MacCormac

"My Father, advised that you suspected me" replies Jason (Looks scared)
Paddy Sheridan has now reached the roof, and can be seen just behind Jason.
"You'll never take me, MacCormac" advises Jason (Looks serious)

Paddy Sheridan moves forward, and a struggle ensues. Paddy brings Jason back down to ground level.
"Are you alright, Sir?" asks Paddy
(Looks concerned)
"I'm getting too old for this"
replies MacCormac
"Sir?" asks Paddy
"I'm alright, Paddy" advises MacCormac (Smiles)
"So, why did you run, Jason?" asks MacCormac
"I thought I was the one you were after" replies Jason

"All we wanted to do was talk, your not a suspect" explains MacCormac

Jason breaks down …
"What's going on?" asks Jason

(Looks intrigued)
"Jason, are you alright?" asks Paddy
"He's had a nasty shock, Sir" explains Paddy

Professor Flinty Lockwood has now arrived on the scene ...

"What's this all about?" asks Professor Lockwood (Looks serious)
"Are you familiar with the words, Sanctum ... Sanctorum, Sir?" asks MacCormac
"It's Latin for the holiest of holies, a shrine, a sanctuary" explains MacCormac
"Why?" asks the Professor (Looks stunned)
"You need to accompany us to the station, Flinty" advises MacCormac
"Whatever for?" asks the Professor (Looks shocked)
"To help in our routine inquiries" explains MacCormac
"Routine inquiries?" asks the Professor (Looks puzzled)
"Are we under suspicion, MacCormac?" asks the Professor
"No, as I said ... just helping us in our inquiries" adds MacCormac
"Do we need a brief?" asks the Professor (Looks serious)
"Only if you think it is necessary, Flinty" adds MacCormac (Looks serious)

"As the Chief Superintendent said, to help in our

inquiries, Sir" advises Sheridan

"Thank you, Paddy" replies MacCormac
Several Police patrol cars are now on the scene.

Professor Lockwood and his son, Jason are led away by the Police officers, where they are driven to Oxford Police Station.
Sheridan and MacCormac follow in the white Audi ...

"There's something not quite right, between those two" advises MacCormac

"Sir?" asks Sheridan (Sounds puzzled)
"Intuition, Paddy ... intuition" explains MacCormac

"I'll drop you off outside of Magdalen College, Paddy ... do a little digging, see what you can find out" adds MacCormac
"What about, protocol, Sir?" asks Paddy (Looks puzzled)

"I'm the Chief Super ... proceed" explains MacCormac (Looks serious)

"What about the Chief Constable, Sir?" asks Paddy
"Leave him to me, Paddy" adds MacCormac

The Chief Superintendent arrives outside of Magdalen College and drops Sheridan near the Gate Keeper's Lodge ...
Paddy Sheridan is met by the Gate Keeper ...

"I'm here to see Sir Robin Moore"
advises Sheridan

"Is he expecting you, Sir?" asks the Gate Keeper

Sheridan flashes his warrant identification card ...
"Inspector Sheridan, Oxford Police" advises Paddy (Looks official)
Chief Superintendent Daniel MacCormac is in interview with Professor Lockwood, and his son, Jason ...
A Police Officer switches on the tape machine ...

"Now, shall we start again?" asks MacCormac (Looks serious)

"I get the feeling your not telling me something" explains MacCormac

"We've told you all we know, Daniel" replies the Professor (Sounds serious)
"Have You?" replies MacCormac
(Looks concerned)
"I wonder?" advises MacCormac
"We've checked out your background, Professor, and history" explains MacCormac
"You'll find nothing there"
advises the Professor
"Are you married?" asks
MacCormac
"I was" advises the Professor

"Was?" asks MacCormac (Looks stunned)

"We separated, last year" explains the Professor

"Do you mind telling me, for the tape, why that happened?" asks MacCormac

A sudden knock at the Interview Room door ...
Enter Professor Lockwood's brief,
Martin Chambers ...
Sorry I'm late" advises the Solicitor
"For the benefit of the tape, Professor Lockwood's Solicitor, Martin Chambers, has entered the meeting" advises MacCormac
"What's going on?" asks the Solicitor (Looks serious)

"We're asking Professor Lockwood, a few

Questions" advises MacCormac

"Is it voluntary?" asks the Solicitor
"Entirely voluntary, Sir" replies
MacCormac
"Don't say another word"
instructs the Solicitor
"All you have is circumstantial evidence, Chief Superintendent ... my client should be allowed to go free, unless you are pressing charges" advises the Solicitor (Looks serious)
Enter, Paddy Sheridan into the meeting ...

"For the benefit of the tape, Inspector Paddy Sheridan, has entered the room" advises MacCormac
Sheridan, whispers into MacCormac's ear ...

"It has come to light, that new evidence has been found, concerning your son, Professor Lockwood" explains MacCormac (Looks serious)
"My Son?" asks the Professor (Sounds stunned)

"What is this all about, Chief Superintendent?" asks the Solicitor

"Please, bear with me, I'm just about to get to that, Sir" adds MacCormac

"Well?" asks Professor Lockwood
"It's about your other son ... Jason's twin brother" explains MacCormac
Professor Lockwood's Solicitor is suddenly overwhelmed by this new information!
"You don't deny then, that you have another son?" asks MacCormac

"No, I don't deny it" replies the Professor (Looks serious)

"Why, didn't you advise that you had twin sons, Professor?" adds MacCormac

The Professor declines to answer the Question ...

"You could have made things easier, now it's complicated" explains MacCormac

Suddenly, the Professor replies, much to the dissatisfaction of his Solicitor ...

"I take it, you've been speaking to Robin Moore?" asks the Professor

Paddy Sheridan confirms the meeting with Sir Robin Moore ...

"Yes, we've spoken to Sir Robin" advises Sheridan

"Ah ... Sir Robin" replies the Professor

"Your former wife is in a relationship with Sir Robin, and he is now the step Father of your other identical Son, Leo" explains MacCormac (Looks serious)

"I'm still his Father" advises the Professor

"That you may be, Sir, but it now puts you both in a very compromising position" explains MacCormac

"What other evidence have you, concerning my client?" asks the Solicitor

"The cryptic crosswords and DNA has led us, directly to him" advises MacCormac (shows proof)

"Does it mean, he is the murderer?" asks the Solicitor

"… and more importantly, can you prove it?" adds the Solicitor

"Sanctum Sanctorum" adds MacCormac

DEADLY ILLUSION

MacCormac and Sheridan track down identical twin, Leo Lockwood, only to find the Professor with his estranged wife.
A plot to capture the murderer is made, and they are lured into a trap!

Will the Police get their man, and does it tie into the four unsolved murders in Oxford, twenty years ago? Chief Pathologist, Mike Mortimer, contacts Chief Superintendent Daniel MacCormac ... with some startling, urgent news ...
The phone rings in MacCormac's office ...
"Mike" answers MacCormac

"I think I've found, the missing link" advises Mike

"Missing link?" replies MacCormac (Looks stunned)

"Yes, to the unsolved Oxford murders" explains Mike
"Past or present, Mike?" asks MacCormac (Looks serious)
"Both" advises Mike
"OK, Mike ... go on, you've got my attention" replies MacCormac

Meanwhile, Paddy Sheridan, tracks down, Marie Lockwood, estranged wife of Professor Simon Lockwood ...

Inspector Sheridan arrives at the home of Sir Robin Moore, where Marie Lockwood also resides. He parks his car in front of the quaint cottage and walks up to the front door. He is greeted by Mrs Marie Lockwood. She is in her late fifties, brunette, and quite attractive …

Paddy knocks on the door …

Mrs Lockwood answers …

"Inspector Paddy Sheridan, Thames Valley Police" advises Sheridan

"Come in, Inspector" advises Mrs. Lockwood

Mrs Lockwood shows Paddy Sheridan into a quaint room …

"Now, what's this all about, Inspector?" asks Mrs Lockwood

"You have twin boys, do you not?" asks Sheridan

"Yes, I do … Jason and Leo … what have they done?" asks Mrs Lockwood

"They are helping us with our inquiries" explains Paddy (Looks serious)

"Your husband" advises Paddy

"Ex-husband" replies Mrs Lockwood (Looks serious)

"What has he done?" asks Mrs Lockwood

"We're looking into the possibility of an old, unsolved investigation" explains Sheridan

"What do you know about Professor

Lockwood's past?" asks Paddy

"His past?" asks Mrs Lockwood (Looks puzzled)

"What about his past?" adds Mrs Lockwood

"We need to eliminate the Professor from our inquiries" explains Sheridan

"He was always devious, quite arrogant, if that's what you mean?" advises Mrs Lockwood (Looks serious)

"It's just a question we need to ask, Mrs Lockwood" advises Sheridan

A sudden phone call is made to Paddy Sheridan's mobile …

"Sheridan" replies Paddy

"Sir?" asks Sheridan

"Yes, I'm with Mrs Lockwood, right now, Sir" explains Sheridan

"Get her statement, Paddy, and then meet me at the White Horse, in an hour" advises MacCormac (Sounds serious)

"Yes, Sir" replies Sheridan

The Inspector concludes his interview with Mrs Lockwood and takes her statement.

Sheridan leaves the quaint cottage, jumps into his car, and makes a dash to meet the Chief Superintendent inside the White Horse pub …

MacCormac is at the bar …

"What'll you have, Sir?"
asks the Barman

"A pint of bitter" advises MacCormac

Inspector Sheridan, suddenly walks into the bar area ...

"Make that two" adds MacCormac
The pub is full of regulars and is quite noisy ...

"Is there somewhere quieter, Sir?" asks Sheridan

MacCormac and Sheridan head out into the beer garden, and find a table, away from the crowd ...
"So, Paddy ... how did you get along with Mrs Lockwood?" asks MacCormac
"She seemed a little anxious, and angry, Sir" advises Sheridan
"Angry ... a woman scorned?" adds MacCormac (Looks serious)
"She thinks her husband used her, Sir" replies Sheridan
"She was always too good for Professor Lockwood" explains MacCormac
"You know her, Sir?" asks Paddy (Looks surprised)
"Yes, she was once a colleague at University, but that was many years ago, Paddy" explains MacCormac
"And ... Lockwood?" asks Paddy
"Flinty was always quite nauseating ...never could see what she saw in him" explains MacCormac (Smiles)

"Status?" replies Sheridan

"Possibly" replies MacCormac

"Any other developments, Sir?" asks Sheridan

"Mike has found a link concerning the old unsolved murders … and today's murders" advises MacCormac (Looks serious)

"In what way, Sir?" asks Sheridan

"He's on his way to join us, Paddy" explains MacCormac

Minutes later, Chief Pathologist, Mike Mortimer joins MacCormac and Sheridan in the beer garden at the White Horse …

"I thought I'd find you in your office, Daniel" quips Mike (Smiles)

"Very funny, Mike" replies MacCormac (Smiles)

"Well, what have you found?" asks MacCormac (Looks intrigued)

Mike Mortimer begins to relay his information.

A call to Paddy Sheridan's mobile from Oxford Police Station increases the tension …

"What's happening, Paddy?" asks MacCormac

"There's been another one, Sir" advises Sheridan (Looks serious)

"Where?" asks MacCormac (Sounds serious)

"At Magdalen College" replies Sheridan

"Not another one," adds Mike

"Luckily though, this time, the victim … is alive" explains Paddy

"Sorry Mike, it'll have to wait … we'll have to

go" advises MacCormac

"Later, Dan" replies Mortimer (Looks serious)

"Mike" nods Sheridan

MacCormac and Sheridan rush to Magdalen College … there is no one at the Gate House …

The victim is coming round on the lawns of the college. They are surrounded by fellow students …

"MacCormac and Sheridan, Thames Valley Police" advises the Chief Superintendent (Looks serious)

Both flash their Police warrant identification cards …

"Did anyone see what happened?" asks MacCormac (Looks serious)

"Are you alright, Miss?" asks Sheridan (Looks concerned)

"Paddy, phone for an ambulance" advises MacCormac

"I'm alright, no ambulance" replies the young woman

"Can you remember what happened?" asks MacCormac (Looks concerned)

"I was on my way to class, when suddenly, I was grabbed from behind, by someone" explains the young woman (Looks serious)

"Anything else?" asks Paddy

"Sorry, all I remember is just coming round, now" adds the young woman

"Sir" advises Sheridan

Paddy hands the Chief Superintendent a

note left at the scene ...
It reads ... QED ... and on the back ... NOW WHAT MACCORMAC?

"QED?" asks Paddy

"It's Latin, Paddy" advises MacCormac (Looks serious)

"Latin for ... Quad Erat Demonstrandum" explains MacCormac (Looks serious)

"It means ... Quite Easily Done, Paddy" adds MacCormac

"I don't follow, Sir?" advises Sheridan

"It means, what was or is to be shown" replies MacCormac

"But your right, Paddy, in one sense it also means the proof of the argument is complete" explains MacCormac

"Hence, it's meaning ... it has been demonstrated" adds MacCormac

"What's it all leading to, Sir?" asks Paddy

"It means they are showing their prowess ... they think they have got one over us, Paddy" replies MacCormac (Looks serious)

"Where's the Gate Keeper?" asks MacCormac

"Why, Sir?" asks Sheridan

(Looks puzzled)

"He's never here" adds MacCormac

"He or She" advises Sheridan

"Right, Paddy ... it could be either, I stand corrected" replies MacCormac

"Who is usually on the Gate?" asks MacCormac (Looks serious)

Several students answer the Question ...

"Tonight, it is Mr Blancton ... but usually it's FitzGibbon" advises a student

"FitzGibbon, that rings a bell, Sir" replies Paddy (Looks puzzled)

"Yes, it ought to, Paddy ... he's the name in the frame" advises MacCormac

"I don't understand, Sir" replies Paddy

"You will, Paddy ... believe me, you will" adds MacCormac (Looks serious)

"OK, get Mike Mortimer, over here, as soon as possible" orders MacCormac

"We need to find Mr Blancton and FitzGibbon" explains MacCormac

"Wasn't FitzGibbon linked to the unsolved murders, Sir?" asks Sheridan

"Spot on, Paddy ... he was" advises MacCormac

"Talk to the college, get their addresses ... we need to move fast on this, Paddy" explains MacCormac (Looks serious)

"Sir?" replies Sheridan

Inspector Paddy Sheridan contacts the Dean of the College, and he helps with Police inquiries.

Chief Pathologist, Mike Mortimer,
rushes to the scene ...

"Daniel" shouts Mike (Smiles)

"Looks like you were right, Mike" advises MacCormac

"See if the DNA and everything else match … let me know as soon as, Mike" asks MacCormac

"And you?" asks Mortimer (Looks serious)

"We're off to arrest the murderer" advises MacCormac

"We've been duped, Paddy" explains MacCormac (Looks stunned)

"Duped, Sir?" asks Paddy (Looks puzzled)

"There are two Magdalen Colleges … one here in Oxford" advises MacCormac

"And the other?" asks Paddy (Sounds serious)

"There is also a Magdalen College … in Cambridge" explains MacCormac

"As we're both in Oxford, I suggest, we check at Cambridge" advises MacCormac

Sheridan and MacCormac make the journey along the A421 and A428 to Cambridge. It takes them over two hours to reach Magdalen College …

Both reach the Gate of the College to find, Derek Blancton in attendance.

"Mr Blancton?" asks MacCormac

"Yes" replies Blancton (Looks stunned)

"MacCormac and Sheridan, Thames Valley Police" advises MacCormac

"I take it, this is about the murders?" asks Blancton

"Yes, it is, as a matter of fact" replies Sheridan

"What do you know about, Matthew FitzGibbon?" asks MacCormac

"He's a wrong one, for sure" replies Blancton

"In what way, Sir?" asks MacCormac (Looks surprised)

The Chief Superintendent is now convinced that he is the suspect, except somehow, Professor Lockwood's name keeps cropping up in their investigation

...

MacCormac and Sheridan arrive back at Oxford Police Station ...

"Bring Professor Lockwood in for questioning, Paddy" orders MacCormac

"OK, Sir ... what about you?" asks Paddy
"I'll confront FitzGibbon" advises MacCormac

Paddy leaves the station and makes his way, by car, to see Professor Lockwood.

The Chief Superintendent goes in pursuit of FitzGibbon, and finds him in an old part of the college in Oxford.

MacCormac suddenly feels a blow to the head ... and eventually comes round, in a daze ...

"You just won't stop, will you, MacCormac?" warns a voice

"I knew it was you, FitzGibbon" replies MacCormac (Looks dazed)

"You have nothing on me" replies FitzGibbon
"We have solid evidence ... we have everything" explains MacCormac

"What if it was me?" replies FitzGibbon (Looks smug)

"It was you, admit it" adds MacCormac (Looks serious)

"OK, yes it was, and I'm not sorry. I did it all" advises FitzGibbon

"Did you get that, Paddy?" asks MacCormac
Step forward Paddy Sheridan out of
the shadows ...

"Yes, loud and clear, Sir" replies Sheridan (Looks serious)

"... and it's all been recorded on my phone" explains Paddy

"I'd say your goose is cooked ... wouldn't you?" asks MacCormac

"Take him away, Paddy" advises MacCormac

DEADLY NIGHTSHADE

Detective Chief Inspector Daniel MacCormac, now Chief Superintendent of Thames Valley Police reports directly to the Chief Constable.

Sergeant Paddy Sheridan, now an Inspector, is based in Oxford, and still an endorsement of his old mentor, the Chief Super!

When a series of poisonings take place in Oxford, concerning ATROPA BELLADONNA, also known as Deadly Nightshade, links are made to several Laboratories in the Oxford area.

MacCormac and Sheridan are assigned by the Chief Constable to find answers!

When Chief Pathologist, Mike Mortimer, comes across a deadly form and highly poisonous plant extract in the Oxford water supply, his life is put in imminent danger.

Can MacCormac and Sheridan prevent more murders, and why is the University Field Laboratory, in Oxford, chief suspect?

RECITAL

New Chamber Opera is a professional Opera company, based in Oxford. It specialises in Chamber Opera and Music Theatre, and produces rarely performed works from the Baroque era to the present.

Chief Superintendent, Daniel MacCormac, is attending one of their last performances of the Summer Baldassaire Galupi La Diavolessa (The She Devil). MacCormac is accompanied by Emily Pearson, a friend who also likes Opera.

Emily is blonde, has green eyes, tall and a former student at Oxford University ... Both meet at The Warden's Garden, New College ...

Drinks are informal and served from early evening ...

"So, what are you called, these days?" asks Emily (Smiles)

"Just call me, Dan or Daniel" replies MacCormac (Smiling)

"Thank you for inviting me, Daniel" advises Emily

"It's a pleasure, Emily, I'm so glad you accepted my invitation" adds MacCormac

"Shall we have some refreshment?" asks MacCormac

"Splendid idea, Daniel" replies Emily

"What time is the recital and opera?" asks Emily (Smiling)

"We've another half hour for socialising" explains MacCormac

"I'm so looking forward to it, Daniel" advises Emily
"Me, too, Emily" replies MacCormac

Emily and Daniel MacCormac select a glass of white wine from the Waiter service.
There is a new seating arrangement in place, and performance of the Opera takes place in a large marquee.
It's an all ticket event. Black tie and formal attire. Daniel MacCormac is in his best black and white dinner suit combo.

Emily is wearing a flowing
red gown ...

"This way, Sir/Madam"
advises an assistant
MacCormac and Emily are shown to their reserved seats in the marquee.
"I'll get a copy of the performance programme" advises MacCormac
"Do you come here often,
Daniel?" asks Emily
"Fairly frequently ... You?"
replies MacCormac
"Yes, as often as I can" advises
Emily (Smiles)

"We'll have to do this, more
often" adds Emily
"Yes, I agree, we must" replies
MacCormac
Everyone is ushered into the Marquee. The performance is about to begin, with an opening recital ...
The Narrator suddenly takes to the microphone ...

"The character of Dorina will be played by Miss Rowena Kendall, for this performance" advises the narrator (Smiling)
Being an Opera, it is also accompanied by the Conductor and Director, as well as a combo Orchestra.
The plot begins sedately, and Dorina is the first to be introduced to the captivate audience.
Suddenly, the performance is interrupted ... a woman faints in the audience.
"Call for a Doctor" asks the Director (Looks concerned)
The Theatre Doctor is quickly on the scene ...

Daniel MacCormac rushes over, and flashes
his Police warrant card.

"Is she going to be alright, Doctor?" asks
MacCormac
"We must get her to hospital" replies the Doctor (Looks serious)

"OK, I'll phone for an ambulance" assures MacCormac (Calls on mobile)
The Responder and Ambulance are quick to

arrive on the scene ...

"Sorry, Emily ... I'll have to go" advises MacCormac

"I understand, Daniel ... call me" replies Emily

The victim seems to be in a state of delirium and having hallucinations.

The ambulance transports the woman to the John Radcliffe Hospital ... blue lights flashing all the way. MacCormac follows in his gleaming white Audi Quattro ...

The Ambulance arrives at Accident and Emergency, where the woman is admitted into Hospital.

"Sorry, Sir ... are you a relative?" asks a Doctor (Looks serious)

MacCormac flashes his Police warrant card ...

"Detective Chief Superintendent Daniel MacCormac, Thames Valley Police" advises MacCormac (Looks serious)

"What's the procedure, Doctor?" asks MacCormac (Looks concerned)

"We're going to have to carry out several tests ... it could be a long wait, Chief Superintendent" advises the Doctor (Looks serious)

"OK, just inform me, if there's any change, Doctor" replies MacCormac

Several hours later, another white coated Doctor speaks to MacCormac.

"... and you are?" asks the Doctor (Looks concerned)

"Chief Superintendent Dan MacCormac, Thames Valley Police" advises MacCormac

"What's the prognosis, Doctor?" asks MacCormac (Looks intrigued)

"We believe it's a poisoning" advises the Doctor (Looks serious)

"A poisoning?" asks MacCormac (Looks stunned)

"Can you be sure ... can you be more specific, Doctor" replies MacCormac

"We've found traces of Atropa Belladonna, in her blood stream" explains the Doctor

"... and the victim?" asks MacCormac (Looks concerned)

"Just hanging on ... it was a lethal dose" advises the Doctor

"What is Atropa Belladonna?" asks MacCormac (Looks serious)

"It's commonly known as, deadly nightshade" explains the Doctor

"... and it lives up to it's name" adds the Doctor (Looks shocked)

"Will she live, Doctor?" asks MacCormac (Looks serious)

"Her life hangs in the balance ... we'll have to wait and see" adds the Doctor

"OK, Doctor ... please keep me informed ... here's my number" replies MacCormac (Sounds serious)

Next day, the Chief Superintendent is summoned into the Chief Constable's office ...

"I hear you were at the Recital, last night?" asks the Chief Constable

"Yes, I was ... with a friend, Sir" replies MacCormac (Smiles)

"I'm putting you and Sheridan on the case" explains the Chief Constable

"Sheridan" replies MacCormac (Looks intrigued)

"Your both renowned for your partnership, and we know you'll deliver results" advises the Chief Constable (Looks serious)

"We don't want a killing spree on our hands" explains the Chief Constable

"Killing spree?" asks MacCormac (Looks puzzled)

"The woman in hospital ... died this morning" advises the Chief Constable

"I'm sorry to hear that, Sir" replies MacCormac (Looks sad)

"It's now a murder investigation, Daniel" adds the Chief Constable

"If you could liaise with Inspector Sheridan, today" asks the Chief Constable

"I'll jump to it, Sir ... and keep you informed, every step of the way" assures MacCormac

"Good man" replies the Chief Constable

The Chief Superintendent links up with Inspector Sheridan at Oxford Police Station ...

"Sheridan" growls MacCormac

"Sir" replies Sheridan

"Good to see you again, Paddy ... how are you?" asks MacCormac

"Very well, Sir ... and You?" asks Sheridan
(Both shake hands)
"The same ... OK you've heard it's a poisoning we're investigating?" asks MacCormac
"Vaguely ... what exactly is deadly nightshade, Sir?" asks Sheridan
"What it sounds like, Paddy ... deadly" advises MacCormac
"It's said to be the property of the devil, meaning that anyone who eats of it's berries or drinks of it's potion will be punished ... by death" explains MacCormac (Looks serious)
"It also represents danger and betrayal" adds MacCormac

"The two most explosive elements in a murder case" advises MacCormac

"Murder?" asks Paddy (Looks stunned)
"We are investigating a murder, Paddy" replies MacCormac
"Where do we start, Sir?" asks Sheridan
"We need a pathologist report. Ask Mike to investigate and to update us as soon as he can" asks MacCormac
"Yes, Sir ... I'll contact him at once" advises Sheridan

"A young Constable knocks on the door of the Chief Superintendent's office ...

"Watkins?" growls MacCormac
"There's been another two poisonings, Sir" advises the young Constable

"Two more?" replies MacCormac (Looks shocked)
"Where, Watkins?" asks MacCormac

"In broad daylight ... inside Oxford covered Market, Sir" explains the young Constable
"OK, we're on our way" advises MacCormac

Sheridan an MacCormac arrive, almost immediately, in the gleaming white Audi

...

The murder scene has been quickly closed off to the public ...

Chief Pathologist, Mike Mortimer, is already at the scene ...

"Mike" shouts MacCormac
"Daniel" replies
Doctor Mortimer
"Hello, Paddy" adds
Mortimer "Mike"
replies Sheridan
"OK, Mike ... what have we got?" asks MacCormac (Looks serious)

The covered market is historic, and houses permanent stalls, in a large structure, located in central Oxford ...
At a Coffee shop in the hall ...

"We have a male and female, both of whom, seemed to have been poisoned" advises Mike
"Was it Atropa Belladonna?" asks MacCormac (Looks serious)

"I see you've done your homework, Dan" replies Mortimer (Looks impressed)

"Not really, Mike ... the Doctor on the case at the Open Air Opera, confirmed it" explains MacCormac
"I'll have to take some tests, but yes it appears to be so" advises Mortimer
"Naturally, Doctor" replies MacCormac
"Time of death, Mike?" asks MacCormac

"You know I can only estimate that, Dan" advises Mortimer (Looks serious)

"Well, give me your best guess, Mike" asks MacCormac
"I would say ... a couple of hours ago, no more than that" advises Mortimer
"Two hours?" asks Sheridan (Looks puzzled)
"We were only notified an hour ago" advises MacCormac (Looks also puzzled)
"That leaves an hour of unknowns" explains MacCormac
"Unknowns, Sir?" asks Sheridan

"That's because we need to fill in the blanks, Paddy" replies MacCormac

Mike Mortimer prepares to leave the scene for his Pathology Lab ...
"I'll be in touch, Dan" advises Mortimer

"We'll await your report, Mike" replies MacCormac (Nods)

Doctor Mike Mortimer, is a Home Office Pathologist. He has little respect for the Police, but is passionate about pathology.

A Police Constable has a word with Paddy Sheridan ...

"Can we re-open the market, Sir?" asks Sheridan

"Have we got everything we need, Paddy?" asks MacCormac

"Yes, Sir" replies Sheridan

"OK ... reopen the market, but keep the coffee shop closed and cordoned off ... it's a murder scene" explains MacCormac (Looks serious)

"Sir" replies Sheridan

Paddy Sheridan instructs the Police Constable to reopen the market area.

"I wonder?" thinks MacCormac (Looks intrigued)

"Sir?" replies Sheridan

"Isn't the University Field Laboratory, near here, Paddy?" asks MacCormac

"Yes, Sir ... it is" replies Sheridan (Looks puzzled)
"Why, Sir?" asks Sheridan

"We may need some advice, Paddy, regarding deadly nightshade ... and they may be able to guide us in solving the case" explains MacCormac
"Do you think it may be relevant?" asks Sheridan

"Very relevant, if we're to find the murderer, Paddy" adds MacCormac

"Yes, I think we'll pay the University Field Laboratory a call" explains MacCormac

"What they tell us could really have some bearing on the investigation, and we may need their advice should more poisonings take place" adds MacCormac

A sudden phone call to Sheridan's mobile ...

"Well, answer it, Paddy" advises MacCormac (Looks serious)

"Mike" advises Sheridan
Right, OK ... I'll inform the Chief Super" replies Sheridan
The call from the Chief Pathologist ends ...

"Well, go on, Paddy, what did Mike say?" asks MacCormac (Looks intrigued)

"Mike confirms that the poisoning of the two victims in the market had been carried out via the water system" advises Sheridan (Looks concerned)

"You mean, contaminated?" asks MacCormac

"Yes, Sir ... it appears so" replies Paddy

"We need to inform the Chief Constable, quickly ... this could easily end up as a killing spree" advises MacCormac (Looks serious)

"I'm on to it, Sir" replies Sheridan

SUSPICIONS

The media are informed, regarding the recent spate of poisonings in Oxford, by the Chief Constable. MacCormac and Sheridan find a leak at Oxford Field Laboratory and Chief Pathologist, Mike Mortimer, uncovers more, when his life is put at risk!
Somewhere in Oxford ... a meeting with the Chief Constable, and the World media is taking place ...
"Is it true, Chief Constable, that several murders have been committed in Oxford, recently?" asks a Reporter (Looks serious)
"Is there any truth, concerning the water supply, that it has been contaminated?" asks another Reporter (Looks equally serious)
"Who is leading the investigation?" asks yet another Reporter
The Chief Constable tries to duck and dive the Questioning, and he is being very tactile with his comments ...
"We have our suspicions" replies the Chief Constable (Looks concerned)
"But we are unable to give any response to who, what or wherefor, at this present time" adds the Chief Constable
"You will be notified, when we have more details" ends the Chief Constable
Meanwhile, Chief Pathologist, Mike Mortimer,

contacts MacCormac ...
"Mike" replies MacCormac
"It seems, a deadly form and highly poisonous plant extract was used in the recent cases, at the market, and in the first murder" advises Mike (Sounds serious)
"Any clues, Daniel, as to who is responsible?" asks Mortimer

"We're pursuing lots of inquiries, Mike" assures MacCormac (Looks serious)

"Maybe, I can help" replies Mike
"Go on, we're listening" advises MacCormac

Sheridan and MacCormac check out the University Field Laboratory in Oxford. Arriving at the Lab, they ask to meet Doctor Brennan.

Brennan is in his mid fifties, has brown hair, green eyes and has a positive de-meaner about him.
Brennan is a prominent Scientist, working in the field of plant extracts ... poisonous species, being a speciality!
Sheridan, MacCormac and Doctor Brennan meet in a side room.
"Doctor Brennan?" asks MacCormac (Looks serious)
"Yes, I'm Brennan" advises the Doctor

"MacCormac and Sheridan, Thames Valley Police" advises MacCormac

Both flash their Police warrant cards to the Doctor.

"We're here to ..." advises MacCormac

"Yes, I know why your here" replies Doctor Brennan

Chief Pathologist, Mike Mortimer, is suddenly taken ill at the Police Pathology Lab.
He is suspected of having a mild
form of poisoning!
A sudden call is made to Sheridan's mobile phone ...
"Sorry ... I'll have to take this" advises Sheridan

When Paddy returns, he advises that another case of poisoning, has materialised.

"Where and when, Paddy?" asks MacCormac

"In the last hour, Sir" replies Sheridan (Looks serious)

"I'm afraid, Chief Pathologist, Mike Mortimer, is the victim" adds Sheridan

"Mike?" replies MacCormac (Looks concerned)
"Why ... why Mike?" adds MacCormac

"We may need to Question you again, Doctor Brennan" advises MacCormac
"You know where to find me" replies
Doctor Brennan
Mike Mortimer is rushed to the John
Radcliffe Hospital.
Sheridan and MacCormac arrive at the complex, and are met by waiting reporters.

"We've got nothing to say" advises MacCormac (Brushes them away)

A white coated Doctor updates them ...

"Doctor Fleming" asks MacCormac
"We met several nights ago, don't you remember?" explains MacCormac
"Ah, yes ... the Police Officer" replies Doctor Fleming
"Chief Superintendent, actually" adds MacCormac (Looks serious)

"Doctor Mike Mortimer ... how is he?" asks MacCormac (Looks concerned)
"Luckily, we got to him in time" advises Doctor Fleming
"Atropa Belladonna?" asks MacCormac (Looks shocked)
"Yes, in plant extract form" replies Doctor Fleming
"Can we see him?" asks MacCormac (Looks concerned)
"He's very weak" adds Doctor Fleming
"I'm sure, Mike will see us" explains MacCormac (Looks serious)
"Very well, ten minutes, maximum" advises Doctor Fleming
"Then, you'll both have to leave" adds Doctor Fleming
"Thank you, Doctor" replies MacCormac
Sheridan and MacCormac

enter a side room.

A nurse is in attendance ...

"We're from the Police"
advises MacCormac

"It's OK, nurse ... let them in"
advises Mike

"Mike ... you had us all worried" adds MacCormac (Looks concerned)

"Don't fuss, Daniel ... you should know, I'm a tough old bird" quips Mike

"That you are, Mike ... that you are" replies MacCormac (Smiles)

"Can you remember what happened, Mike?" asks Paddy (Looks serious)

"All I remember is, someone coming into the Pathology Unit ... then the lights went out" replies Mike

"I'm not surprised, you've taken a lethal dose, Mike ... any more and you wouldn't be here" advises MacCormac (Looks serious)

"Job's comforter, as always, Paddy"
replies Mike (Smiles)

Paddy Sheridan laughs at Mike's
sense of humour.

"Ask the Chief Constable to take extreme measures, now, Daniel" asks Mike

"Remember, to be for warned is to be for armed" quips Mike

"I'll ask the Chief Constable to make the public aware of what we're dealing with, Mike ... don't worry" replies MacCormac (Looks serious)

"… and my involvement in all of this?" asks Mike (Looks puzzled)

"You were near the truth, Mike" replies MacCormac (Looks serious)

"In the wrong place at the wrong time" quips Mike

"Yes, it appears so" adds MacCormac

"We'll get a uniformed officer to keep watch" explains Paddy

"You take care, Mike" advises MacCormac

"Don't worry, I will be up and about again, in a matter of no time" replies Mike

"Thank you, Daniel" adds Mike (Shouts)

"See you soon, Mike"
advises Paddy

"Count on it" quips Mike
(Smiles)

Sheridan and MacCormac leave the Radcliffe …

"We need a breakthrough, Paddy" advises MacCormac (Looks serious)

"Any suggestions, Sir?" asks Sheridan

"Perhaps if we retrace our steps … somehow I think we've missed something" replies MacCormac (Looks puzzled)

"Missed something, in what way, Sir?" asks Sheridan

"As complex as it sounds, Paddy, the answer could be staring us right in the face" explains MacCormac

"We need to re-evaluate our way of thinking" adds

MacCormac

"Something tells me that the University Field Laboratory know more than they are letting on" advises MacCormac (Looks cautious)

"Do you think, Brennan is a suspect?" asks Paddy (Looks serious)

"Everyone is, at the moment, Paddy" adds MacCormac

"You'd better put us both down" advises MacCormac

"How far do you think they will go, Sir?" asks Sheridan

"No doubt, all the way" replies MacCormac

"We may need to set a trap to catch them, Paddy ... they are very cunning" explains MacCormac (Looks serious)

"Check other Laboratories, in the area, and in particular those who deal with Atropa Belladonna" advises MacCormac

"On to it, Sir" replies Sheridan

"Let me know when you have something, Paddy" asks MacCormac

"... and where will you be?" asks Sheridan

"You'll find me back at the Station, Paddy" adds MacCormac

A young Constable, on the beat, near the Bodleian Library, comes across a young woman, being accosted, by a man in black suit...

"Stop ... Police" shouts the young Constable

The young Officer blows his whistle ... then calls for assistance on his radio ...

"Back up required" advises the young Constable (Looks concerned)
"Broad Street, near the Bodleian Library ... a young woman has been assaulted" advises the young Constable
The Bodleian Library is the main research Library of the University of Oxford, and is one of the oldest Libraries in Europe. It is well known to Oxford scholars as "Bodley" or the "Bod".
The Bodleian operates, principally, as a Reference Library.

Paddy Sheridan returns to Oxford Police Station and begins to update Chief Superintendent, Daniel MacCormac in his office ...
"Well, Paddy ... what did you find out?" asks MacCormac

Paddy opens his black notebook and begins to reel off information concerning the investigation ...
"It appears, several Research Laboratories are linked to the University Field Laboratory, Sir" advises Sheridan (Looks serious)
"... and they all specialise in plant extract" adds Sheridan
"Very interesting, Paddy" replies MacCormac (Looks serious)
"That's not all" advises Sheridan
"Go on" adds MacCormac (Looks intrigued)

"A young woman was recently assaulted near the Bodleian Library" explains Sheridan
"That's close by, Paddy" replies MacCormac (Looks startled)
"Is she alright?" asks MacCormac (Looks concerned)
"Luckily, a young Constable saved her" explains Sheridan
"In time?" asks MacCormac
"Just in the nick of time, I'd say, Sir" advises Sheridan (Looks serious)
"She's given us a statement" adds Sheridan
"Anything else, Paddy?" asks MacCormac
"Her attacker was trying to inflict a dose of deadly nightshade, by needle" explains Paddy (Looks shocked)
"Luckily, the young Constable, heard her scream, and came to help her" adds Sheridan
"Any other witnesses, Paddy?" asks MacCormac

"Not yet, Sir, no one has come forward" advises Sheridan

"We're checking CCTV footage, right now, Sir" adds Sheridan (Looks serious)

"I think it's time we paid another visit to see the illustrious, Doctor Brennan,
Paddy" advises
MacCormac
"Tonight?" asks
Sheridan
"First thing, tomorrow morning, Paddy … get some

sleep, you look awful" adds MacCormac
"What about you, Sir?" asks Sheridan

"Just one or two things to tidy up, then I'll make my way home" advises MacCormac (Smiles)
"Fancy one for the road, Paddy?"
asks MacCormac
"Not for me, Sir" replies Sheridan
"I know what your thinking, Paddy" replies MacCormac

"Don't worry, I think I'll leave the Audi here tonight, Paddy, I'll get a taxi home" adds MacCormac (Looks serious)
Paddy Sheridan leaves Oxford Police Station
and makes his way home. A taxi arrives at the
Station for Daniel MacCormac as arranged.
"Where to, Sir?" asks the Taxi driver (Smiles)
Fifteen minutes later, the taxi arrives at the Chief Superintendent's home on the outskirts of Oxford.
"Thank you, Sir ... don't I know you?" asks the Taxi driver

"Quite Possibly" replies MacCormac (Looks intrigued)
"Good night" advises MacCormac
"Night, Sir" replies the Taxi driver

The taxi cab drives off into the distance.

MacCormac stumbles across the pebbled driveway. He fumbles with his keys and tries to open the door of his house.
Suddenly, a blow to the head. MacCormac keels over.

Unbeknown to him, a lethal dose of deadly nightshade has been injected into his left arm ...
MacCormac starts to come round ... in
John Radcliffe Hospital!
"Sir, Sir ... are you alright, Sir?" asks a voice
"Paddy ... where am I?" asks MacCormac (Looks serious)
"Don't you remember, Sir?" asks Sheridan (Looks concerned)
"If I remembered, I wouldn't be asking, would I?" replies MacCormac
"Right, that's enough of that" advises a Doctor
"Doctor?" asks MacCormac (Looks shocked)

"You are in the Radcliffe, Mr MacCormac" advises the Doctor

"Tell him, Doctor" asks Sheridan
"Tell me what, Paddy?" asks MacCormac

"Your lucky to be alive ... some would say very lucky

indeed" explains the Doctor

"If your Inspector, hadn't been passing your home" adds the Doctor

"My God, Paddy ... I owe you my life" replies MacCormac

"Good man, Sheridan" adds MacCormac (Shakes hands)

Chief Pathologist, Mike Mortimer, arrives on the scene.

"Mike?" asks MacCormac

"It looks like you've had a dose of what I've had" advises Mike

"You'll have to rest" insists another Hospital Doctor (Looks concerned)

"... but I've a murderer to catch" replies MacCormac

"Daniel ... let Paddy do it ... you can liaise with him" advises Mike

"Doctor?" asks MacCormac (Looks stunned)

"I'm afraid Mr Mortimer, is right ... it could be several weeks before you can carry on with your duty" explains the Doctor (Sounds serious)

"Several weeks ... not on your nelly" replies MacCormac

"Sheridan" shouts MacCormac

"Sir" replies Sheridan

BREAKTHROUGH

With Chief Superintendent Daniel MacCormac, now sidelined in the Radcliffe, Paddy Sheridan takes over the investigation, and finds incriminating evidence ... but is MacCormac, off the hook?
Why does the attacker, now have it in, for the Police?

Inspector Paddy Sheridan, decides to cross check, the University Field Laboratory, with other Laboratories, on the outskirts of the city.
Sheridan is astonished, at what he finds ...
Oxford City Police Station ...

"Is that the Department of Plant Science?" asks Sheridan

"Who is calling?" asks the Receptionist (Sounds inquisitive)

"Inspector Sheridan, Thames Valley Police" advises Sheridan
"I'm making several inquiries into Atropa Belladonna, and the recent murders in Oxford" explains Sheridan (Sounds serious)
"You'll need to make an appointment to see Professor Noel Chambers" advises the Receptionist
"OK, I'll be along later today" advises Sheridan
"I've made an appointment for you" explains the

Receptionist

A young Constable enters Chief Superintendent MacCormac's office ...

"I've brought this, for the Chief Super" advises the young Constable

"Sorry, no tea today lad, the Chief Super is in hospital" replies Sheridan

"I also have this for him" adds the young Constable
"What is it?" asks Sheridan (Looks intrigued)

"It arrived a few minutes ago, by courier, Sir" explains the young Constable

"OK, I'll deal with it" adds Sheridan
The Inspector opens the package in MacCormac's absence ...

A cryptic message, written on a piece of white paper is enclosed. The message reads ...

WHEN IS BELLADONNA NOT POISONOUS?
Sheridan asks the young Constable to have the note and the contents of the package checked for fingerprints.
"Let me know if the lab find anything as soon as possible?" asks Sheridan
"Yes, Sir" replies the young Constable
Meanwhile, back at John Radcliffe Hospital, MacCormac is his usual cantankerous self, and decides to discharge himself from the ward!

"You should be taking it easy, Mr MacCormac" advises a Doctor (Looks serious)

"I've got a murder investigation to solve, Doctor" replies MacCormac

"If Atropa Belladonna, was a woman, you'd treat it with care, wouldn't you?" asks the Doctor

"That's it, Doctor" advises MacCormac (Looks excited)

"A woman ... the She Devil and the Devil's plant with deadly berries" explains MacCormac (Looks serious)

"Sorry, I don't understand, Mr MacCormac" replies the Doctor (Looks puzzled)

"They are all connected ... maybe this is the breakthrough we've been looking for" advises MacCormac

"I still don't follow" replies the Doctor (Looks surprised)

"A match?" explains MacCormac

The Chief Superintendent shakes the Doctor's hand ...

"Thank you, Doctor ... for everything" adds MacCormac

"Remember, what I told you" explains the Doctor

The Chief Superintendent phones Paddy Sheridan on his mobile phone and explains his theory, and a possible breakthrough concerning the investigation.

"We need to speak to Mike ... where are you, Paddy?" asks MacCormac

"On my way to see, Professor Noel Chambers, at the Department of Plant Science" replies Sheridan

"What about you, Sir?" asks Sheridan

"Don't worry about me ... I've discharged myself from the Radcliffe" explains MacCormac

"Discharged yourself ... was that wise, Sir?" asks Sheridan (Sounds concerned)

"Don't you start, Paddy ... I've had enough of Doctor's" advises MacCormac

"I'll meet you at the Plant Science Laboratory, in half an hour" adds MacCormac

"Sir?" replies Sheridan (Sounds puzzled)

"We need Mike to accompany us" advises MacCormac

"OK, I'll pick him up" replies Sheridan

All three eventually arrive at the Department of Plant Science on the outskirts of Oxford ...

"Highly irregular, all of this, Daniel" advises Mike (Looks serious)

"It may well be, Mike ... but I think we're on to something" advises MacCormac

"Such as?" asks Mike (Looks stunned)

"A breakthrough ... don't you want to know who poisoned you?" asks MacCormac

"Yes, of course ... and why" replies Mike (Looks stunned)

Sheridan, MacCormac and Chief Pathologist, Mike Mortimer arrive at reception ...

"We're here to meet Professor Noel Chambers" advises MacCormac

"… and you are?" asks the Receptionist
"MacCormac and Sheridan, Oxford Police, Thames Valley … this is Mike Mortimer, Chief Pathologist" explains MacCormac (Looks official)
Suddenly, another voice intervenes in the conversation …

"It's alright, Samantha … they are here to see me" advises the voice

"Professor Chambers?" asks MacCormac

"Yes, I'm Doctor Chambers" advises the Professor "A woman" replies Sheridan
"I take it you were expecting, a man?" asks the Professor
"Well" replies MacCormac
"As you can see … I'm sorry to disappoint you" advises the Professor (Smiles)

"We thought Noel was a man's name?" asks MacCormac (Looks stunned)

"My name is pronounced … Noelle" explains the Professor
"That's enough, Daniel" replies Mike

A sudden call comes through on Paddy Sheridan's mobile phone …

"Sorry, I'll have to get this" advises Sheridan (Looks serious)
The Professor shows MacCormac and Mike Mortimer into her study …

"We understand you are dealing with herbaceous plants, here, in the nightshade family?" asks MacCormac (Looks inquisitive)
"Amongst others" replies the Professor

Paddy Sheridan knocks and enters the Professor's study ... he whispers into MacCormac's ear ...
"It appears we have new evidence, concerning the murders and poisonings in Oxford, Professor" advises MacCormac
"How exactly does it link to this facility, Chief Superintendent?" asks the Professor
"It links it to DNA found at the scene, and the initiated doses of poisoning" advises MacCormac (Sounds serious)

"I'm afraid you'll have to accompany us to the Station, madam" adds MacCormac (Looks serious)
"On what charge, Chief Superintendent?" asks the Professor
"Assisting us with our inquiries" replies MacCormac
"Daniel?" asks Mike
"Doctor Mortimer is keen, as I am, to know who gave us a deadly potion" explains MacCormac
"If you can help in identifying the Solanaceous plant, we would appreciate your advice" explains MacCormac (Looks official)
"OK, Chief Superintendent … I'll accompany you to the station … do I need a Solicitor, present?" asks the Professor
"Your not under any caution, madam … you are simply helping us with our inquiries" assures MacCormac
"Very well, now I understand" replies the Professor (Looks relieved)
"Doesn't Belladonna mean beautiful lady, in Latin?" asks MacCormac
"Yes, I believe it does" advises Professor Chambers
"What does that have to do, with the investigation?" asks the Professor
"Perhaps, everything, Mrs Chambers" replies MacCormac
"… and it's Miss, actually" advises the Professor

"I see ... so your not married then?" asks MacCormac (Stands corrected)

"No ... obviously not" adds the Professor
"My profession wouldn't allow any domestic issues to get in the way" explains the Professor (Looks serious)
"I'm a Scientist first, and foremost" adds the Professor

Meanwhile, at Oxford Police Station, Chief Superintendent MacCormac continues to question Professor Chambers, at length. A brief is at her side ...
A Police Constable switches on the recording machine ...

"We need to ascertain your whereabouts and your connections with Oxford Field Laboratory, Professor" asks MacCormac (Looks serious)
"My whereabouts?" replies Professor Chambers (Looks confused)
"I take it you mean, my alibi?" asks the Professor
"Putting it that way ... yes your alibi" replies MacCormac

As the Professor begins to detail her whereabouts ... Paddy Sheridan enters the room ...
"For the benefit of the recording, Inspector Paddy Sheridan, has just entered the interview room ...
Paddy whispers into MacCormac's ear ...

The Police Constable stops the recording on the

Chief Superintendent's advice.

"It seems, new evidence has come to light" advises MacCormac
"Your free to go, Miss Chambers" adds MacCormac

"Am I to understand, there are no charges, Chief Superintendent?" asks the Professor (Looks relieved)
"We may need to Question you again, Professor" explains MacCormac
"Thank you for your co-operation" adds MacCormac
Professor Noelle Chambers and her Solicitor leave the Interview room and make their way out of the Police Station.
Paddy Sheridan begins to update the Chief Superintendent ...
"I've been in contact with the Chief Constable" advises Sheridan
"What are his instructions, Paddy?" asks MacCormac
"The Chief Constable agrees. I've obtained a warrant as instructed" advises Sheridan (Shows warrant to MacCormac)
"Ask Chief Pathologist, Mike Mortimer, to join us at Oxford Field Laboratory" advises MacCormac
The Police Laboratory informs MacCormac that deadly nightshade ranks amongst the most poisonous plants in Europe.
All parts of the plant are poisonous, they contain tropane alkaloids!

On arrival at the Laboratory, MacCormac and

Sheridan are waiting in Reception to see Doctor Brennan.

After a rigorous check, it appears that Brennan and Chambers were not only Scientists of Plant extract but were also more than just friends!

Doctor Brennan walks into the Reception area to greet the Police.

"This way, Chief Superintendent" asks Doctor Brennan

"Well, what can I do for you, this time?" asks Brennan (Sounds annoyed)

"I take it you know, Professor Noelle Chambers?" asks MacCormac

"Yes, we know each other ... we both work together in Plant Extracts" explains Brennan

"... Atropa Belladonna?" asks MacCormac (Looks serious)

"Yes, amongst others, Chief Superintendent" replies Brennan

"Deadly Nightshade?" adds MacCormac

"Yes, it's compounds are poisonous" explains Brennan

Doctor Mike Mortimer, arrives in Reception and joins the meeting ...

"We've met before, haven't we, Doctor Brennan?" asks Mike (Looks serious)

"Sorry, I don't recall" replies Brennan (Looks sheepish)

"... but I remember you, and Miss Chambers" advises Mike

"Are you still working on a Scientific breakthrough?" asks Mike

"Scientific breakthrough?" asks Brennan (Looks stunned)

"Please, enlighten us, Doctor" asks MacCormac

Professor Chambers, enters the room ...

"Please join us, Professor" greets MacCormac

"Doctor Brennan was just about to tell us about a Scientific breakthrough" advises MacCormac

"Please, go on, Doctor" adds MacCormac (Looks serious)

"I don't have to" replies Brennan

"Why?" asks MacCormac (Looks cautious)

Brennan, pulls out a gun, from under his jacket ...

"Ah ... now I see" replies MacCormac

"I take it, money is the motivator, in all of this?" asks MacCormac

"You'll never know now, Chief Superintendent" advises Brennan

Paddy Sheridan tries to catch the Doctor off guard ...

"Stand back" orders Brennan

"Why Ben, why?" asks Professor Chambers (Looks stunned)

"It's the only way ... my experiments ... all my achievements" replies Brennan

"Your warrant is useless, MacCormac" adds Brennan
"We know, you were the perpetrator, Doctor Brennan" replies MacCormac
"Tropane alkaloid is related to Cocaine, and Scopolamine ... they are both notorious for their psychotic effects" explains MacCormac
"It's true, Brennan" advises Mike

"Their pharmacological properties can act as a stimulant" explains Mike Mortimer
"We found all of this in the Pathology Lab ... it had to come from here" explains MacCormac
"The death's were regrettable" advises Brennan

"... and the Devil's extract?" asks MacCormac (Looks serious)
"Something that went wrong" adds
Brennan
"... and the She Devil?" adds
MacCormac
"That'll be me, Chief Superintendent" replies Professor Chambers
"Professor Chambers ... who else?" asks MacCormac

STAND OFF

With MacCormac, Sheridan and Doctor Mike Mortimer, backed into a corner at the Oxford Field Laboratory ... Brennan takes to the roof and holds MacCormac hostage ... can Paddy Sheridan save the day?

Professor's Brennan and Chambers confirm their plot ...

"It's true, Ben and I, are lovers" advises Professor Chambers (Looks serious)

"Why the experiment with Atropa Belladonna?" asks MacCormac

"It was never meant to cause harm" replies Brennan

"... but it's a notorious poisonous extract" explains MacCormac

"You may call it that ... we were experimenting with life and death" adds Professor Chambers (Looks serious)

"You caused the deliberate deaths of several members of the public, all in the realms of dealing with science" advises MacCormac (Looks angry)

Armed Police Officers arrive on the scene at Oxford Field Laboratory, with the Chief Constable ...

The area is quickly
cordoned off ...

Brennan becomes
edgy ...

"The She Devil was the fruit of the berries" explains Brennan

"It was our code for the extract" advises Professor Chambers (Looks serious)

"You see I was never the She Devil … that was in your mind" explains Professor Chambers

"I knew you were trying to foil the Police" adds the Professor

"MacCormac?" asks Mike

"Very clever … you planned a take over?" advises MacCormac

"… but why use the water supply?" asks Mortimer (Looks puzzled)

"That was an error of judgement" replies Professor Chambers

"We were meant to flush it away, but somehow it entered the water supply" adds Brennan

"It was an accident … an unfortunate accident" explains Brennan

"Except for one thing" replies MacCormac (Looks serious)

"What do you mean?" asks Brennan

"One of your ex-partners is alive, Doctor" advises MacCormac

Brennan wonders who it can be …
Enter, Rowena Kendall …

"Hello, Ben" advises Rowena (Smiles)

"The actress?" asks Paddy Sheridan

"Yes, Paddy ... and funnily enough, she played the part of the She Devil, at an Opera I recently attended" advises MacCormac (Looks serious)
"There was a link" explains MacCormac
"Clever, MacCormac ... bravo" adds Brennan (Claps)

"So now, there's three in the equation?" asks Sheridan (Looks puzzled)

"Three?" asks Mike (Looks equally puzzled)
"Sir?" replies Sheridan

"Yes, Doctor Brennan, Professor Chambers ... and Miss Kendall" replies MacCormac
"Daniel, I'm confused" advises Mike

"You, soon won't be, Mike ... bear with me" replies MacCormac

"Miss Kendall was not only a gifted actress, but an ex-student of Professor Brennan" explains MacCormac
"I was, much more than that Chief Superintendent" replies Miss Kendall
Suddenly, the Chief Constable enters the room ...
"I take it, your the man in charge?" asks Brennan

"Well, the Chief Superintendent is actually in charge of the Investigation, but I am in overall command, if that's what you mean?" asks the Chief Constable

"What about a deal?" asks Brennan (Sounds serious)
"We don't do deals, Sir ... we're the Police" advises MacCormac (Sounds serious)

"The evidence is clear, your are the perpetrator" adds MacCormac

"Why, Doctor Brennan ... why?" asks the Chief Constable

"Ask MacCormac, he has all the answers" replies Brennan

"No more Questions" advises Brennan

"May I remind you, I hold the balance of power" adds Brennan (Shows the gun)

Doctor Brennan orders Chief Superintendent MacCormac to walk in front of him, out of the room ...

"Remember, MacCormac, I have a gun on you" advises Brennan

MacCormac is told to climb several flights of stairs on to the roof ...

MacCormac looks over the edge of the building ...

"It's a long drop to the ground ... six flights up" explains Brennan

The Chief Superintendent is clearly petrified ...

Several Police cars are below in the grounds, blue lights flashing ...

"Come on, MacCormac ... over here, where I can see you" orders Brennan

The Chief Superintendent is dragged across the roof by Doctor Brennan ...

"What's the matter, Chief Superintendent, are you afraid your going to die?" asks Brennan

MacCormac doesn't reply, but begins to sweat profusely ...
"You are ... I believe your afraid of dying" adds Brennan
"Well, this is your day" explains Brennan
"My day, for what?" asks MacCormac

"For the truth, Chief Superintendent ... the truth, and for the reckoning" replies Brennan

"It's you and me, against the World, MacCormac" explains Doctor Brennan

"Your mad, Brennan ... quite mad" answers MacCormac

"Who are you working for?" asks MacCormac

"For me ... I'm working for me, MacCormac" advises Brennan

"Now, I have you" adds Brennan (Looks serious)

"Your up here, all alone ... and there's nothing you can do about it" laughs Brennan

Suddenly, another voice is heard, on a speaker ...

"Come down, Doctor Brennan ... it's all over" advises the Chief Constable

"If I go, MacCormac will too" replies Brennan (Shouts)

Paddy Sheridan is now, somewhere near the top of the roof, and has been given explicit instructions by the Chief Constable to bring Brennan and MacCormac down, in one piece ...

"Remember, tread carefully, Paddy" advises the Chief Constable

"Sir?" asks Sheridan

"You know how, MacCormac can be, in this situation" explains the Chief Constable (Looks concerned)

"Oh, yes ... I know, Sir" replies Sheridan

"Don't worry, I'll get them both down" advises Sheridan

Paddy Sheridan begins to climb the stairs to the top of the roof ...

MacCormac is pinned down ... while Doctor Brennan is parading around ...
The Chief Superintendent can see that Paddy Sheridan is now on the roof, and he tries to keep Doctor Brennan's attention ...
"Think man, your not going to achieve anything up here" advises MacCormac
"Why did you poison all those people?" asks MacCormac

"I told you, it was a mistake, MacCormac ... the extract entered the water system ... I couldn't retract it" replies Brennan (Looks serious)
"You can claim diminished responsibility for all your actions" explains MacCormac
"They'll call me a mad man, MacCormac" advises Brennan (Laughs)
"Then prove your not mad, and do the right thing" adds MacCormac
The Chief Constable is now speaking on a loud hailer ...
"Doctor Brennan, we have someone here who wants to talk to you" advises the Chief Constable
Step forward, Professor Noelle Chambers ...

"Please do as the Police ask, darling" advises the Professor

"It's too late ... far too late" replies

Brennan (Shouts)
Paddy Sheridan lies in wait on the roof, for the right moment and opportunity to catch Doctor Brennan off guard.
MacCormac nods to Sheridan ...

Suddenly, Paddy Sheridan decides
to make his move ...

"It's all over, Doctor Brennan"
advises Sheridan
"Reinforcements ... maybe you will be saved after all, MacCormac?" advises Doctor Brennan
"Come on, Sir, do the right thing ... let the Chief Superintendent, go" asks Sheridan
" ... your playing mind games, Inspector Sheridan" replies Brennan
"There are no mind games, Doctor Brennan" advises MacCormac
"It's the right thing to do" explains MacCormac
"This is the day, MacCormac" replies Brennan
"The day?" asks Sheridan

"The day, and hour of shadows" adds Doctor Brennan

"What do you mean, Doctor Brennan?" asks MacCormac

"Now is the hour, the time for the truth" adds Brennan
The Chief Constable is growing anxious and looking for alternatives ...
Suddenly another voice, enters ...

"He'll come down for me"
advises the voice
"Miss Kendall?" asks the Chief
Constable
"Just, do as I ask" advises
Rowena Kendall
"Miss Kendall/Miss Chambers ... what's going on?" asks Paddy Sheridan
"Don't you see, a love tryst, Paddy" advises MacCormac
A love tryst is a meeting arranged by lovers, especially a secret one. It is an agreement/pact to meet at a time and place. It can also mean the coming together of several individuals.
"A pact" adds MacCormac
(Looks serious)
"Pact?" asks Sheridan (Looks
stunned)
"Yes, between the Devil and the She Devil" explains MacCormac
"So, there was more than one of them?" asks Sheridan
"Yes, Paddy ... there was always more than one" advises MacCormac

"You see, it's quite true, when they say ... the devil is in the detail, isn't that right Doctor Brennan?" explains MacCormac
" ... and the deadly nightshade?" asks Sheridan (Looks puzzled)
"Atropa Belladonna was a lethal potion" adds

MacCormac
"... and all of it links together" advises MacCormac
"Bravo ... Chief Superintendent ... bravo" replies Doctor Brennan
"You think your so clever, don't you?" asks Brennan
Doctor Brennan points the revolver at the Chief Superintendent ... then on himself!
Doctor Brennan squeezes the trigger, falls back from the fatal gunshot saying ...
"I'm sorry" advises Brennan
Doctor Brennan falls over the side of
the building ...
Paramedics and several Ambulances
arrive at the scene.
Doctor Brennan is pronounced dead.
"Are you alright, Sir?" asks
Paddy Sheridan
"I'll live" replies MacCormac
"Is there anything, I can you for you, Sir?" asks Paddy

"Just get me off this roof, back to ground level, Paddy" asks MacCormac

Sheridan grabs hold of the Chief Superintendent and guides him back down the flights of stairs to ground level, where he is greeted by the Chief Constable ...

"Are you alright, Chief Superintendent?" asks the Chief Constable
"As I said to, Sheridan ... I'll live, Sir" replies MacCormac

"A very unsavoury state of affairs, Daniel"

advises the Chief Constable

"Very, Sir" advises MacCormac

"So many people dead, all because of a mad man" explains MacCormac

"Sadly, there are mad men, everywhere" replies the Chief Constable

Chief Pathologist, Mike Mortimer, arrives on the scene ...

"Are you alright, Dan?" asks Mortimer (Looks concerned)

"Stop fussing, Mike" replies MacCormac

"What about, if I buy you a drink?" asks Mike

"That'll be a first, Mike" replies MacCormac (Smiles)

"Will you join us, Paddy?" asks MacCormac

"Don't mind if I do, Sir" replies Sheridan

THE PLETHRON CONNECTION

Detective Chief Inspector Daniel MacCormac, now Chief Superintendent of Thames Valley Police, reports directly to the Chief Constable.

Sergeant Paddy Sheridan, is now an Inspector in Oxford, but is still an endorsement of his old mentor, the Chief Super!

When a murder is committed in Oxford, all roads lead to a suspect within closed doors!

A riddle of texts are found at the murder scene, prompting the Chief Constable to put MacCormac and Sheridan on the case, to decipher their meaning.

A pattern emerges, when the Chief Superintendent, links the murder to a Greek tragedy, and the four texts of Socrates!

The investigation leads MacCormac and Sheridan to College ... and it involves ... Euripides, Aristophanes, Socrates and Sophocles, which are all connected to the murder!

Will the Chief Superintendent, and Sheridan, identify the murderer, and why are mystic Greek tragedies involved?

Are they the answers, to the crime?

It turns out to be MacCormac's most complicated investigation.

CONNECTION

Similarities, between the trial of Socrates, and the trial of Jesus, have been discussed, since the age of, the Apologists!

Daniel, a first degree student at Magdalen College, is attending an Evening of Greek Philosophy, with fellow student, Emma, and several College friends.

The new Dean of Divinity at the College, is Reverend Doctor Steven Naylor.

The renowned Oxford educated Doctor is now on stage, reciting to the students

...

"I am extremely happy to announce, that I will be joining Magdalen College, as the next Dean of Divinity" advises Doctor Naylor (Smiles)
Applause from students ...

"The College has an extraordinary history of excellence, across the spectrum of academic scholarships" adds Doctor Naylor
"The Chapel has been the heart of the College, for generations" explains Doctor Naylor (Looks pleased)
"I will try to ensure it remains a place of welcome, worship, lively discussion and pastoral care" advises Doctor Naylor (Sounds serious)
More applause from students ...

"I am a firm admirer of the philosophy of Socrates. He believed that it was impossible, for anyone, to engage in behaviour that was wrong. Socrates believed, a person must have thought he was doing right" explains Doctor Naylor (Looks serious)

After the meeting, the new Dean, invites all the students into the Main Hall. Doctor Naylor, momentarily, leaves the room.

Several students, including Daniel, rush forward into another room where they make a grisly find!

Emma is on the floor, face down,
motionless. Suddenly, a moan
from someone in a dark corner …

It's Doctor Naylor … with a large knife in his hands … and on his face, an expression of despair …

"My God … get the Dean" asks a student (Shouts)

"… but the Dean?" replies another student (Looks concerned)

"No … Doctor Morris … fetch him at once" adds yet another student

The Police are called, and they quickly arrive on the scene.

A number of texts are found, written on several sheets of paper …

The Police are baffled, by the evidence, left at the scene.

The Chief Constable instructs Chief Superintendent, Daniel MacCormac to investigate …

"Sir, I'll leave for the scene, at once" advises MacCormac (Looks serious)

"Paddy Sheridan, is already at the scene, Daniel" advises the Chief Constable

"Sheridan?" asks MacCormac

"I'd like you both to work on this, Daniel" adds the Chief Constable

"It's sensitive, so remember to tread carefully" explains the Chief Constable

"Yes, Sir … don't worry, we'll use the kid gloves approach" replies MacCormac

The Chief Superintendent jumps into his gleaming white Audi and arrives quickly on the scene, at Magdalen College.

MacCormac joins Paddy Sheridan, in the Main Hall …

"Paddy" advises MacCormac (Both shake hands)

"Sir" replies Sheridan (Looks stunned)

"We've been drafted in by the Chief Constable, Paddy" explains MacCormac

"OK, what have we got?" asks MacCormac (Looks serious)

Paddy Sheridan shows Chief Superintendent MacCormac the texts and a witness advises how they saw the new Dean, holding a knife, over the body.

"Damn peculiar, this, Paddy" advises MacCormac (Looks shocked)

"What do you make of it?" asks MacCormac

"All roads, lead to Socrates" replies Sheridan (Looks puzzled)

"Socrates ... a bit high brow for you isn't it, Paddy?" asks MacCormac
"What has a Greek Philosopher, got to do with this?" adds MacCormac
Paddy Sheridan shows MacCormac the texts ...
"Ah ... now I see" replies MacCormac (Looks surprised)

"What is the link between now and Socrates, Sir?" asks Sheridan (Looks baffled)

"Socrates belonged to a time when Athens was moving through a phase of transition, Paddy" explains MacCormac (Looks clever)

"With uncertainty about the future" adds MacCormac

"What does it have to do with the murder?" asks Paddy (Looks puzzled)

"That's what we've got to find out, Paddy" replies MacCormac
"How?" asks Sheridan (Looks puzzled)

"The Chief Constable has asked us to tread lightly on this case, Paddy" advises MacCormac (Looks serious)
"Where's the suspect?" asks MacCormac
"I'm afraid ..." replies Sheridan
"Go on, Paddy ... spit it out" adds MacCormac (Looks concerned)
"He's under protection" advises Sheridan
"Protection ... by whom?" asks

MacCormac (Looks stunned)
"He's behind closed doors, Sir" explains Paddy
"Don't tell me he's got diplomatic immunity" asks MacCormac
"In a way, he has, Sir" advises Sheridan

"That's preposterous" adds MacCormac (Looks annoyed)

" ... he was in possession of the murder weapon" explains MacCormac

The Chief Constable arrives on the scene ...
"Chief Superintendent" bellows
the Chief Constable
"Sir?" replies MacCormac
"I warned you about treading carefully" advises the Chief Constable (Sounds serious)

"Look at the evidence ... I'm sure you'll be able to decipher clues from the texts, Daniel" adds the Chief Constable (Looks serious)
"We need to Question the suspect, Sir"
replies MacCormac
"All in good time, Daniel" advises the
Chief Constable
"You need to think logically, on this one" explains the Chief Constable
"Sir?" asks MacCormac (Looks baffled)
"We have to work within the legal boundaries, Daniel" adds the Chief Constable
"The suspect is under restrain ... he's going no where" advises the Chief Constable (Looks serious)
"Now, get the evidence we need, to lock him away, Daniel" explains the Chief Constable
"What's the connection?" asks the Chief Constable

"Socrates, and the words of the text, all lead to a cover up" replies MacCormac

"Cover up?" replies the Chief Constable (Looks

puzzled)

"Doctor Naylor, is a man of the cloth" advises the Chief Constable

"Now, I see, why we have to tread carefully, Sir" replies MacCormac

"Indeed ... he is protected by the hierarchy of the Church" adds the Chief Constable (Looks concerned)

"Church?" asks MacCormac

"The Church of England, Daniel" replies the Chief Constable

"We'll need special dispensation to gain admittance" advises the Chief Constable

"From, whom, Sir?" asks MacCormac (Looks suspicious)

"The Arch Bishop of Canterbury" explains the Chief Constable

"Now, I see the need for diplomacy, Sir" replies MacCormac

"I'm sorry, Daniel ... but our hands are tied, but I'll get on to it ... let me know when you have anything regarding the texts" advises the Chief Constable

"Dan" says the Chief Constable on leaving the scene

"Sir" replies MacCormac

The Chief Constable is driven away from Magdalen College ...

MacCormac and Sheridan, decide to decipher the texts, back at Oxford Police Station ...

The Chief Superintendent looks puzzled at the texts,

but soon comes to a conclusion ...
"We've been deceived, Paddy" advises MacCormac (Looks serious)
"Sir?" asks Sheridan (Looks puzzled)
"The wording is not a text, but part of the seven Greek Tragedy plot outlines" explains MacCormac
"They are over views" adds MacCormac (Sounds serious)

"What do they have to do with the murder?" asks Sheridan

"Perhaps nothing ... perhaps everything" replies MacCormac
"Someone wants to lead us on into a suppliant of meanings" explains MacCormac (Looks serious)
"I don't get it, Sir?" replies Sheridan (Looks puzzled)

"Neither do I, Paddy ... but somehow, they are all connected" adds MacCormac

"The real murderer left them, at the scene" explains MacCormac
"The real murderer?" asks Sheridan

"Are you saying that Doctor Naylor, may not be the one?" adds Sheridan

"Maybe, Paddy ... maybe" advises MacCormac (Looks cautious)
"What happened at Magdalen College was merely a diversion, as to the real murderer" explains MacCormac
"... and Doctor Naylor?" asks Paddy (Looks serious)

"We'll need to Question him, of course ... but I doubt whether he is the one we're looking for" adds MacCormac

"Have the documents checked for DNA, Paddy" asks MacCormac

The Chief Superintendent hands over the texts in their clear plastic wallets to Paddy Sheridan.

"I doubt whether it will match Doctor Naylor" advises MacCormac

"And?" asks Sheridan

"I'll let you know, when the Chief Constable gives us the go ahead ... I'll brief him on our thoughts" explains MacCormac (Look serious)

"Paddy" shouts MacCormac

"Sir?" replies Sheridan

"We'll need to speak to the deceased's friend, Daniel" asks MacCormac

"To eliminate him from our inquiries?" asks Sheridan

"Yes, also the Dean of the College" adds MacCormac (Looks serious)

"I'm on to it, Sir" replies Sheridan

"Wait till morning, Paddy ... let them stew over things tonight" advises MacCormac

"We'll both have clear heads, tomorrow" adds MacCormac

"My office, 9am sharp" advises MacCormac

"Sir" replies Paddy

The Chief Superintendent and Paddy leave Oxford Police Station, and go their separate ways, but unbeknown to them, they are being watched by a possible suspect ...

Will Chief Superintendent MacCormac crack this complicated investigation? The answer lies in possible Greek tragedies, and they may well point the way to the murderer!

A BRILLIANT DEDUCTION

As the Chief Constable gives permission for MacCormac and Sheridan to question Doctor Naylor, a dramatic chain of events brings forward another Greek tragedy ... does MacCormac find blood on the hands of yet another suspect?

Thames Valley Police HQ, Chief Superintendent Daniel MacCormac's office ...

"Good morning, Sir" greets Sheridan

"Morning, Paddy" greets MacCormac

"Any thoughts regarding the investigation, Paddy?" asks MacCormac

"Somehow, Greek tragedies are involved" advises Sheridan

"Your not wrong, Paddy ... your not wrong" replies MacCormac

The phone begins to ring in the Chief Superintendent's office ...

It's the Chief Constable ...

"I'll get the coffee's, Sir" advises Sheridan (Smiles)

"Stay, Paddy" replies MacCormac

The Chief Superintendent is on the phone for several minutes, then suddenly puts the phone down ...

"Well?" asks Paddy

"OK, we're clear to investigate, and question,

Doctor Naylor" advises MacCormac (Looks serious)

"Has the Chief Constable pulled a few strings, Sir?" asks Sheridan

"I would say so ... but we still have to tread carefully, Paddy" explains MacCormac
The Chief Superintendent, suddenly, jumps out of his chair ...
"Where next, Sir?" asks Sheridan
"Magdalen College ... there's no time like the present, Paddy" replies MacCormac
The Chief Superintendent and Paddy Sheridan leave the Police Station, and jump into MacCormac's gleaming white Audi Quattro.
Both proceed to Magdalen College ... where they are granted access to see Doctor Naylor.
Magdalen, pronounced Maudlen, has some of the most beautiful buildings in Oxford. Some of the buildings are new, while others are ancient. The College is set in a hundred acres of grounds, which include the deer park, and Addison's riverside walk.
It houses an undergraduate body of about four hundred students. The College is also conveniently located, about ten minutes from the high street, and a ten minute walk from the town centre, University Libraries and the Science area.
In a secluded meeting room ... Doctor Naylor enters, with his Secretary ...
"Good morning, Doctor Naylor" greets MacCormac (Flashes warrant card)

"My name is Detective Chief Superintendent, Daniel MacCormac, this is Inspector Sheridan" advises MacCormac (Sheridan flashes warrant card)

"I take it, you've been briefed by the Chief Constable?" asks MacCormac

"Yes, both the Chief Constable and the Arch Bishop" replies Doctor Naylor

"If we may question you, under caution, Sir?" replies MacCormac

"I understand, Chief Superintendent" advises Doctor Naylor

"What exactly happened, last night?" asks MacCormac (Looks serious)

"Can you give us your views on the situation?" adds MacCormac

Doctor Naylor ponders the question, then gives his response ...

"I really can't remember, Chief Superintendent" advises Doctor Naylor

"Try, man, try" replies MacCormac

"I was giving a lecture to the students ... I left the room, the next thing I was in a trance" adds Doctor Naylor

"A trance?" asks Sheridan (Looks puzzled)

"You were found, holding the murder weapon that killed Emma Lloyd" explains MacCormac (Looks serious)

"Don't you remember, Doctor Naylor?"
asks MacCormac

"Sir?" reminds Sheridan
"Alright, Paddy" replies MacCormac

"I think that's quite enough, Chief Superintendent" advises Doctor Naylor's Secretary (Looks anxious)
"We are in the middle of a very serious murder investigation" explains MacCormac (Looks concerned)
"Someone seems to be mimicking Greek tragedies" advises MacCormac
"Greek tragedies?" replies Doctor Naylor (Looks puzzled)
"In what way, Chief Superintendent" asks Naylor

"As a way of identity, and connection to the investigation" adds MacCormac

"We are being left a trail of written texts ... they obviously mean something" explains MacCormac
"What?" asks Doctor Naylor

"That's what I intend to find out. Somehow they are all connected" adds MacCormac
The Chief Superintendent continues to push Doctor Naylor for answers ...
"Are you a teacher of Greek Mythology, Doctor Naylor?" asks MacCormac
"No ... my role is as Dean of Divinity at the College" advises Doctor Naylor
"I know nothing about Greek tragedies or mythology" explains Naylor
"Is that all, Chief Superintendent?" asks Doctor Naylor's Secretary

"Yes, that's all for now, Doctor Naylor ... but we may need to question you again sometime ... if only to eliminate you from our inquiries" explains MacCormac

"I understand" replies Doctor Naylor

MacCormac and Sheridan leave the meeting, and begin walking across the University campus ...

"Well, what do you think, Sir?" asks Sheridan

"He's not our man, Paddy" replies MacCormac
"But all the evidence, points to him" explains Sheridan

"Circumstantial, it's not conclusive, Paddy" replies MacCormac (Looks serious)

"... and the knife?" asks Sheridan
"Have we had the results back from the Lab?" asks MacCormac
"I'll get on to it, Sir" replies Sheridan
"What do you think?" adds Sheridan (Looks suspicious)

"I doubt it will link, Doctor Naylor, to the murder, Paddy" advises MacCormac

Sheridan and MacCormac return to Oxford Police Station.
The results are in concerning the murder weapon ...
Paddy Sheridan updates the Chief Superintendent ...
"Well, Paddy?" asks MacCormac (Sounds serious)

"It's come back ... negative, Sir" replies Sheridan (Looks surprised)
"See, Paddy ... I told you" advises MacCormac (Looks smug)
"How did you know?" asks Sheridan

"A simple case of deduction ... Doctor Naylor was set up, by fear" explains MacCormac
"You mean, he may have seen the real murderer?" asks Sheridan

"I'd say so ... but he froze in fear, and the real culprit left him at the scene of the crime" adds MacCormac
"To carry the can?" replies Sheridan

"Well, yes, Paddy ... as you put it, to carry the can" replies MacCormac

A sudden knock on the Chief Superintendent's door ... A young Constable enters, with the morning mail ...

One envelope is personally addressed to, Chief Superintendent MacCormac.

Paddy Sheridan passes the envelope carefully to his boss ...

The envelope contains another written text.

It reads as follows ...

"The trial of Socrates focusing on four major works of Ancient Greek Literature particularly on his trial, defence, and the charges against him" advises MacCormac (Looks puzzled)
"I don't get it, Sir?" replies Sheridan

"We're being taunted, Paddy ... by the real killer"

explains MacCormac

"You need to have a fundamental understanding on the thoughts of Socrates, in relation to the truth" adds MacCormac (Sounds serious)

"So, if the real murderer isn't Doctor Naylor … who is it?" asks Sheridan

"Pearls before swine … Plato and Aristophanes" advises MacCormac

"What, two murderers" asks Sheridan (Looks baffled)

"No, Paddy … an apology of Socrates" explains MacCormac

"Now, you've lost me, Sir?" adds Sheridan (Looks stunned)

"Find the answer of the four texts … and we find our killer" adds MacCormac

"Where?" asks Sheridan

"Behind closed doors" advises MacCormac

"Magdalen College?" asks Sheridan

"We need hard evidence, Paddy" adds MacCormac

"What else do we have to go on?" asks MacCormac

"I believe the Lab have done a DNA test on Emma Lloyds clothing, Sir" advises Sheridan

Another knock at the Chief Superintendent's door …

Enter, Chief Pathologist, Mike Mortimer

"Daniel" greets Mike (Smiles)

"Mike, what have you found out?" asks MacCormac (Looks serious)

"Let me get in the door, won't you?" replies Mike (growls)
Paddy Sheridan smirks ...

"It's not meant to be funny, Paddy"
adds MacCormac

"Sorry, Sir" replies Sheridan
"OK, Mike ... " asks MacCormac
The Chief Pathologist starts to go into raptures ...

"Can we have the simple version, in plain English, Mike?" asks MacCormac

"Well, DNA was found on the girl's clothing, which doesn't match her own" advises Mike Mortimer
"Possibly the killer?" asks
MacCormac
"Possibly" replies Mike (Looks concerned)
"We need to find a match" advises
Paddy Sheridan
"That we do, Paddy" replies
MacCormac
"Find the match, and I suspect you'll find your killer, Daniel" explains Mike
"Thanks, Mike ... we'll bear that in mind" quips MacCormac
"These damn Greek tragedies are somehow

connected, Paddy" explains MacCormac (Looks shocked)
"We need to question the Dean" advises MacCormac
"Doctor Naylor?" asks Sheridan
"No, Paddy ... the Dean of the College" explains MacCormac
"We may find some answers there" adds MacCormac
"Do some digging, Paddy" asks MacCormac
"Sir?" asks Sheridan

"If we look closer, Paddy ... there our treasure will be found" advises MacCormac (Smiles)
"On my way ... I'll let you know when I have something, Sir" replies Sheridan
Several hours later, Paddy Sheridan finds out that Latin and Greek are both taught at Magdalen College in a Socrative style.
The Sub Dean is Anthony Summerscales.

Paddy Sheridan reports back to the Chief Superintendent ...

"Well, what have you found out, Paddy?" asks MacCormac

Sheridan opens his black note book and begins to read from it.
"The Sub Dean is one Anthony Summerscales ... and that's not all, Sir" replies Sheridan
"Go on, Paddy" advises MacCormac (Looks intrigued)

"He offers courses at Magdalen College in Latin and Greek" replies Sheridan

"As in Socrates style, and seminar discussions" explains Sheridan
"Socrates ... Paddy?" asks MacCormac

"Look for gold and there you'll treasure find?" adds Sheridan

Suddenly, the Chief Superintendent jumps out of his chair ...
"That's it, Paddy ... the connection" advises MacCormac (Looks pleased)
"Right, we need to question the Sub Dean again, he may be able to help us" explains MacCormac
Sheridan and MacCormac arrive back at Magdalen College and walk up to the Gate Keeper's Lodge ...
"We're here to see Doctor Summerscales" advises MacCormac
Sheridan and MacCormac flash their Police warrant cards ...

"Chief Superintendent MacCormac and Inspector Sheridan" advises MacCormac

"Thames Valley Police" adds Sheridan
The Gate Keeper allows entry into the College grounds ...

"Across the yard and in the next building" points the Gate Keeper

"Thank you" replies MacCormac
"Paddy, be prepared for surprises" advises MacCormac (Looks anxious)

"Surprises?" asks Sheridan (Looks puzzled)
"Anything, out of the ordinary, Paddy"
adds MacCormac
"Understood, Sir" replies Sheridan
MacCormac and Sheridan knock and enter Doctor Summerscales study, to find him seated, reading over several College Lecture assignments.
"Doctor Summerscales?" asks MacCormac

"Yes, I'm Summerscales, how can I help you" replies the Sub Dean

"Detective Chief Superintendent MacCormac, and Inspector Sheridan ... Thames Valley Police" advises MacCormac (Both flash their Police warrant cards)
"What can I do for you, gentlemen?"
asks the Sub Dean
Paddy Sheridan notices a bust of
Euripides on a side board.
"I see that you are a tutor of Greek tragedies, Sir?" asks MacCormac

"Yes, I am ... as you see, Euripides along with Aeschylus and Sophocles ... I am a scholar of Mythology" replies the Sub Dean (Sounds serious)
"So, I see, Doctor Summerscales" adds MacCormac

"How can I help you, Chief Superintendent?" asks the Sub Dean

"We're investigating the murder, of one of your students ... Emma Lloyd" explains MacCormac
"Murder?" asks the Sub Dean (Looks stunned)
"Did you teach her ... and did you know her, Sir?" asks Sheridan

"I teach many students here at Magdalen … but yes, it is possible, she was one of my students" replies the Sub Dean (Looks sheepish)
"Possible?" asks MacCormac

"I can't be certain" replies Doctor Summerscales

"You, do have, records, Sir?" asks MacCormac
"Can you tell me your whereabouts, the night before last?" adds MacCormac
"Yes, I was attending a Lecture, here at the College" advises the Sub Dean
"Were you in attendance, on the evening, of the murder?" asks Sheridan
"You mean, was I in the same meeting?" replies the Sub Dean
"Well … were you?" asks MacCormac

"No … but I was aware of the poor girl's unfortunate death" adds Doctor Summerscales
"How did you know, she was killed?" adds MacCormac
"Or murdered?" asks Sheridan
"I assumed" replies the Sub Dean

"You assumed … yet you claim not to know the victim" explains MacCormac

"It's the truth, Chief Superintendent" advises the Sub Dean
"Very well, Doctor" replies MacCormac

The Chief Superintendent ponders the response,

and scratches his head …

"Would you mind giving my Inspector, a sample of your DNA?" asks MacCormac

"My DNA … why?" asks the Sub Dean (Looks to be on his guard)
"To eliminate you from our inquiries, Sir" explains MacCormac
"Obviously, of your own free will" adds MacCormac
The Sub Dean mulls over the request, then gives a sharp response …
"Chief Superintendent" bellows the Sub Dean (Looks serious)
"Yes, Sir" replies MacCormac (Looks equally serious)

"You'll need to have more than circumstantial evidence for me to co-operate with that" explains the Sub Dean
"I'll be talking to the Chief Constable" adds the Sub Dean

"Now, if you both don't get out of here fast" growls the Sub Dean

MacCormac and Sheridan leave Doctor Summerscales study, with a flea in their ear.
"We'll be hearing about that one, Sir"
advises Sheridan
"That we will, Paddy … that we will"
replies MacCormac

SMOKE SCREEN

New evidence comes to light when it is presented to the Chief Constable.

Chief Superintendent MacCormac and Paddy Sheridan are led into a trap by way of a web of lies and deceit!

Can MacCormac and Sheridan flush out the murderer?

The Chief Superintendent and Inspector Paddy Sheridan are both summoned to the Chief Constables office …

"What the hell were you playing at with Doctor Summerscales at Magdalen College, Daniel?" asks the Chief Superintendent (Looks serious)

"I was trying to get to the truth, Sir" replies MacCormac (Looks equally serious)

"We needed to question the Doctor, and that's all we did" adds MacCormac

"Well, Daniel … he has friends in powerful places … and I'm afraid we need something concrete to charge him" explains the Chief Constable

"I understand, Sir" replies MacCormac (Looks serious)

"What about you … Inspector?" asks the Chief Constable (Looks serious)

"We were only fulfilling our duty, Sir" replies Sheridan

"Loyal ... your loyal, I will say that for you, Sheridan" adds the Chief Constable

"Thank you, Sir" adds Sheridan (Smiles)

"Magdalen College" advises the Chief Constable

"What about the College, Sir?" asks MacCormac (Looks intrigued)

"New evidence has come to light" adds the Chief Constable

"New evidence?" asks Sheridan (Looks stunned)

"Yes, concerning Emma Lloyd, Inspector" replies the Chief Constable

"... and Magdalen College" adds the Chief Constable

"Yes, Sir ... we are fully aware of the College" adds MacCormac

"No, Daniel ... this concerns Magdalen College in Cambridge" advises the Chief Constable (Looks serious)

"Cambridge ... how is it related?" asks MacCormac (Looks concerned)

"The old College archives are full of collections of rare books ... as in the four texts of Socrates" advises the Chief Constable (Looks intrigued)

"My God ... it's been staring me in the face, all along" advises MacCormac

"What has?" asks the Chief Constable (Looks stunned)

"The connection" replies MacCormac (Looks surprised)

"That's it, Sir" adds MacCormac
(Looks serious)
"Daniel?" asks the Chief Constable
(Looks intrigued)
"Sorry, Sir ... we have to go ... I'll be in contact" advises MacCormac

Sheridan and MacCormac leave Oxford Police Station and jump into the white Audi ...
"We've been taken for a ride, Paddy" advises MacCormac (Looks annoyed)
"How?" asks Sheridan
"A smoke screen ... and it's clouded my judgement" explains MacCormac
"I still don't get it, Sir" replies Sheridan (Looks puzzled)
"Don't you see, Paddy ... the murder may have been committed in Oxford, but the suspect or murderer, may well have been linked to Magdalen College in Cambridge" adds MacCormac (Looks serious)
"A pattern is emerging" replies Sheridan

"We've been fed a web of lies and deceit" advises MacCormac

"Come on, Paddy ... next stop, Cambridge" adds MacCormac

It's over a two hour drive from Oxford to Cambridge by car.
Like Oxford, the city of Cambridge is a University place of distinction. It is just fifty five miles from London.
Magdalen College is a constituent College of the

University of Cambridge. It has a medieval hall, and it has been a continuous tradition of academic study at the site for over six hundred years.

"So what's the plan, Sir ... we can't just go in unannounced, can we?" asks Sheridan (Looks puzzled)

"What would the Chief Constable say?" adds Sheridan

"Don't worry about him ... he knows we're on to something" advises MacCormac

Sheridan and MacCormac speed towards Cambridge, and are met by the Gate Keeper of the College ...

"Good afternoon, gentlemen ... how can I help you?" asks the Gate Keeper

"Detective Chief Superintendent MacCormac and Inspector Sheridan, Thames Valley Police" advises MacCormac (Flash warrant cards)

"Do you have an appointment, Sir?" asks the Gate Keeper

"We don't need one ... we're the Police" replies MacCormac

"But ..." replies the Gate Keeper (Looks surprised)

Someone else, suddenly arrives, at the Gate ...

"OK, Roberts ... I'll deal with this" advises a voice

"Well, gentlemen, I take it your here to see the Master of Magdalen College ... Sir Jason Templeton?" adds the voice

"Yes, we would appreciate a meeting, with the Master" replies MacCormac
"... concerning?" asks the voice
"Greek tragedies, and the murder of a young woman at Magdalen College, Oxford" explains MacCormac (Looks serious)
"Yes, I can see the similarity" adds the voice
"I'll arrange for you to see the Master" advises the voice

"When?" asks MacCormac (Looks serious)

"Tomorrow" replies the voice

"Sorry, Sir ... we need to see him now" explains MacCormac (Sounds serious)

The Chief Superintendent flashes his warrant card. Paddy Sheridan follows suit.

"I'll see what I can do ... please wait here in the Great Hall" adds the voice

" ... and you are?" asks MacCormac (Looks intrigued)

"Jasper Roache ... I'm a Professor at the College" advises Roache (Smiles)

"Thank you, Professor" replies MacCormac
Several minutes pass then suddenly, Professor Roache returns ...

"The Master will see you now" advises the Professor

"I thought he might" adds MacCormac (Looks smug)

"Thank you" replies MacCormac
Sheridan and MacCormac enter a stately room, and introductions are made ...

"Chief Superintendent Daniel MacCormac and Inspector Paddy Sheridan, Thames Valley Police" advises MacCormac (Flash warrant cards)
All three shake hands, and begin their official inquiries ...

"I'm Jason Templeton, Master of the College, how can I help you, Chief Superintendent?" asks

Templeton (Sounds official)
The Chief Superintendent explains the intricate details concerning the death of Emma Lloyd in Oxford.
"We have reason to believe, that somehow, Magdalen College in Cambridge, is involved" advises MacCormac (Looks serious)
"Do you have any evidence regarding that?" asks Templeton (Looks smug)
"No … but I'll get it" assures MacCormac (Sounds annoyed)
"We think someone is being shielded from our inquiries" adds Sheridan
"We believe, Greek tragedies are the key to our investigation" explains MacCormac (Sounds serious)
"How, have you come to that conclusion, Chief Superintendent?" asks Templeton (Sounds intrigued)
"Let's say we have been given certain information relative to the investigation" advises MacCormac (Looks serious)
"I'm afraid you'll have to do better than that, Chief Superintendent" replies Templeton (Sounds pompous)
"If I need to get a warrant, I'll get it" explains MacCormac (Sounds official)
"From whom?" asks Templeton (Looks intrigued)
"The Chief Constable" replies MacCormac

Jason Templeton pauses for a moment, then

answers MacCormac's response.

"I think you should understand the implications, Chief Superintendent" advises Templeton (Sounds arrogant)

"Now let's be rational" replies MacCormac

"If you co-operate with our inquiries, we'll do our level best to keep your voluntary information, under wraps" explains MacCormac (Looks serious) "Do I have your word on that, Chief Superintendent?" asks Templeton

"Yes, and Inspector Sheridan's word too" adds MacCormac

Paddy Sheridan shrugs at the Chief Superintendent's remarks …

"We'll talk the matter over with, the Chief Constable" assures MacCormac

Jason Templeton begins to express remorse at the victims death, and decides to co-operate with MacCormac and Sheridan.

"Well, there's been some strange things here, that have been let's say, out of the ordinary" advises Templeton (Sounds incriminating)

"Out of the ordinary, in what way, Sir?" asks MacCormac (Looks intrigued)

The Professor decides to explain all to the Chief Superintendent and Inspector Sheridan.

Back at Oxford Police Station, another calling card has been left on the Chief Superintendent's desk.

MacCormac and Sheridan arrive back at the Station in the white Audi, and head for the office for an update concerning the investigation.
Paddy Sheridan draws MacCormac's attention to an envelope on his desk, marked personal.
"Sir?" asks Sheridan (Holds up envelope)
"Yes, Paddy" replies MacCormac
"I think you'd better take a look at this" advises Sheridan
MacCormac picks up the letter and reads it …
"My God, Paddy … another Greek tragedy" advises MacCormac (Looks concerned)
The Chief Superintendent reads out the contents of the letter …

"The slaughter committed by Clytemnestra is acting together with her new lover, Aegisthus … also slaughtered is an innocent victim, the Princess Cassandra" advises MacCormac (Looks puzzled)
Clytemnestra, in Greek mythology, was the wife of Agamemnon, King of Mycenae and half sister of Helen of Troy. She murders Agamemnon, said by Euripides, to be her second husband.
"What do all these Greek quotes and tragedies mean, Sir?" asks Sheridan
"The death of Cassandra is one of the most poignant moments in the tragedy" advises MacCormac (Looks serious)

"It means, there could be another death, or murder" explains MacCormac

"Where?" asks Sheridan (Looks stunned)
"In Oxford or Cambridge?" adds Sheridan

"Yes, exactly, Paddy" replies MacCormac (Looks serious)

"Get on to the Deans of both Colleges" advises MacCormac

"Alert them about the contents of the letter, and the possibility of maybe another victim" explains MacCormac (Sounds concerned)

"I'm on to it, Sir" replies Sheridan

A young Police Constable knocks on the Chief Superintendent's door and enters the room …
"What is it, Larkins?" asks Sheridan

"There's been another one, Sir" replies the young Constable (Looks serious)

"What, another victim?" asks MacCormac
"Yes, Sir" advises the young Constable
"Where man … where man?" asks Sheridan
"Magdalen College in Oxford" advises the young Constable
"Thank you, Larkins" replies MacCormac
"Right, I'll call the Chief Constable, and put him in the picture" advises MacCormac (Picks up mobile phone)
"Get over there, Paddy … I'll join you within the

hour" adds MacCormac

"Within the hour, Sir?" asks Paddy (Looks stunned)

"Something has been staring me in the face ... I've been so stupid ... leave your phone on, Paddy ... I'm going to look into a lead" advises MacCormac

"Do you need back up, Sir?" replies Sheridan (Looks concerned)

"Ask for a squad car to follow me ... I may need their assistance" advises MacCormac (Looks serious)

"Sir" replies Sheridan

Inspector Sheridan leaves Oxford Police Station, and arrives at Magdalen College ... the scene of the crime ...

The area has been cordoned off by the Police ...

Chief Pathologist, Mike Mortimer, is already at the scene ...

"Mike ... what have we got?" asks Sheridan

"A male victim" replies Mike
(Looks serious)

"Male?" asks Sheridan

"I think, the Chief Superintendent, was expecting a female" adds Sheridan

"Why?" asks Mike (Looks concerned)

"To tie in with our latest Greek tragedy warning" advises Sheridan

"Well, sorry to disappoint you, but it's definitely male" explains Mike (Sounds facetious)

"Do we have a name, Mike?" asks Sheridan

"One David Maxman" replies Mike

"Maxman?" asks Sheridan
(Looks concerned)

"Wasn't he tied into the first victim, Emma Lloyd?" asks Mike

"Yes, Mike ... he was" explains Sheridan

"Time of death?" asks Sheridan

"Sorry, not sure yet" replies Mike
(Looks daggers)

"What about an estimated guess, Mike?" asks Sheridan

"About two to three hours ago" replies Mike
"Where's Dan MacCormac?" asks Mike (Looks around)
"Oh, he's on his way to Cambridge, Mike" advises Sheridan
"My God … no" replies Mike (Looks concerned)
The Chief Constable now arrives at the scene of the crime …

"I've issued a warrant for Professor Jasper Roache" advises the Chief Constable
"We've checked into his background, … it's bogus" adds the Chief Constable
"Oh no" replies Sheridan (Looks serious)
"What's wrong, Sheridan?" asks the Chief Constable (Looks concerned)

"Chief Superintendent MacCormac is on his way there, Sir, to confront him with evidence" explains Sheridan
"Right on your way … I'll request full back up" replies the Chief Constable
"MacCormac, could be in grave danger" explains the Chief Constable

TRAGEDY

Chief Superintendent, Daniel MacCormac, arrives in Cambridge and makes his way to Magdalen College.

The Police squad car following him has been detained en-route ... Inspector Paddy Sheridan and the Chief Constable make a dramatic dash.

Will they arrive in time, to save MacCormac, from impending doom?

The Chief Superintendent arrives at Magdalen College in Cambridge, and makes a call to Paddy Sheridan's mobile phone. He leaves a message, then enters the grounds of the College ...

MacCormac arrives at the Gate Keeper's Lodge ...

"Chief Superintendent Daniel MacCormac, Thames Valley Police ... I'm here to see Professor Jasper Roache" advises MacCormac (Flashes warrant card)

"I'm afraid, Professor Roache has been detained, elsewhere, Sir" replies the Gate Keeper

"I'll wait" replies MacCormac (Looks official)

"You can wait, in his study, Sir" adds the Gate Keeper

MacCormac agrees, and follows the Gate Keeper to Professor Roache's quarters, where he is shown into his study.

The Chief Superintendent sits down in a comfy

chair ... where he is met with a sudden blow to the head.
MacCormac falls to the floor and is dazed with the blow ...
Suddenly, another voice greets MacCormac, and gets his attention.
"You see, I knew you were on to me, Chief Superintendent" advises the voice
"Professor Jasper Roache" replies MacCormac (Looks stunned)
Blood is now pouring from the wound on the Chief Superintendent's head.
"Your the one who sent the red herrings, concerning Greek tragedies" advises MacCormac (Looks serious)
"Your very clever, Chief Superintendent ... but not quite clever enough" adds the Professor (Looks pompous)
Jasper Roache pulls MacCormac across the floor ...

Suddenly, the Professor begins to pour inflammable liquid all over the floor. MacCormac is in concussion.
"You'll never get away with it" advises MacCormac (Looks serious)

"I've already got away with it, Chief Superintendent, and there's nothing you can do about it" adds the Professor (Sounds smug)
Roache continues to pour inflammable liquid all over the furniture.

The sudden arrival of a Police car, followed by the Chief Constable and Inspector Sheridan's vehicles into the College, breaks the silence ...

The Chief Constable and Sheridan rush to MacCormac's aid.

"Call them off, MacCormac ... or your a dead man" advises Professor Roache

MacCormac shouts out aloud ...

"Hold your pursuit" advises MacCormac
"It sounds like the Chief Superintendent" replies the Chief Constable (Looks serious)

Both look into the Professor's study, to see MacCormac on the floor, with his head bleeding, and Jasper Roache, standing over him, with a drum of inflammable liquid ...
"See if you can get in behind them, Sheridan" orders the Chief Constable
"I'll try to negotiate with the Professor" adds the Chief Constable
"Be careful, Sheridan, we don't want any more tragedies" advises the Chief Constable (Looks serious)
"Sir" replies Sheridan

MacCormac is obviously feeling the strain, and dizziness due to his injury.
"You thought you were so clever, MacCormac" advises Roache (Sounds pompous)
The Chief Superintendent manages to steady himself against a chair ...
"Why did you murder, Emma Lloyd?" asks MacCormac
"She got in the way" replies Professor Roache (Sounds annoyed)

"Got in the way of what?" asks MacCormac (Looks surprised)
"The four texts of Socrates" adds Professor Roache (Sounds arrogant)

"You see, Chief Superintendent, it was going to be a tragedy" explains Professor Roache
"Your a madman" replies MacCormac

Paddy Sheridan manages to get through an outside window into the back of the room ...
"What the hell have I got to do with it?" asks MacCormac (Looks serious)
"Don't you see, your part of the tragedy?" advises Professor Roache
"In what way?" asks MacCormac (Sounds cautious)

"Euripides, Aristophanes, Socrates and Sophocles, they are all tied into it, too" explains Professor Roache
" ... and now I have to kill again" explains Professor Roache
"Who did you kill?" asks MacCormac (Looks serious)
"David Maxman" replies Professor Roache
"Maxman, why for God's sake?" adds MacCormac

"Just like you, Chief Superintendent, he got too close to the truth" replies Professor Roache
The Chief Constable begins to address the Professor with a loud hailer ...
"This is the Chief Constable" advises the voice
"Tell your man, to hold off, MacCormac" orders

Professor Roache

"I'm alright, Sir ... please do as I say ... no more hailing" asks MacCormac

Jasper Roache reaches into his pocket, and brings out a lighter ...

"Tell them I mean business, Chief Superintendent" orders Roache

Paddy Sheridan is now in Jasper Roache's study, and the suspecting Professor warns MacCormac ...

"OK, tell your man to back off, MacCormac" orders Roache

"Sheridan" shouts MacCormac (Sounds official)

"Hold your position" orders MacCormac

"Are you alright, Sir?" asks Sheridan (Looks concerned)

"He's alright for as long as I want him to be" advises Roache (Sounds pompous)

"Do as he says, Sheridan" orders MacCormac

"You see, MacCormac ... I'm finally in control, not you or your men" adds Roache

Paddy Sheridan becomes concerned for the Chief Superintendent's life ...

"You're not thinking straight, Sir" advises Sheridan (Looks serious)

"For God's sake, man" replies MacCormac (Sounds concerned)

Paddy Sheridan makes a mobile call to the Chief Constable, and asks them to hold their position. The Professor is obviously barking mad, and still quoting from Greek tragedies. The Chief Constable has ordered two Police snipers to take up their position.

Jasper Roache is unaware of their presence ...

"It all ends, today, Chief Superintendent" advises Roache

"Everything" adds Roache (Sounds annoyed)

"We can help you" advises MacCormac

"No one can help me, MacCormac ... I've already killed twice, and I'll take you with me, if I have to" explains Roache

Suddenly, Emily Sandler appears with Paddy Sheridan ...

"Jasper?" asks Emily (Looks stunned)

"Emily" replies Roache
(Looks surprised)

"Please, do as they ask"
advises Emily

"It's too late, Emily"
advises Roache

"It's never too late, Jasper" replies Emily

A sudden movement makes MacCormac uneasy ...

The Police snipers are given orders by the Chief Constable.

"Hold your position ... await further orders" advises the Chief Constable

The Chief Superintendent is now sweating profusely, due to his head wound ...

"What's the matter, Chief Superintendent ... are you afraid of dying?" asks Roache (Sounds arrogant)
"Jasper, let the Chief Superintendent, go" asks Emily

"All the Greek tragedies can't bring anyone back" adds Emily

"Why did you do it?" asks Emily (Looks serious)
"Why did you take those two lives?" adds Emily
"They got in the way" advises Roache
"In the way of what?" asks Emily

"The truth, Emily ... the truth" explains Roache (Sounds serious)

"Now I must end it all" adds Roache
Paddy Sheridan calls out to the Chief Superintendent ...
"Are you alright, Sir?" asks Sheridan
"Yes, Paddy ... I'm still here" replies MacCormac

The Chief Superintendent has now become the victim of a re-enacted Greek tragedy, and more and more incriminating evidence comes to light ...
"Beware of Greek's bearing gifts, Chief Superintendent" advises Professor Roache (Sounds serious)
"What do you mean?" asks MacCormac (Looks intrigued)

"I was a Scholar of Ancient Greece, at the College" advises Roache

"... and the connection?" asks MacCormac (Sounds suspicious)

"The Plethron Connection, of course" replies Roache
Paddy Sheridan decides to try and free the Chief Superintendent by trying another method of escape.
"The Plethron connection?" asks MacCormac (Sounds intrigued)
"A unit of measurement?" adds MacCormac
"The connection of time, Chief Superintendent ... and mine is running out" explains Roache
"We can sort this out, Jasper" advises Emily

"Sorry, but I don't think we can, Emily" replies Roache

The Police snipers advise the Chief Constable that they may have a clear shot at Jasper Roache ...
"On my command, wing the Professor" advises the Chief Constable
"Sir" replies a Police Officer
Paddy Sheridan advises the Chief Constable, that he is now in a position where he may be able to take out Professor Roache.
The Chief Constable contacts the Police snipers ...

"Hold your fire ... stand down" orders the Chief Constable (Sounds serious)

The Police snipers suddenly disappear, and head back to their Unit.
The Chief Superintendent sees that Paddy Sheridan

may be in a position to take down the Professor, and tries to keep the conversation flowing.

"Greeks bearing gifts, a proverb and a warning?" asks MacCormac

"That's right, Chief Superintendent" replies Roache

"It's a warning to be wary about reasons and ulterior motives" adds MacCormac

"You were liked and had no enemies … why?" asks MacCormac

"The prophecy" replies Roache

"What prophecy?" asks MacCormac (Sounds serious) "The priest of Troy and the tragedies" advises Roache "Beware of Greeks bearing gifts" adds Roache

"Or … a rival enemy … be suspicious of their motives" explains Roache

"We are not your enemy, Professor" replies MacCormac

Professor Roache produces the lighter from his pocket and prepares to light it. Suddenly, Paddy Sheridan lunges forward, holds on to the Professor, and knocks the lighter out of his hand.

As the Professor falls, he hits his head on the concrete floor. He is pronounced dead on impact.

Paddy Sheridan, MacCormac and Emily leave the Professor's study, to be greeted by the Chief Constable.

"Are you alright, Daniel?" asks the Chief Constable (Looks serious)

"Yes, Sir" replies MacCormac (Still bleeding)

"He was a madman" advises the Chief Constable

"The victim of a Greek tragedy, and the Plethron connection, Sir" explains MacCormac

"The what?" asks the Chief Constable

(Looks surprised)

"I'll explain it to you one day, Sir"

replies MacCormac

The Chief Superintendent and Paddy Sheridan leave the scene.

"I'm not keen on your new aftershave, Sir" advises Sheridan

"Very funny, Paddy … I do smell a bit though … petrol fumes are not very becoming" adds MacCormac (Sounds pompous)

"Where to now, Sir?" asks Sheridan

SUBTERFUGE

Chief Inspector, Daniel MacCormac, is now Chief Superintendent of Thames Valley Police. He reports directly to the Chief Constable.

Former colleague, Sergeant Paddy Sheridan, is now an Inspector in Oxford, Both are reunited by the Chief Constable, when the city centre becomes involved in trickery, deception and double dealing.

A murder, committed at the Opera, involves several high profile people, that were tricked by a deceptive strategy, putting them all at the scene of the crime!

To break the case, Chief Superintendent MacCormac has to find a way of infiltrating the murderer's craftiness and guile.

When a bluff encounter occurs after a pretence, and fraudulent, sophisticated plan, MacCormac and Sheridan know they are dealing with no one ordinary!

A trick of sharp practice lures MacCormac into the frame.

Can MacCormac outwit the cunning deceit of the murderer, and ultimately bring them to justice?

SUBTERFUGE

EVASION

The Sheldonian Theatre, Oxford.

The audience arrive for the production of Puccini's tragic Opera ... Tosca. Daniel MacCormac is in attendance with an unknown woman.

"Comfortable?" asks MacCormac (Sounds charming)
"Yes, are you?" asks the young
woman (Smiling)
"Very much so" adds MacCormac
(Smiles)
"It's one of my passions" adds MacCormac

"And your other passions?" asks the
young woman (Smiles)

"Beautiful ladies, naturally" explains
MacCormac (Laughs)
The lights go down, and the first movement of the Opera begins ...
Several movements in, and a loud scream, suddenly rings out.
Daniel MacCormac jumps from his seat in the stalls
...

A young woman is lying face down at the back of the auditorium ...

MacCormac makes his way to the back of the theatre.

"Excuse me ... excuse me" asks MacCormac (Looks serious)

The Chief Superintendent flashes his warrant card to the Theatre Manager.

MacCormac checks for a pulse ... and finds a faint beating ...

"Is there a Doctor in the house?" shouts MacCormac (Looks around)

Someone rushes forward to help ...

"She needs to be admitted to hospital" advises the Doctor

The Theatre Manager phones for an ambulance.

MacCormac's date has now joined him at the back of the theatre.

"Full of surprises, aren't you, Daniel?" advises the young lady (Smiling)

MacCormac smiles, then stands up ...

Someone from the audience responds.

"Did someone say, MacCormac?" asks the voice

Step forward, Chief Pathologist, Mike Mortimer ...

"Mike?" answers MacCormac (Looks stunned)

"Yes, it's me, Daniel" replies Mike

(Smiles)
"I didn't know you were an Opera fan, Mike?" asks MacCormac
"There's a lot you don't know about me, Daniel" replies Mike (Laughs)
The responder ambulance arrives on the scene, and swiftly transports the victim to the John Radcliffe Hospital.
The Chief Superintendent walks up the staircase on to the stage to update the audience.
"May I have your attention please?" asks MacCormac (Sounds official)

"My name is Chief Superintendent Daniel MacCormac, Thames Valley Police" advises MacCormac (Looks serious)
"I'm afraid tonight's performance is cancelled" explains MacCormac
Paddy Sheridan and an array of Police officers arrive on the scene.
"If you could please bear with us, and help in anyway you can" adds MacCormac
"Sir?" asks Sheridan
"Paddy ... the Chief Constable wants us to work together, on this one" advises MacCormac
"Together?" asks Sheridan (Looks stunned)

"Get the details of all attending ... I'll get over to the Radcliffe" replies MacCormac (Sounds serious)
Paddy Sheridan asks the Police officers to follow the Chief Superintendent's orders.

"Well, go on then, do as the Chief Superintendent asks" orders Sheridan

"Silly old sod, still thinks I'm his Sergeant" adds Sheridan (Smiles)

"I heard that, Paddy" replies MacCormac (Sounds pompous)

The Chief Superintendent leaves the Opera House, and drives for three miles out of Oxford. He enters the John Radcliffe Hospital complex, where he is sent to Intensive Care.

MacCormac enters the Intensive Care Ward, and flashes his warrant card.

"Well, Doctor … is she going to live?" asks MacCormac (Looks concerned)

"I'm afraid, your guess is as good as mine, Chief Superintendent" replies the Doctor (Sounds official)

"Does she have any belongings, Doctor?" asks MacCormac

A nurse hands over a bag to MacCormac.

The Chief Superintendent checks it's contents, and finds a driving licence.

"Madeline Brooks" advises MacCormac (Looks at contents)

"We've got a name, Doctor" adds MacCormac

Suddenly, the machine in Intensive Care goes off …

"I'm afraid you'll have to leave the ward, Chief

Superintendent" advises the Doctor (Looks serious)
"Crash Team?" shouts the Doctor
The Crash Team enter the ward ...
"Hurry ... she's flat lining" advises the Doctor (Looks concerned)
The Crash Team try everything but it's too late ...
"I'm afraid she's dead" explains the Doctor (Looks serious)
"OK, mark it, date and time" adds the Doctor (Looks concerned)
The Chief Superintendent is waiting outside the ward.
"I'm sorry, the victim died" advises the Doctor (Looks serious)
"We'll get in contact with the next of kin, Doctor" replies MacCormac
Next day, the death is all over the Oxford news ...

KILLER AT OPERA ON THE LOOSE

Paddy Sheridan joins MacCormac at Oxford Police station.

"Just like, old times, Sir" advises Sheridan (Smiles)
"Not quite, Paddy" replies MacCormac (Looks serious)
"How did you get on last night with statements?" asks MacCormac

Paddy Sheridan hands the Chief Superintendent a coffee, then sips his own ...

"We got everyone's details, as you requested, Sir" advises Sheridan

"Everyone?" asks MacCormac (Looks serious)
"Everyone, Sir" adds Sheridan

"All but one, Sir" explains Sheridan

"Whom?" asks MacCormac
(Looks concerned)

"The Killer" replies Sheridan
"Maybe, he's one of them, Sir?" adds Sheridan

"Maybe he is, Paddy" replies MacCormac

"We'll check, thoroughly, Sir" explains Sheridan

A call from the Chief Constable advises that several of the audience fell victim to trickery, by way of, a deceptive strategy, at the performance.

"The case has taken on another level, Paddy" advises MacCormac

"In what way, Sir?" replies Sheridan (Looks puzzled)

"A certain number of the audience were taken for a ride, last night" adds MacCormac

"How?" asks Sheridan (Looks concerned)

"It seems the killer, or murderer, has more than one face" explains MacCormac

"He's a deceptive fraudster … of the highest level, Paddy" adds MacCormac

"Christ Church College, for one" adds

MacCormac (Looks serious) "How is it linked to the performance, Sir?" asks Sheridan
"The Dean ... Sir Edwin Kennedy" replies MacCormac
"What about him?" asks Sheridan (Still puzzled)
"He was one of those, duped" explains MacCormac (Looks concerned)
"Several others were also in the frame, Paddy" adds MacCormac
"There is no relation to anyone, no common denominator" advises MacCormac
"No link, in any shape or form" explains MacCormac (Looks suspicious)
"Where do we start?" asks Sheridan (Looks puzzled)

"You contact, Professor Magnus Lindsay and Cannon Jonathan Smythe" advises MacCormac
"I'll make contact at the University with Sir Edwin Kennedy" explains MacCormac
"OK, Paddy ... I'll meet you back here around four" adds MacCormac
"Sir" replies Sheridan
MacCormac leaves Oxford Police Station, and they go their separate ways. The Chief Superintendent drives away in his white Audi, and pulls up in the court yard of Christ Church College University, Oxford.
The Chief Superintendent walks away from his car towards the Gate Keeper's Lodge.
"Yes, how can I help you?" asks

the Gate Keeper MacCormac flashes his warrant card.

"Chief Superintendent MacCormac, Thames Valley" advises MacCormac

"I'm here to see, Sir Edwin Kennedy" adds MacCormac (Sounds official)

"Is, Sir Edwin expecting you, Sir?" asks the Gate Keeper (Looks puzzled)

"Naturally, what other reason would I be here?" asks MacCormac

"Very well, Sir ... I will contact Sir Edwin" replies the Gate Keeper

"Thank you" adds MacCormac

"Don't I know you ... I've seen you somewhere before?" asks MacCormac

"Come to think of it, weren't you at the Opera, the other night?" adds MacCormac

"You were there?" asks the Gate Keeper (Looks shocked)

"Don't look so surprised, yes I was, obviously" explains MacCormac

"A partaker in the arts?" asks the Gate Keeper

"Yes, you could say that ... and I never forget a face" adds MacCormac

"Sorry, your name?" enquires MacCormac

"Charles Pemberton" replies the Gate Keeper

"Have you worked here long, Mr Pemberton?" asks MacCormac

"Yes, for many years ... and my father before me" replies the Gate Keeper

Mr Pemberton takes a phone call.
"You may now go in, Sir Edwin is expecting you" advises Pemberton
"Floor two, Room 532" adds Pemberton
"Thank you" replies MacCormac

The Chief Superintendent leaves the Gate Lodge and makes his way across the lawns towards the meeting room.
MacCormac notices something on the way ... someone darting through the grounds in a hooded coat.
MacCormac arrives at room 532, and knocks on the door.
"Come in" advises a voice
The Chief Superintendent enters Sir Edwin's room.

"Well, I never ... Daniel MacCormac" advises Sir Edwin (Looks surprised)

"Do you know me?" asks MacCormac (Looks stunned)
"Of course ... don't you remember, I was John F Kennedy at College?" adds Sir Edwin
"Oh, now I remember ... still a college boy, Daniel?" asks Sir Edwin
"Hardly ... I'm a Police Officer" replies MacCormac
"A high ranking one too, Daniel?" asks Sir Edwin

"Well ... if you say so" adds MacCormac (Looks smug)

"So, why do you want to see me?" asks Sir Edwin

"I'm here about the deception and murder of Madeline Brooks" replies MacCormac

"Murder?" asks Sir Edwin (Looks stunned)

"What have I got to do with it, Daniel?" asks Sir Edwin "Perhaps nothing, Sir Edwin, it's all part of our inquiries" replies MacCormac

"Do you think I've got something to do with it, Daniel?" asks Sir Edwin

"We have to keep open minds, at this stage" adds MacCormac

"Now the deception?" asks MacCormac

"How did you find out, Daniel?" asks Sir Edwin

"We have our ways, Sir Edwin" advises MacCormac

"Well?" asks MacCormac (Looks serious)

"It's true, I and several others were taken in at the Opera" replies Sir Edwin

"How, exactly?" asks MacCormac (Looks intrigued)

"Quite easily, I'm afraid" adds Sir Edwin

"Please enlighten me" adds MacCormac

"Research at Christ College ... I and others were asked to donate a large amount of money" explains Sir Edwin

"When … at the Opera?" asks MacCormac
"No, prior to that … but it was at the Opera when we all received a text, confirming the deception" adds Sir Edwin
"A scam?" asks MacCormac (Looks serious)

"Yes, if you want to put it that way … it was a scam" advises Sir Edwin

"You gambled … and lost" asks MacCormac
"Big time, Daniel" replies Sir Edwin

"How big?" asks MacCormac
(Looks serious) "We each lost 200,000" explains Sir Edwin "That's big" replies MacCormac

"Now, that's deception on a massive scale" adds MacCormac

"Have you reported it to the Police?" asks MacCormac

"What do you think?" replies Sir Edwin

"What does it have to do with murder, Daniel?" asks Sir Edwin

"Perhaps nothing, perhaps everything … we must check" replies MacCormac

"However, you and your fellow victims, are placed at the scene of the crime" explains MacCormac

"Surely, you don't think …" replies Sir Edwin

"I'm not paid to think, but to find answers, Sir" adds MacCormac

"Then find them, Daniel" asks Sir Edwin
"Rest assured, I will, Sir Edwin" advises MacCormac

ENCOUNTERS

A fraudulent and sophisticated plan has been put in place.

Chief Superintendent Daniel MacCormac and Inspector Paddy Sheridan know they are dealing with someone out of the ordinary!
Sharp practice takes place, leaving Paddy Sheridan with egg on his face!
Oxford Police Station, Chief Superintendent Daniel MacCormac's office ...
"Paddy" shouts MacCormac (Looks serious)
"Yes, Sir" replies Sheridan

"I've just had a call from the Chief Constable, and he's not happy with our progress, or my little talk with, Sir Edwin Kennedy" advises MacCormac

"Why, Sir?" asks Sheridan (Looks stunned)
"Harassment" replies MacCormac

"We've been told to lay off ... for now" explains MacCormac

"Do you have anything, Paddy?" asks MacCormac
"Some cases remain unsolved in Oxford" replies Sheridan
"Cases?" responds MacCormac (Looks shocked)
"Yes, but ..." advises Sheridan

"Go on, man" adds MacCormac

"I found one in particular" advises Sheridan

"And?" asks MacCormac (Sounds serious)

"Sir Edwin's name, is all over it" explains Sheridan

"Is it now ... that's uncanny, Paddy" replies MacCormac (Looks intrigued)

"Yes, I'd say it is, Sir" adds Sheridan
"Look, it's getting late, Paddy, you get off home to your wife and kids" advises MacCormac
"What about you, Sir?" asks Sheridan

"Leave me the file, and we'll reconvene here, tomorrow morning" replies MacCormac
"Good night, Sir" advises Sheridan (Smiles)
"Night, Paddy" replies MacCormac

The Chief Superintendent peruses the file, where he finds a certain link to Sir Edwin, and a series of scandals linked to Christ Church College, several years ago.

Next day, Inspector Paddy Sheridan is back at his desk.

Chief Superintendent, Daniel MacCormac enters the office.

"Morning, Sir ... coffee" asks Sheridan (Smiles)

"Morning, Paddy ... yes, thank you" replies

MacCormacPaddy Sheridan brings MacCormac a coffee from the drinks machine.

"This stuff gets worse every time I have it" advises MacCormac

"Sorry, best I can do, Sir" replies Sheridan

"Do we have anything, Paddy?" asks MacCormac (Looks serious)

"We've got a lead on the murder case, Sir" advises Sheridan

"... and I'm going to see a Walter Townsend, later" adds Sheridan

"Walter Townsend?" asks MacCormac (Looks intrigued)

"I know that name from somewhere" adds MacCormac

"You?" asks Sheridan

"I've checked the file, over and over, and Sir Edwin is certainly in the frame, but somehow he's never been brought to book, Paddy" advises MacCormac

"How has he managed to evade matters, Sir?" asks Sheridan

"Friends in high places?" adds Sheridan (Looks puzzled)

"Yes, I'd say so, Paddy" replies MacCormac

"You know the type ... you scratch my back, I'll scratch yours" explains MacCormac (Looks serious)

A young Constable knocks on the Chief Superintendent's door and enters the room ...

"Yes, what is it lad?" asks Sheridan

"There's been another one, Sir" advises the young Constable (Looks shocked)

"Where?" asks MacCormac (Looks serious)
"Close to the Bodleian, Sir" replies the young Constable

MacCormac and Sheridan, dash out of Oxford Police Station and jump into the white Audi. It takes a matter of minutes to reach the Bodleian.
The Police have already cordoned off the area. The Audi pulls up sharply in front of the Bodleian Library.
Over thirteen million items are held in the Bodleian Libraries, including special collections.
The Chief Superintendent and Inspector Sheridan liaise with several uniformed Police Officers, and high ranking officials.
The body of a young girl has been found
close to the Bodleian.
Chief Pathologist, Mike Mortimer is
already at the scene.
"What have we got, Mike?" asks MacCormac
"Anything distinguishing?"
adds MacCormac
"Maybe ... maybe not, Dan"
replies Mike
"Well?" asks MacCormac
(Looks serious)
A Police Officer hands over the girls bag to Paddy Sheridan, and he begins to check it's contents

thoroughly …

"I've found the girls identification, Sir" advises Sheridan

"Well, Paddy … who is she?" asks MacCormac

"Tracey Stevens" replies Sheridan
(Looks serious)

"How old?" adds MacCormac

"Twenty five, Sir" replies Sheridan

Chief Pathologist, Mike Mortimer adds his comments …

"I estimate the time of death to be approximately, 9pm, Daniel" advises Mike

"I'll let you know the rest after the postmortem" adds Mike

"When?" asks MacCormac

"As soon as possible" replies Mike

"Don't let the Chief Superintendent boss you around, Paddy" adds Mike

"As if I would?" replies MacCormac (Smiles)
Paddy Sheridan laughs at
Mike's comments.
The Chief Pathologist leaves
the library.

"We also found this, Sir" advises Sheridan

"What is it, Paddy?" replies MacCormac (Looks intrigued)

"It looks old, and official" adds

Sheridan
Paddy Sheridan hands the evidence to the Chief Super ...

"It's out of the Bodleian" advises MacCormac

"I didn't know you could take away rare books, Sir?" replies Sheridan

"You can't, Paddy ... they must remain on site" adds MacCormac

"We'd better look into it" advises MacCormac

"I'll see to it, Sir" replies Sheridan

"So far, we've uncovered two murders, deceit and trickery, at the highest level, Paddy" explains MacCormac

"By who?" asks Sheridan

"Whom, Paddy ... by whom" adds MacCormac

"Well?" asks Sheridan

"They are always a step ahead of us ... but somehow it's almost as if they want to be caught" advises MacCormac (Looks serious)

"... and we're the bait, Paddy" adds MacCormac

"I get it ... if we lure them in, we just might get lucky" replies Sheridan

"Precisely" replies MacCormac (Looks candid)

"To trap a murderer you have to beat them at their own game" explains MacCormac

"Where to now, Sir?" asks Sheridan

"Back to the Nick ... we've overlooked something" replies MacCormac

"We'll trawl through what we've got, back at the office, and see what else we can put together" explains MacCormac
The Chief Superintendent calls into a newspaper shop on his way back to Oxford Police Station.
Paddy Sheridan returns in his own car.
Suddenly, another voice greets him in the newspaper shop ...
"Daniel?" asks the voice (Looks stunned)
"Well I never" adds the voice
"Geoffrey Bates ... how long has it been?" asks MacCormac (Smiles)
"Too many years, Daniel" replies Geoffrey (Smiling)
"What are you up to these days?" asks MacCormac

"I'm retired now, although I do a bit of this and a bit of that" advises Geoffrey

"I know what you do, Daniel" adds Geoffrey (Looks serious)
"Your Chief Inspector, here in Oxford" explains Geoffrey

"I've recently been promoted, I'm now Chief Superintendent" informs MacCormac
"In Oxford?" asks Geoffrey (Looks intrigued)

"Well, the whole of the Thames Valley, actually" advises MacCormac
Geoffrey shows the Chief Superintendent the latest Oxford newspaper.
"Another murder" advises Geoffrey (Looks stunned)
"Are you working on that, Daniel?" asks Geoffrey

"Afraid so ... I've been drafted in by the Chief Constable" advises MacCormac

"I've got theories of my own, Daniel" adds Geoffrey
"Would you like to hear what I've got to say?" asks Geoffrey (Looks serious)
"Go on, I'm listening" replies MacCormac (Looks intrigued)
"Do you remember Tim Reynolds?" asks Geoffrey
"Old swarthy Reynolds" adds Geoffrey (Smiles)
"Vaguely ... why?" asks MacCormac (Looks serious)
"He's back in Oxford ... and a real strange type" explains Geoffrey
"Strange in what way, Geoffrey?" asks MacCormac
"I saw him the other day, near the Bodleian" advises Geoffrey
"He was super strange ... hiding a secret I'd say" adds Geoffrey
"How do I find, Reynolds?" asks MacCormac
"I think he's staying with relatives in Jericho" advises Geoffrey

"Thank you ... I'll make it a priority to check him out" adds MacCormac

Suddenly, the Chief Superintendent's mobile phone begins to ring.

"Excuse me Geoffrey, I'll have to take this" advises MacCormac

"MacCormac" growls the Chief Superintendent
"Your sure?" replies
MacCormac
"Yes, Sir" advises
Sheridan
"I'll meet you at Christ Church College, Paddy" replies MacCormac
"Sorry ... have to go Geoff" advises MacCormac (Smiles)
"Here's my card ... we'll get into old times again" adds MacCormac
The Chief Superintendent leaves the newspaper shop in the centre of Oxford, jumps into his white Audi, and heads towards Christ Church College.
Inspector Paddy Sheridan is waiting outside of the Gate Keeper's Lodge.
"We've got a suspect" advises Sheridan (Looks serious)
"Who?" asks MacCormac
(Looks intrigued)
"Don't you mean, whom, Sir?"
asks Sheridan
"Very funny, Paddy ... whom?" adds
MacCormac (Smiles)
"If you follow me, Sir" adds Sheridan
"Evidence?" asks
MacCormac
"Circumstantial"

advises Sheridan

"It may not be enough, Paddy" advises MacCormac

"We need hard evidence" explains MacCormac (Looks serious)

"Remember, don't jump before you leap, Paddy" adds MacCormac

"Sir?" replies Sheridan (Looks stunned)

"We don't want to end up with egg on our faces do we?" asks MacCormac

CHICANERY AND SHARP PRACTICE

As more evidence comes to light, MacCormac and Sheridan track Tim Reynolds to Jericho.
Another suspicious death follows by asphyxia ... and DNA matches the killer to the scene of the crime!
"So what's all the fuss about, Paddy?" asks MacCormac (Looks serious)
"There seems to be some sort of sharp practice going on at the College, Sir" replies Sheridan
"Do we have anyone in the frame?" asks MacCormac (Looks intrigued)
"Yes, someone called, Sean Baptiste, Sir" adds Sheridan
"I've never heard of him" replies MacCormac
"Apparently, he's a brilliant scholar, Sir" explains Sheridan
MacCormac and Sheridan begin interviewing the Gate Keeper.
Both flash their Police warrant cards.
"We're looking for a certain Sean Baptiste, does he reside here?" asks MacCormac
"No, I believe he lives in Jericho, Sir" advises the Gate Keeper

"That's twice Jericho has been mentioned" adds Sheridan (Looks suspicious)

"Now we have two suspects" replies MacCormac
"I know it may sound a bit wild, Sir" explains Sheridan
"Go on, Paddy, I'm listening" replies MacCormac
Sheridan whispers into the Chief Superintendent's ear …
"That's it, Paddy … good man … we're not looking for two men but one man with two names" adds MacCormac (Looks stunned)
The Gate Keeper looks baffled and surprised at the comments.
As MacCormac and Sheridan prepare to leave, two more characters appear on the scene.
"It's alright Davies, we'll handle it" advises a voice

"Good evening gentlemen … I'm Professor Magnus Lindsay and this is Cannon Jonathan Smythe … can we help?" asks the Professor (Smiles)
"MacCormac and Sheridan, Thames Valley Police" replies MacCormac

"If you could both accompany us to my study, we can be more comfortable there" adds Professor Lindsay (Points the way)
MacCormac and Sheridan follow both distinguished gentlemen into the Professor's study.
"So Chief Superintendent, how can we help you?" asks the Professor
"Perhaps you can … what do you know about a certain individual called, Sean Baptiste?" asks MacCormac

"I personally don't know him" replies the Professor (Looks stunned)
"Who is he?" asks the Cannon
"Apparently he is a student here" advises Sheridan

"Does the name, Tim Reynolds, mean anything to you?" asks MacCormac

"Yes" replies the Professor
"Old Reynolds … swarthy Reynolds" adds the Professor (Looks serious)
"Did you say your name was MacCormac?" asks the Professor
"Yes, I did, Sir" replies MacCormac

"Weren't you at Saint John's College?" adds the Professor (Looks intrigued)

"Yes, I won a scholarship to study there" explains MacCormac

"So you have a secret hiding in the past?" asks the Professor

"It's no secret … everyone knows I'm Oxford educated" adds MacCormac

"… and now Chief Superintendent of Police" adds the Professor

"Yes … investigating a murder, Sir" replies MacCormac (Looks serious)

A sudden call on Sheridan's mobile breaks the silence.

Paddy Sheridan whispers into the Chief Superintendent's ear.

"I'm afraid we have to go, gentlemen"

advises MacCormac

"But, as they say in the movies ... please don't leave town, I may need to Question you both again, later" explains MacCormac (Looks serious)

The Chief Superintendent and Paddy Sheridan leave the college, and jump back into the white A4 and head into town.

"Cheeky so and so's" advises Sheridan (Laughs)

"They tried to put you down, Sir" adds Sheridan (Looks serious)

"Tried, being the word, Paddy" replies MacCormac (Laughs)

"Where to now, Sir?" asks Sheridan

"Jericho" replies MacCormac (Looks serious)

"Do you think we'll find both men there, Sir" adds Sheridan

"I think we may be in for a surprise, Paddy" replies MacCormac

Jericho is an historic suburb of Oxford. It's streets are bounded by the Oxford canal, Worcester College and various roads into the city centre.

MacCormac and Sheridan arrive at an address in Jericho.

Paddy Sheridan knocks on the door of number 11, but there is no reply.

"Try the next one, Paddy" shouts MacCormac (Points)

Someone answers the door at
number 9 ...

"Yes?" asks a voice
"Sam Baptiste?" asks Sheridan (Sounds serious)

"Who wants to know?" replies the voice

"Tim Reynolds" replies MacCormac (Looks serious)
"Chief Inspector MacCormac, is that you?" asks the voice
"Yes, and it's Chief Superintendent, now" explains MacCormac
"Why are you here?" asks the voice
"You see, Paddy ... Baptiste and Reynolds are not two men but just one" adds MacCormac (Looks serious)
"How did you know?" asks Sheridan (Looks puzzled)

"Intuition, Paddy ... intuition" replies MacCormac (Looks smug)

"Well, go on Reynolds, tell the Inspector why" asks MacCormac

Reynolds invites them into the house ...
"It's a long story, Chief Superintendent" replies Reynolds

"I'm afraid you'll have to do better than that, your involved in chicanery and sharp practice, and your in the frame for two murders" explains MacCormac "Where's your evidence?" asks Reynolds (Looks serious)
"We'll get it" adds MacCormac

"So what you mean is you don't have it already" replies Reynolds (Looks smug)

"You still haven't answered the Question"

advises MacCormac

"What Question?" asks Reynolds (Sounds evasive)

"Why Baptiste, and your real name? Replies MacCormac

Reynolds is stunned into an eery silence.

"Your a crook, aren't you, Reynolds?" asks MacCormac (Looks serious)

"That's how he makes a living, Paddy" adds MacCormac

"He blackmails others" explains MacCormac

"You mean ..." asks Sheridan (Looks stunned)

"Yes, Reynolds is the one who blackmailed all those people at the Opera" replies MacCormac (Looks serious)

"Why?" asks Sheridan (Looks puzzled)

"The well to do ... they can afford it" replies Reynolds (Smiles)

"Call me a modern day, Robin Hood" adds Reynolds (Laughs)

"I get it ... you take from the rich and give to the poor" replies Sheridan

"Only, there's no poor, Paddy ... Reynolds pockets the lot" explains MacCormac

"... and the two murders?" asks Sheridan (Looks intrigued)

"I told you, MacCormac ... I didn't do it" replies

Reynolds

"Well, persuade me Reynolds, why we shouldn't take you down the station righ now" asks MacCormac (Looks official)
"Alibi ... I have alibi's" adds Reynolds (Looks serious)
"You, an alibi?" replies MacCormac (Looks in disbelief)
"Yes, an alibi for the evenings when the murders took place" explains Reynolds
"How?" asks Sheridan
"... not how, but where" replies Reynolds (Looks smug)
"Well, where then, man?" asks MacCormac
"I'm a Porter at the Radcliffe" advises Reynolds

"You a Porter?" replies MacCormac (Looks intrigued)

"Check it out, Paddy" advises MacCormac
Inspector Sheridan phones the Management Section at the Radcliffe.
"Well?" asks MacCormac (Looks official)
"I'm afraid it's true, Sir ... he's telling the truth" replies Sheridan

"See I told you, MacCormac ... now are you going to leave here or do I get you done for Police harassment?" adds Reynolds (Looks serious)
"You see, I know my rights" explains Reynolds

MacCormac and Sheridan leave with their tails between their legs.

"Well, a fat lot of good that did us" advises MacCormac (Looks suspicious)

"We were barking up the wrong tree" replies Sheridan

"Not necessarily, Paddy" adds MacCormac (Looks serious)

MacCormac and Sheridan jump back into the white A4 and head into town.

"Now where, Sir?" asks Sheridan

"Back to see, Mike Mortimer" replies MacCormac

"Why, Mike?" adds Sheridan (Looks puzzled)

"DNA results ... to track the killer" advises MacCormac

"It may help ... a modern day miracle" explains MacCormac (Looks serious)

"It just might lead us to the murderer" adds MacCormac

While the Chief Superintendent and Sheridan return to Police HQ, another report comes in.

Someone has been found hanged by asphyxia in Jericho.

The Chief Constable knocks and enters Daniel MacCormac's office ...

"Daniel ... Daniel" shouts a voice

"Sir" replies MacCormac

"Reynolds" advises the Chief Constable

"What about, Reynolds, Sir?" asks MacCormac

"He's committed suicide ... death by hanging" explains the Chief Constable

"My God ... we've just seen Reynolds" advises Sheridan (Looks shocked)

"Our boys are at the scene now, Dan" adds the Chief Constable

"Where's Doctor Mortimer?" asks MacCormac

"He's also at the scene" replies the Chief Constable (Looks serious)

MacCormac and Sheridan head back to Jericho ... Police are everywhere, and a cordon holds back the public.

Chief Pathologist, Mike Mortimer is checking the body for possible cause of death.

"Well, Mike?" asks MacCormac

"Definitely, death by asphyxia ... however ..." replies Mike (Sounds official)

"However?" asks MacCormac (Looks intrigued)

"There are other distinguishing marks on the body, Daniel" replies Mike

"How fresh?" asks Sheridan

"Very fresh" advises Mike (Looks serious)

"Time of death?" asks MacCormac (Looks serious)

"In the last hour" replies Mike

"The victims body is still warm" adds Mike (Looks

serious)

"You see, Paddy ... yet more chicanery and sharp practice" replies MacCormac

"Nothing is as it seems" adds MacCormac (Looks suspicious)

"You are right, Dan" replies Mike Mortimer

"Something is wrong" adds Mike

"In what way, Mike?" asks Sheridan (Looks puzzled)

"I'll have to run tests, and have a postmortem" explains Mike

"I'll be in touch when I know more" adds Mike (Sounds official)

"Mike" replies MacCormac (Nods)

"Daniel" replies Mike Mortimer (Nods)

The Chief Pathologist prepares to leave the scene.

"You see, I told you, Paddy ... nothing's straight forward" advises MacCormac

"When it comes to murder" adds MacCormac (Looks suspicious)

"Motive?" asks Sheridan

"Everything's implicated ... it's like something I've never seen before" explains MacCormac (Looks stunned)

"In what way, Sir?" asks Sheridan

"Let's see what DNA comes up with" replies MacCormac

"If it matches the scene of the crime?" adds

MacCormac (Looks serious)

"and if not?" asks Sheridan
"Then we're still looking for the killer" replies MacCormac

CUNNING DECEIT

MacCormac and Sheridan find out that circumstantial evidence puts someone else in the frame ... are they about to find the real murderer? Back at Oxford Police Station ... the Chief Superintendent and Sheridan await the post mortem results from Chief Pathologist, Mike Mortimer.

Daniel MacCormac scratches his head ...

"It's like I've overlooked something, Paddy" advises MacCormac (Looks puzzled)

"I know what you mean, Sir ... something doesn't add up" replies Sheridan

"Three murders and the chief suspect dead" adds MacCormac (Looks suspicious)

"We've missed something, Paddy" explains MacCormac

The Chief Super looks towards files that are stacked on top of set of filing drawers.

"Please bring me the files, Paddy" asks MacCormac

Sheridan gets up from his desk and hands the files to the Chief Superintendent.

"You check those, and I'll check these" advises MacCormac (Looks serious)

"... but I've got a bigger pile" replies Sheridan (Smiles)

"Your more cut out for it ... I'm a thinker, Paddy" explains MacCormac (Smiles)

"Thank you very much" laughs Sheridan
They both start to go through the bundles of files.

The Chief Constable suddenly makes an impromptu visit.

"Daniel ...hows it going?" asks the Chief Constable (Looks serious)

The Chief Superintendent begins to explain the unfolding situation ...

"One hell of a mess, but it's not your fault" advises the Chief Constable

"Sir?" replies MacCormac (Looks serious)
"I think we're on to something" advises MacCormac

"Yes, I know you are ... you've certainly ruffled a few feathers, though" replies the Chief Constable (Looks serious)

"Everyone is now implicated in the smoke screen" adds the Chief Constable

"Smokescreen?" asks Sheridan (Looks stunned)

"Yes, I'd say they are ... how to change their tactics?" asks the Chief Constable

"Do you have something we don't know about, Sir?" asks MacCormac

"Yes, and more" replies the Chief Constable (Looks suspicious)

"Go on" adds MacCormac

"Sir Edwin Kennedy, the Dean" advises the Chief Constable

"What about him, Sir?" asks MacCormac (Looks intrigued)
The Chief Constable hands over a file to MacCormac.
"It's all here in the file ... classified government information" advises the Chief Constable (Looks official)
"Is he the murderer, Sir?" asks MacCormac (Looks serious)
"I'll let you decide on that, Daniel" adds the Chief Constable
"Remember, we need hard evidence" explains the Chief Constable

"What we have is not enough" advises the Chief Constable (Looks serious)

"Don't worry, we'll find it, Sir" replies MacCormac (Looks assuring)
"You can rely on us" adds Sheridan (Looks serious)

"Thank you, Sheridan" replies the Chief Constable (Smiles)

"I'm glad your both on to it, let me know when you have anything" adds the Chief Constable
"Sir" replies MacCormac

The Chief Constable leaves Dan MacCormac's office and wanders back to his own office.
An hour later, Chief Pathologist, Mike Mortimer arrives at the Chief Superintendent's office.
"Mike" greets MacCormac (Smiles)

"Well, did the postmortem throw anything up,

Mike?" asks MacCormac (Sounds serious)

"Not just the postmortem, Dan" replies Doctor Mortimer (Looks serious)

"Go on" adds MacCormac (Looks intrigued)
"It turns out, Tim Reynolds was murdered with a lethal dose of strychnine" advises Doctor Mortimer (Looks serious)

"Strychnine?" replies Sheridan (Looks stunned)

"Yes, a highly toxic dose ... it was poisoning" explains Mike

"So it wasn't asphyxia" asks MacCormac (Looks stunned)
"No, it was made to look like suicide ... as if he had taken his own life" explains Mortimer
"That's not all" adds Doctor Mortimer

"Go on" asks MacCormac (Looks intrigued)

"The DNA we found was not just his but the killer's too" adds Doctor Mortimer

"Find the killer and that will match" advises Doctor Mortimer (Looks serious)

"That's the evidence we've been looking for, Paddy" advises MacCormac

Paddy Sheridan checks the file brought in by the Chief Constable ...
"Sir, there's also something else"
advises Sheridan (Looks at file)
"Go on, Paddy" replies MacCormac

"Sir Edwin Kennedy" replies Sheridan (Looks serious)
"What about him?" asks MacCormac
"He's Tim Reynold's brother" advises Sheridan
Daniel MacCormac looks puzzled
...
"How?" asks MacCormac (Looks intrigued)
"Apparently he changed his name in his twenties" explains Sheridan
"That's why we were thrown ... no connection" replies MacCormac
"It also says that he is a Mason ... and a high ranking one too" adds Sheridan

"I'll bet you all those at the Opera, that fateful night, were all Masons, too" adds MacCormac (Looks suspicious)
"I'll check on it" replies Sheridan
Dan MacCormac turns to Doctor Mortimer ...

"Mike, as always, your information has proved to be invaluable" advises MacCormac (Look serious)
"A compliment" replies Doctor Mortimer (Smiles)
"Thank you, Daniel" adds Doctor Mortimer
The Chief Superintendent turns towards Paddy Sheridan ...

"Paddy it's time we paid another visit to see Sir Edwin at Christ Church College" advises MacCormac

The Chief Superintendent is adamant that Kennedy is their man, but things may become a little awry for MacCormac and Sheridan, and Sir Edwin is not playing ball this time!

MacCormac and Sheridan arrive at the College and are confronted by the Gate Keeper.

"I'm afraid Sir Edwin has given strict instructions not to be disturbed today, gentlemen" advises the Gate Keeper (Looks serious)

"He'll see me" replies MacCormac (Looks annoyed)

"But I've been given instructions" replies the Gate Keeper

"Do you want to be implicated in a murder, and are you stopping us from carrying out our investigations?" asks MacCormac (Sounds serious)

"We're in the middle of a murder investigation" adds Sheridan (Looks serious)

MacCormac budges past the Gate Keeper followed by Paddy Sheridan. The Gate Keeper then waves them through.

MacCormac and Sheridan enter Sir Edwin's room unannounced ...

A meeting is taking place between several students and scholars of the University ...

"Forgive the intrusion, Sir Edward" advises MacCormac (Sounds official)

"I gave strict instructions at the gate" replies Sir Edwin (Sounds serious)

"I'm afraid I have a warrant for your arrest" explains MacCormac (Looks serious)

"A warrant ... on what grounds?" asks Sir Edwin (Sounds stunned)

"Deception, for one thing" advises MacCormac (Sounds serious)

"Deception?" puzzles Sir Edwin

"Your not really who you say you are ... Sir Edwin" replies MacCormac

Sir Edwin dismisses everyone from the meeting.

"Well, Chief Superintendent, how long did it take you to find out?" asks Sir Edwin (Looks surprised)

"Not long, after some digging and delving, Sir" replies MacCormac

"You do know that your brother, Tim Reynolds, has been murdered, don't you?" asks MacCormac (Sounds serious)

"Murdered ... how?" asks Sir Edwin (Looks stunned)

"Someone slipped him a lethal dose of strychnine" advises Sheridan

"Where were you a few hours ago?" asks MacCormac (Sounds serious)

Sir Edwin is silent and still pondering his response.

"The games up Kennedy ... where were you?" adds MacCormac

"... or should I call you Tim Reynolds?" asks MacCormac (Looks serious)

"You think your very clever don't you, Chief

Superintendent?" asks Sir Edwin

"I work with facts ... only facts, Sir Edwin" replies MacCormac

"Then I suggest that you get your facts straight" adds Sir Edwin

"What do you mean?" asks MacCormac (Looks serious)

"If you had properly done your homework ..." advises Sir Edwin

"Go on" replies MacCormac (Sounds intrigued)

"You'd see that I am one of triplets" explains Sir Edwin

"Triplets?" asks Sheridan (Looks stunned)

"I wanted my old life to go away" adds Sir Edwin (Looks serious)

"Hence the name change?" asks MacCormac

"Yes, naturally" replies Sir Edwin

"John Reynolds, he's the jealous one ... he's the one you want" explains Sir Edwin (Looks concerned)

"And where exactly can we find him, Sir?" asks MacCormac

"Last known whereabouts?" asks Sheridan

"Jericho, but also Wolvercote" replies Sir Edwin

"Get on to it, Paddy" adds MacCormac

"You've not heard the last of this Chief Superintendent ... I'm contacting the Chief Constable" advises Sir Edwin (Looks serious)

"Be my guest" replies MacCormac (Looks unprovoked)

"It was the Chief Constable who sanctioned your warrant and arrest" explains MacCormac (Looks serious)

Kennedy is taken by surprise at the Chief Superintendent's remarks.

"So, what happens now?" asks Sir Edwin (Looks stunned)

"We'll investigate your brother ... what's his address?" asks MacCormac

Sir Edwin hands MacCormac his current address.

"Just one other thing, Sir Edwin" asks MacCormac

"Don't leave the country or Oxford, for that matter" advises MacCormac (Sounds serious)

MacCormac and Sheridan hurry over to the address in Wolvercote in the white Audi, which is three miles north west of the city centre of Oxford.
They pull in near the Church
of Saint Peter.
"Pretty village, Sir" advises
Sheridan
"Looks can be deceptive, Paddy" replies MacCormac (Looks serious)
Sheridan jumps out of the Chief Superintendent's white Audi and asks a local man for directions.
MacCormac and Sheridan drive off the road to an old disused farm building just outside of Wolvercote.
Someone is working on the land
close to the house.
The Chief Superintendent confronts John Reynolds. "Mr Reynolds?" asks MacCormac
(Looks serious)
Reynolds makes a run for it ...

"Cut him off, Paddy" shouts MacCormac

The Chief Superintendent goes in the opposite direction to Paddy Sheridan.

Suddenly MacCormac is hit from behind with a tree branch. John Reynolds is stood over him.
"You just won't give up will you?" shouts Reynolds (Looks angry)
"Why did you do it, Reynolds?" asks MacCormac (Looks stunned)

"I had my reasons" advises Reynolds

"Reasons ... you killed three times" replies MacCormac

Paddy Sheridan approaches from behind, and radio's for help ...

"Now it's your turn to pay MacCormac" advises Reynolds

Reynolds drags the Chief Superintendent towards the river Thames.

"So, your going to kill me too?" replies MacCormac (Looks serious)

"That's the general idea" replies Reynolds

"You'll never get away with it" advises MacCormac (Looks stunned)

Paddy Sheridan suddenly lunges at Reynolds, and takes him out.

Reynolds is laid out cold.

"Are you alright, Sir?" asks Sheridan (Looks concerned)

Paddy Sheridan pulls up the Chief Superintendent to his feet.

"Thanks to you, Paddy ... I am" replies MacCormac

Police units arrive on the scene, and they take away John Reynolds.

Back in Oxford, MacCormac and Sheridan receive commendations from the Chief Constable for a job well done!

PARASYMPATHETIC REBOUND

Chief Inspector Daniel MacCormac, now Chief Superintendent reports directly to the Chief Constable. Inspector Paddy Sheridan, a former colleague, is now based at Oxford, and still a protege of his mentor, the Chief Super!

MacCormac and Sheridan are asked to investigate by the Chief Constable, when an unusual murder has been committed in Oxford.

This investigation turns out to be no ordinary murder. The victim received a shock to their body, which stopped their heart from beating, due to the severity of the attack.

When, Chief Pathologist, Mike Mortimer informs MacCormac that it was a parasympathetic rebound death, caused by an autonomic imbalance of congestive heart failure, he knows that this is no ordinary murder investigation.

MacCormac and Sheridan find there is very little evidence and reports of side effects stemming from this condition.

Did the victim die after being
simply, scared to death? But what
caused it to happen?

When MacCormac and Sheridan look deeper into the case they find that strong emotions such as fear can induce death.

Is there something more sinister concerning the condition?
Why is Daniel MacCormac being targeted?
Could he be the next victim?

When another victim dies of the same condition, MacCormac and Sheridan set out to trap whoever is responsible!

PARASYMPATHETIC REBOUND HALLOWEEN PARADE

Friday evening, Oxford town centre.

The annual Oxford Halloween event is taking place ... floats and marching bands are taking part in a eye opening spectacle.

Lots of people are congregating along the route which has been closed off to normal traffic.
Best friends, Maeve and Gemma, are both Medical students at one of the Universities (Oxford Medical School).
"Where's Dom?" asks Gemma (Looks around)

Gemma is in her mid twenties and brunette. Her face has been painted, and she is dressed in a scary outfit for Halloween.
"He should be here" replies Maeve (Looks around)

Maeve is also in her twenties, has long blonde hair, and is dressed as a scary Doctor in white outfit. She also has her face painted for Halloween.
"I'm here" replies a voice in the crowd

"You almost scared us to death" replies Gemma (Laughs)

Dom is also in his early twenties, but he is dressed as a scary Vampire.

"No guessing whom you've come as" adds

Maeve (Looks impressed)

"Why, Count Dracula, naturally" replies Dom (Looks smug)

"Naturally" adds Gemma
Several Halloween floats pass by ...
Dom suddenly, jumps on to one of them ...
"Come on girls" shouts Dom (Motions to girls)
"Later, Dom" replies Gemma (Smiles)

"We'll catch up with you, later" adds Maeve (Laughs)
"Welcome Count Dracula" greets a woman on the float (Looks impressed)
"Who have you come as?" asks Dom
"I'm a naughty Devil Woman" replies the woman
"Naughty?" asks Dom (Looks intrigued)
"Wait and see" replies the woman (Laughs)

Maeve and Gemma head for a town centre pub, but decide to make detour through the grounds of the University ...
The Gate to the University is unmanned.

"Looks as if Soames is away from his usual spot" advises Maeve (Shouts)

"Maybe he's decided to join the parade, Gemma" adds Maeve (Laughs)

"I doubt it, that's way too much excitement for Soames" replies Gemma

"He's like our Grandad" adds Maeve (Smiles)
Both girls leave the Gate Keeper's Lodge and begin to

walk through the dimly lit University grounds. Gemma suddenly advises that she needs to go to her room.

"I'll only be a few minutes, meet you back here then Maeve" advises Gemma

"OK, don't be long, Gem" replies Maeve (Smiles)
"Back in a jiffy" adds Gemma (Smiling)

Maeve begins to look into her compact mirror, and notices someone in the bushes.
"Who's there?" asks Maeve (Looks scared)

"I know your there" adds Maeve
(Looks around)

No one responds.
Suddenly, a loud scream …

Gemma rushes back to Maeve, but it's too late, she's lying motionless on the ground.
The Gate Keeper, Soames, calls the local Police.

The area is quickly cordoned off, and Chief Pathologist, Mike Mortimer is at the scene, assessing what happened …
Minutes later, a familiar white Audi
arrives on the scene …
"Mike" responds MacCormac (Looks serious)
"Daniel, Paddy" replies Doctor Mortimer

"What have we got, Mike?" asks MacCormac (Looks concerned)

"All I can tell you is that there are no wounds" advises Doctor Mortimer

"Time of death?" asks MacCormac
"Within the last hour" adds Doctor Mortimer

"I'll need to do a full postmortem, but she may have literally been scared to death" adds Doctor Mortimer (Looks serious)

"Scared to death, Mike?" asks MacCormac (Looks stunned)

"How?" asks Sheridan (Looks puzzled)

"A possible delayed over reaction of the nervous system" explains Doctor Mortimer (Sounds serious)

"What does that mean in simple English, Mike?" asks MacCormac

"Have you heard of parasympathetic rebound?" asks Doctor Mortimer

"Never heard of it" replies Sheridan (Still puzzled)

"Thank you, Paddy" adds MacCormac

"I've heard of it, but never expected a case concerning parasympathetic rebound" explains MacCormac (Looks serious)

"What does it mean, Sir?" asks Sheridan (Looks stunned)

"Literally, as I said, Paddy ... the victim was scared to death" adds MacCormac

"Well, it is Halloween" replies Sheridan
"Halloween, is that all you can think of Paddy?" asks MacCormac (Looks serious)

"I'll be in touch, gentlemen" advises Doctor Mortimer (Leaves the scene)

"In the morning?" asks MacCormac
"As soon as I have answers" replies Doctor Mortimer
"Thank you, Mike" adds MacCormac MacCormac and Sheridan head back to Oxford Police Station.

In the Chief Superintendent's office …

"A sorry state of affairs, Paddy" advises MacCormac (Looks serious)

"Your right, Sir it is" replies Sheridan
"Parasympathetic rebound?" adds Sheridan (Looks in disbelief)
"Who would have thought it" replies MacCormac
"The murderer obviously did, Sir" advises Sheridan

"Obviously, we're both in agreement about that" agrees MacCormac

"We haven't much to go on, Sir" replies Sheridan
"Check on the victim, Paddy … there must be something on her" asks MacCormac
"And Mike?" asks Sheridan (Looks serious)

"No doubt he'll come up with some fandangled story" replies MacCormac

"I'll check in with the Chief Constable" advises MacCormac
"He'll want some answers, Paddy" explains MacCormac (Looks serious)

"Do some digging in the morning ... see what you can find" adds MacCormac

"... and you?" asks Sheridan

"I'll be in contact after talking to the Chief Constable" replies MacCormac

Next day, Chief Pathologist, Mike Mortimer, has some evidence and DNA from the victim.

Mike arrives at Oxford Police Station and enters the Chief Superintendent's office.

"Morning Mike" greets MacCormac (Smiles)

"Morning ... I thought you'd like to know, Daniel, sooner than later" advises Doctor Mortimer (Looks serious)

"Know what?" replies MacCormac
(Looks intrigued)

"The name of the victim" adds Doctor Mortimer (Sounds serious)

"Go on, Mike, who was she?" replies MacCormac (Looks attentive)

"She was known as Maeve Quinn, twenty one, attending Oxford Medical School" advises Doctor Mortimer (Looks at notes)

"Here in Oxford?" asks MacCormac

"Yes, Daniel, here in Oxford" replies Doctor Mortimer

Enter Paddy Sheridan ...

"Morning, Paddy" greets MacCormac

"Morning, Sir ... Mike" replies Sheridan (Smiles)

"I've been doing some digging, Sir" adds Sheridan

"Hold on, Paddy" replies MacCormac

"What else, Mike?" asks MacCormac (Looks serious)

"Just a thought ... death by parasympathetic rebound ... she was literally scared to death" adds Doctor Mortimer (Looks equally serious)

"Scared to death ... by whom?" adds MacCormac (Looks puzzled)

"That's your job, Daniel ... I've done mine ... everything is in the autopsy report

... I suggest you read it" replies Doctor Mortimer (Looks serious)

"Thank you Mike, we will" advises MacCormac (Looks glum)

"That's not all, Sir" replies Sheridan

"OK, what is it, Paddy" asks MacCormac (Looks puzzled)

"I found out that the dead girl was at Oxford Medical School" informs Sheridan

"That we do know" replies MacCormac
"Anything else?" adds MacCormac

"She was Professor Quinn's niece" confirms Sheridan

"Quinn ... as in Peter Quinn?" asks MacCormac (Looks surprised)

"Yes, Sir ... the very same ... do you know of him?" asks Sheridan (Looks stunned)

"You could say that our paths have crossed, in the past" advises MacCormac

"Well, well ... things are beginning to add up, Paddy" adds MacCormac

"What next, Sir?" asks Sheridan

"I think we'd better pay Doctor Quinn a visit" replies MacCormac (Looks serious)

The Chief Superintendent and Sheridan leave Oxford Police Station and jump into MacCormac's white Audi. They make a short trip to Oxford Medical School, which is situated centrally in the University.

On arrival in the grounds of the College, MacCormac and Sheridan jump out of the Audi, and enter the gated area.

Both wander towards the Gate Keeper's House.

"Can I help you?" asks a voice

"We're here to see Professor Quinn" advises MacCormac (Flashes warrant card)

"Sorry, he's not taking any visitors, Sir" replies the Gate Keeper

"He'll see me" replies MacCormac

The Chief Superintendent and Sheridan flash their respective Police identity cards.

"Shall I advise who's looking for him, Sir?" asks the Gate Keeper

"No thanks ... we prefer to go in

unannounced" adds MacCormac
The Gate Keeper points the way to Professor Quinn's quarters.
"Room C15" advises the Gate Keeper (Looks serious)
MacCormac and Sheridan take several flights of stairs.
"This is it, Sir" advises Sheridan
Paddy Sheridan knocks
on the door.
An old Professor
answers.
"Yes?" asks the voice

"Police" replies MacCormac (Sounds serious)

"Why it's you ... Daniel" replies Doctor Quinn (Looks surprised)

"You know each other?" asks Sheridan (Looks stunned)
"Not only do we know each other, but we studied together" replies Doctor Quinn
"Well, I never" adds Doctor Quinn (Smiles)

"This is Inspector Paddy Sheridan" replies MacCormac (Smiling)

"I've heard great things about you Daniel" advises Doctor Quinn
"I hear your in the upper echelons now?" adds Doctor Quinn (Looks serious)
"Chief Superintendent indeed" advises Doctor Quinn

"I guess this isn't a social call, Daniel … what can I do for you?" asks Doctor Quinn (Looks concerned)

"You haven't heard?" asks Sheridan (Looks serious)

"Heard what?" replies Doctor Quinn (Looks stunned)

"A young student was found dead" advises Sheridan

"Who was she?" asks Doctor Quinn

"I'm sorry to advise you … it was your niece … Maeve Quinn" replies MacCormac (Looks serious)

"Maeve … surely not?" replies Doctor Quinn (Looks stunned)

"I'm afraid it's true, Peter" explains MacCormac

"My God" adds Doctor Quinn (Looks shocked)

"How … why?" asks Doctor Quinn (Falls back into chair)

"Apparently it was due to parasympathetic rebound" advises MacCormac

"She was literally frightened to death" explains MacCormac (Looks serious)

"Where is she now?" asks Doctor Quinn (Looks stunned)

"In the mortuary, Doctor" replies Sheridan

"Thank you, Paddy" replies MacCormac (Looks concerned)

"Any idea how it could have happened?" asks MacCormac

"None whatsoever" replies Doctor Quinn (Looks puzzled)

"Maeve was such a head strong girl" adds Doctor Quinn

FRIGHTENED TO DEATH

Chief Superintendent Daniel MacCormac and Inspector Paddy Sheridan, retrace the steps of Maeve Quinn ... will MacCormac be the next victim? Early evening, Daniel MacCormac's residence on the outskirts of Oxford.
Suddenly the doorbell rings ...
Daniel MacCormac checks the phone ...

"What the hell" asks MacCormac
(Looks surprised)

The doorbell rings a second time
...
Daniel MacCormac gets up from his chair and opens the door to see a familiar face greeting him ...
"Paddy ... what a pleasant surprise" greets MacCormac (Smiles)
"Sir" replies Sheridan (Smiling)
"Come in ... come in" adds MacCormac (Looks relaxed)

Sheridan follows the Chief Superintendent back into the room ...

"Would you like a drink, Paddy?" asks MacCormac
"No I'd better not, still on duty" replies Sheridan

"Sorry to disturb you, Sir" adds Sheridan (Looks serious)

"OK, Paddy ... what's on your mind?" asks MacCormac

"I thought you'd like to know ..." replies Sheridan
"Couldn't it have waited till the morning?" asks MacCormac
"Afraid not, Sir" advises Sheridan (Looks serious)
"The Chief Constable asked me to contact you directly, Sir" replies Sheridan
"Well, go on man ... what's it all about?" replies

MacCormac (Looks puzzled)
"Professor Quinn" advises Sheridan
"What about Professor Quinn?" asks MacCormac (Looks serious)
"I'm afraid he's been found dead, Sir" explains Sheridan
"Dead ... of what?" adds MacCormac (Looks shocked)
"The same as his niece" adds Sheridan
"Parasympathetic rebound" replies Sheridan
"Where's the body?" asks MacCormac (Looks stunned)

"Still at the crime scene ... the Chief Constable is there, awaiting your arrival" adds Sheridan
"That's all I need" replies MacCormac (Looks serious)
The Chief Superintendent gets his jacket.
"Come on, Paddy ... time is of the essence" advises MacCormac

Sheridan and MacCormac jump into the Chief Superintendent's white Audi and speed along to the crime scene with blue lights flashing. They arrive fifteen minutes later.
The University of Oxford, Medical School.

MacCormac and Sheridan walk through the grounds, enter the Police cordoned off area, and are met by the Chief Constable.

"A very sorry state of affairs, Daniel" greets the Chief Constable (Looks concerned)
"Indeed, Sir" replies MacCormac

"We only met with the Professor earlier today" adds Sheridan

"Well, that may be the case, Paddy, but now we have another victim" replies MacCormac (Looks serious)
"Not only that, Daniel, but now the story has become political" advises the Chief Constable
"Political?" asks MacCormac (Looks stunned)
"Prominent people in Government want to know what's going on" adds the Chief Constable (Looks serious)
"I wish, I knew, Sir" replies MacCormac (Looks equally serious)

Chief Pathologist, Mike Mortimer is already at the scene, and steps in ...

"Well, Mike?" asks MacCormac
"Same as last time, Daniel" replies Doctor Mortimer (Looks serious)

"I can give you the long or short version of events" adds Doctor Mortimer

"Keep it short, Mike" asks MacCormac
"I think we already know the answer" adds MacCormac
"Go on" replies MacCormac (Sounds serious)
"Parasympathetic rebound?" asks Sheridan (Looks serious)

262

"Correct" replies Doctor Mortimer
"Exactly the same circumstances as his niece" explains Doctor Mortimer
"Exactly?" asks the Chief Constable (Looks intrigued)
"Except for this" replies
Doctor Mortimer Mike
produces a Halloween mask
...
"Frightening isn't it?" asks Doctor Mortimer (Looks serious)
"If you say so, Mike" replies MacCormac (Looks sceptical)
"Could this have been the cause for both deaths?" asks MacCormac
"Maybe" replies Doctor Mortimer (Looks suspicious)
"OK, Mike ... let us know when you've carried out the postmortem ... we need answers" advises MacCormac (Looks authoritative)
"... and the press?" asks Sheridan (Looks puzzled)
"I'll take care of them" advises the
Chief Constable
"Daniel ... we need some answers ... and snappy" adds the Chief Constable
"Yes, I'm aware of that, Sir" replies MacCormac (Looks serious)
The Chief Constable leaves the crime scene and talks to the waiting press ...
MacCormac turns to Sheridan ...

"Do we have anything else to go on, Paddy?" asks MacCormac

"I've spoken to Gemma Lane" advises Sheridan

"Who's she?" asks MacCormac (Looks puzzled)

"She's a friend of the dead girl, Maeve Quinn … and" replies Sheridan

"Go on" adds MacCormac (Looks intrigued)

"She's identified a male friend, called Dom (Dominic Slater), who just happens to be a fellow student at the Medical School" advises Sheridan

"He was with both of them on the night of the murder, Sir" explains Sheridan

"Interesting, Paddy" replies MacCormac (Looks serious)

"Good work, Paddy" adds MacCormac

"Gemma says Dom was in costume early evening Halloween, and then left them to go on one of the Parade floats" explains Sheridan

"Was he wearing a mask?" asks MacCormac

"If he was we'll need to check it for DNA" replies Sheridan (Looks serious)

"OK, Paddy … get on to it" advises MacCormac

"Then, maybe we can track down the killer" explains MacCormac

"I'll give them, snappy, indeed" adds MacCormac (Looks smug)

"Oh and Paddy" shouts MacCormac

"Sir?" replies Sheridan (Looks back)

"I think we'd better check with Oxford Medical School for possible matches" explains MacCormac
"OK, on to it, Sir" replies Sheridan

Next day, Chief Pathologist, Mike Mortimer, arrives at Oxford Police Station and enters the Chief Superintendent's office.
"Morning, Mike" greets Sheridan (Smiles)
"Paddy" replies Doctor Mortimer (Nods)
"Mike" adds MacCormac
"Well, what have you found out, Mike?" asks MacCormac (Looks serious)
"Don't tell me ... parasympathetic rebound, again?" adds MacCormac
"I'm afraid so, Daniel" replies Doctor Mortimer
"... but in addition to finding the mask and during the postmortem of the victim, we found two bruises on the back of the neck" explains Doctor Mortimer
"Bruises?" asks Sheridan (Looks intrigued)
"I'd say, the victim, Maeve Quinn, shows all the signs of being strangled" adds Doctor Mortimer
"So, not parasympathetic rebound, after all?" asks Sheridan

"No ... now it's murder, Paddy" advises MacCormac (Looks serious)

"What about Professor Quinn ... do you think it may be the same, Mike?" asks MacCormac
"I've already checked, Daniel ... yes same marks, same area" adds Doctor Mortimer

"So now we have two murders?" replies Sheridan (Looks serious)

"Yes, I'm afraid so" explains Doctor Mortimer

"And we have a serial killer on the loose" replies MacCormac

"OK, we'll take it from here, Mike" adds MacCormac

"Thanks, Mike" advises MacCormac (Nods)

"High praise indeed, Daniel" replies Doctor Mortimer (Smiles)

"Your always highly praised by me, Mike" adds MacCormac (Laughs)

The Chief Pathologist leaves the Police station.

"So, what now, Sir?" asks Sheridan

"Now I'll brief the Chief Constable, Paddy" replies MacCormac

"You head over to see Gemma Lane ... she could be the next victim" explains MacCormac (Looks serious)

"On my way, Sir" advises Sheridan

Paddy Sheridan arrives at Oxford University and enters the Medical School. He is met by the Gate Keeper.

Sheridan flashes his Police identification card ...

"Is Gemma Lane on campus today?" asks Sheridan (Sounds serious)

"I believe she is in the Biomedical Sciences

department, Sir" replies the Gate Keeper (Points direction)

"Did you say Biomedical Sciences?" asks Sheridan (Looks stunned)

"Yes" replies the Gate Keeper

"So, it's not just a Medical School?" asks Sheridan

"No, it's part of Oxford College" advises the Gate Keeper

Paddy Sheridan enters the Medical School grounds and eventually catches up with Gemma Lane.
"Miss Lane?" asks Sheridan

"Yes" replies Gemma (Looks surprised)

"I'm Inspector Paddy Sheridan, Oxford Police" advises Sheridan

"I believe you were a friend of Maeve Quinn?" asks Sheridan

Gemma breaks down and begins to cry ...
Sheridan looks for somewhere
they can both talk.
"This way, we can talk here"
advises Gemma
"Please sit down" asks Sheridan
(Looks concerned)
"Poor Maeve" replies a teary
Gemma (Looks sad)
"Sorry to ask you this, but do you know why anyone would want to kill her?" asks Sheridan (Looks serious)
"Kill her ... I thought her death was down to

parasympathetic rebound?" replies Gemma (Looks shocked)

"I'm afraid new evidence has come to light ... Miss Quinn was murdered ... as was her Uncle, Professor Quinn ... in exactly the same way" advises Sheridan "Murdered?" replies a shocked Gemma

"Do you know of anyone who would want to harm her?" asks Sheridan

"No ... she was loved by everyone" replies Gemma

"What about Dominic Slater?" asks Sheridan (Looks serious)

"What about Dom?" adds Gemma (Sounds shocked)

"You don't think he's the killer, do you?" replies Gemma

"We're not paid to think, Miss Lane, we rely on hard evidence" explains Sheridan (Sounds serious)

"Do you have evidence?" asks Gemma

"We're looking at all possibilities" adds Sheridan

"So, your a student of Medicine?" asks Sheridan

"No, we focus on how cells, organs and systems function in the human body" replies Gemma (Looks serious)

Paddy Sheridan receives a call on his mobile phone.

"Sorry, Miss ... I have to take this"
advises Sheridan
"OK, I'm on my way" replies
Sheridan
The call ends.

"Sorry, I have to go ... I may need to talk to you again" advises Sheridan

"Please find Maeve's killer, Inspector" asks Gemma (Looks sad)
"Don't worry, we will" assures Sheridan
Paddy Sheridan returns to Oxford Police Station, and is met by the Chief Superintendent ...
"A sudden development, Paddy" advises MacCormac (Sounds serious)
"Sir?" replies Sheridan (Looks stunned)
"The DNA from the mask seems to match that of Dominic Slater" explains MacCormac (Looks optimistic)
"Bring him in" advises
MacCormac
"Where will you be, Sir?"
asks Sheridan
"If you need me, I'll be at home"
replies MacCormac
"At home?" asks Sheridan (Looks stunned)
"An appointment with a friend, Paddy" adds MacCormac (Sounds coy)

The Chief Superintendent takes the road out of Oxford into the suburbs and arrives home. He finds a parcel awaiting on his doorstep.

MacCormac opens the parcel to find inside a mask similar to the one with DNA on it, and a chilling note ...

YOUR NEXT!!!

THE NEXT VICTIM

When Chief Superintendent, Daniel MacCormac realises he could be the next victim, he shrugs off the warning, and continues to look for the murderer with Paddy Sheridan.
When they find a "death mask" bearing the face of Daniel MacCormac they know this is no ordinary murderer.
A plan is set in motion to draw out the killer.

Daniel MacCormac's apartment on the outskirts of Oxford.

Paddy Sheridan arrives, followed by the Chief Constable, and Chief Pathologist, Mike Mortimer.
"Are you alright, Sir?" asks Sheridan (Looks concerned)

"Perfectly alright, Paddy … did you speak to Gemma Lane?" replies MacCormac

"Yes, and she knows Dominic Slater … we've got him in custody, down at the station" advises Sheridan
"Excellent work, Paddy … I'll be along as soon as I've sorted this out" advises MacCormac
"What's that, Sir?" asks Sheridan (Looks surprised)

The Chief Superintendent hands over the parcel, and Paddy Sheridan takes a look inside.
"Why, it's you, Sir" advises Sheridan
(Looks stunned)
Suddenly, the Chief Pathologist, Mike

Mortimer, chips in ...
"Spitting image, I'd say" replies Doctor Mortimer (Smiles)
"Thank you, Mike" advises MacCormac
The Chief Constable arrives on the scene, and looks at the mask.
"I think someone has a grudge against you, Chief Superintendent" advises the Chief Constable (Looks concerned)
"If you say so, Sir" replies MacCormac

"I do say so, Daniel ... and it's getting personal ... we may have to take you off the case" explains the Chief Constable (Looks serious)
"There's no need for that, Sir, surely" replies MacCormac (Looks concerned)

"OK, we'll go with it for now ... I'll blind side the press, but tread very carefully, Daniel" adds the Chief Constable (Looks reassuring)
"Sir" replies MacCormac

The Chief Constable leaves the room and talks to the waiting press. Chief Pathologist, Mike Mortimer discusses the note and mask with MacCormac and Sheridan.
"Well, Mike ... what do you make of it?" asks MacCormac

"A very true likeness, Dan ... we'll get it checked for DNA ... as for the note, tread carefully" replies Doctor Mortimer (Sounds concerned)
"Not you too, Mike" adds MacCormac

"I'll get back to you, tomorrow" adds Doctor Mortimer (Nods)

"Mike" replies MacCormac
"Daniel" replies Doctor Mortimer

"Right, Paddy … there's not a moment to waste … Dominic Slater" advises MacCormac (Sounds serious)
Back at Oxford Police Station, in a nearby custody interview room, Dominic Slater is waiting …
MacCormac and Sheridan begin the interview …
"For the benefit of the tape, Chief Superintendent Daniel MacCormac and Inspector Paddy Sheridan are interviewing Dominic Slater under caution … the time is now 10.20am" advises Sheridan (Sounds official)
"Now, Mr Slater, do you know … sorry, did you know the deceased victim, Maeve Quinn?" asks MacCormac (Sounds serious)
"Yes, we were both at Medical School, together" replies Slater

"Where were you on the night of the murder?" adds MacCormac (Looks serious)
Dominic Slater continues to advise
his version of events.
All of a sudden, a brief enters the
room …
"Tape stopped at 10.30am" advises Sheridan

"… and you are?" asks MacCormac (Looks serious)

"David Whitaker … I'm Mr Slater's Solicitor"

advises Whitaker (Sounds pompous)
MacCormac nods to Sheridan ...

"Tape restarted at 10.33am" adds Sheridan

The Chief Superintendent continues to question Dominic Slater.

He is eventually released, with no charge, but asked to co-operate if required.

Dominic Slater and his Solicitor leave the Police station.
MacCormac and Sheridan head back to their office ...

"Well, Paddy ... what did you make of it?" asks MacCormac (Sounds serious)

"I think he was hiding something, Sir" replies Sheridan (Looks puzzled)

"That's exactly what I was thinking too, Paddy" adds MacCormac
It is now early evening. The Chief Superintendent bids Sheridan farewell and heads for a local pub.
MacCormac has a couple of drinks then leaves the pub, but is suddenly jumped upon from behind, by someone dressed in black.
A sack is put on his head.

"What the hell?" shouts MacCormac (Sounds stunned)

"Do exactly as I say ... and you'll come to no harm" advises a voice

"Alright" replies MacCormac (Sounds gruff)
"Walk this way" insists the voice

Suddenly, the Chief Superintendent's mobile begins to ring …

"It's Sheridan" advises MacCormac
"Don't answer it" instructs the voice

"Who are you?" asks MacCormac (Sounds fraught)

"Why are you doing this?" adds MacCormac (Sounds serious)

The mobile phones continues to ring out.
Paddy Sheridan becomes suspicious and heads back to the pub, but there is no sign of Daniel MacCormac. Sheridan thinks that MacCormac may have taken a taxi home, and waits outside the Chief Superintendent's residence in his car, but he never returns.
Sheridan radio's into Oxford Police Station …
The desk Sergeant takes the call …

"Possible abduction" advises Sheridan (Sounds serious)

"Of whom?" asks the Sergeant (Sounds serious)

"Chief Superintendent MacCormac" explains Sheridan (Sounds anxious)

The desk Sergeant contacts the Chief Constable …

"OK, Sergeant … put Inspector Sheridan through" advises the Chief Constable

Sheridan explains the current situation involving the Chief Superintendent's abduction to the Chief

Constable.

Meanwhile, Daniel MacCormac is blind folded and bound in sack cloth, then bundled into a van and driven out of Oxford to a disused care home.

"They'll never find you here" advises the voice

"I wouldn't bet on it" replies MacCormac (Sounds positive)

Paddy Sheridan and the Police check on the position of MacCormac's mobile phone ...

"Come on man, time is of the essence" advises Sheridan (Looks anxious)

Location details are passed over to the Inspector ...

"OK, contact the Chief Constable, and arrange for Police teams to go to the search area" orders Sheridan (Sounds official)

The location radiating from the Chief Superintendent's mobile phone is traced to Wolvercote, a village that is part of the city of Oxford.

It is about three miles north west of the city centre ... the area pinpointed is close to Wolvercote Common.

Paddy Sheridan liaises with the
Chief Constable.

Armed Police Units now flank the
area.

The Police Commander in control, issues orders from a specifically designed Police vehicle ...

"Gold and Silver Units ... copy?"
asks the Commander

"Gold copy ... in position" advises the Unit Officer

"Silver copy ... in position" replies another Unit Officer

"Await instructions and order" replies the Commander (Sounds serious)

"Copy" advise both Units

The Chief Constable arrives on the scene.

Paddy Sheridan updates the Chief Constable regarding the unfolding situation.

"Any news about the Chief Superintendent?" asks the Chief Constable (Looks anxious)

"Do you have any idea where he is located, Paddy?" adds the Chief Constable

"We have the situation and area under control, Sir" replies Sheridan

"The Chief Superintendent's mobile indicates a nearby barn" adds Sheridan

"Have you spoken to the Commander in charge?" asks the Chief Constable

"Only to await instructions" replies Sheridan (Looks serious)

"OK, Paddy ... I'll speak to them" adds the Chief Constable (Sounds anxious)

"Sir?" adds Sheridan (Looks stunned)

Paddy Sheridan hands his mobile phone over to the Chief Constable which is directly linked to the Unit Commander.

"Watch Commander" asks the Chief Constable (Sounds serious) "Sir" replies the Commander

"Await instruction and orders ... hold position until advised" adds the Chief Constable

"Affirmative ... await instruction and orders" replies the Unit Commander

The Police Commander issues further instructions to the armed Police units.

"Await instructions and order" advises the Unit Commander (Sounds official)

"Copy, Sir" reply both Police armed Units.

Meanwhile, Chief Superintendent, Daniel

MacCormac is becoming impatient ...
"So, what do you intend to do?" asks MacCormac (Looks anxious)
The abductor offers no response to that Question.

MacCormac still has the sack cloth hood over his head, and his feet and hands are tied. He starts to shout for help.
"Can anyone hear me?" shouts MacCormac

Paddy Sheridan thinks he heard something, and advises the Chief Constable.
"Did you hear that, Sir?" asks Sheridan (Looks towards the barn)

The Chief Superintendent calls out for a second time ...

"Is there anyone there?" shouts MacCormac
"MacCormac?" advises the Chief Constable (Looks anxious)
"Use the loud haler" replies Sheridan
The Chief Constable issues orders to the armed Police units to proceed with caution, into the barn ...
"Copy, Sir" replies the Unit Commander (Slowly moves forward)
The Police Commander gives the order to the armed officers ...
"Gold/Silver units" advises the Unit Commander
"Copy, control" reply Gold/Silver Units

"Move forward ... hold on fire" adds the Unit Commander

"Affirmative" reply Gold and Silver Units
"Well, Paddy?" asks the Chief Constable (Looks serious)
"I think it's the right thing to do, Sir" replies Sheridan
Gold/Silver Units go into the barn, and find the hooded figure of Daniel MacCormac, alone …
"Will someone please take this damn hood off me?" asks MacCormac
An armed Police officer removes the hood …
"Thank you" advises MacCormac

Paddy Sheridan rushes into the barn and begins to untie his colleague …

"Are you alright, Sir?" asks Sheridan (Looks serious)
The Chief Superintendent's answer is as expected, under the circumstances …
"Do I look alright, Paddy?" replies MacCormac (Sounds pompous)
"Where is he?" adds MacCormac (Looks around)
"Where's who, Sir?" asks Sheridan
"My abductor?" replies MacCormac (Sounds concerned)

"We're the only ones here, Sir … apart from our fellow Officers" explains Sheridan
"I think, I've an idea, Paddy … who it is" adds MacCormac
"How?" asks Sheridan (Looks puzzled)

"Voice recognition" replies MacCormac (Looks serious)

"The blighter is more slippery than an eel ... he certainly caught me out" explains MacCormac (Sounds fraught)
"He took you by surprise?"
asks Sheridan
"Exactly, Paddy" replies
MacCormac
"Now, we must set a trap to capture him" adds MacCormac

ENTRAPMENT

MacCormac and Sheridan set out to finally trap those responsible ... a surprise lead ... will the murderer be caught or will they escape?

November 4th, Mischief Night ...

The Chief Superintendent and Paddy Sheridan are now back at Oxford Police Station.
Chief Pathologist, Mike Mortimer, enters the Chief Superintendent's office.
"Mike" greets Sheridan (Nods)
"Well, Mike?" asks MacCormac (Looks serious)

"Are you alright, Daniel ... you look as if you've had a fright" replies Doctor Mortimer (Looks stunned)
"Parasympathetic rebound?" adds Doctor Mortimer (Sounds official)
"Quite" adds MacCormac (Sneers)
"Only ... I hope I'm not a sufferer, Mike" advises MacCormac (Looks puzzled)
"You were right about the DNA" explains Doctor Mortimer
"Was I?" asks MacCormac (Looks surprised)
"Yes, both match" replies Doctor Mortimer (Sounds official)
"Now, all you have to do is catch the murderer" adds Doctor Mortimer

"Do you know who it is, Daniel?" asks Doctor Mortimer (Looks serious)

"We've got an idea, Mike" replies MacCormac

"What's the plan, Sir?" asks Sheridan (Looks serious)

"We've already met him, Paddy" advises MacCormac

"Have we?" replies Sheridan (Sounds suspicious)

"Yes, but he didn't stand out" explains MacCormac

"How do you know it's the right man, Daniel?" asks Doctor Mortimer

"Voice recognition, Mike ... and I'll bet his DNA matches" replies MacCormac

"Will it stand up in court, Sir?" asks Sheridan (Looks concerned)

"Naturally ... we have DNA on the murder victims, and now on the hooded sack cloth" explains MacCormac

"We've got him" advises Sheridan (Looks serious)

"Now, all we need to do, is set a trap, Paddy" replies MacCormac

"Well, the suspect does seem to be infatuated with you, Sir" adds Sheridan

"Yes, I'd say so, Paddy ... I'll be the bait" explains MacCormac (Looks serious)

"What again?" asks Doctor Mortimer (Looks stunned)

"It's the only way, Mike" advises MacCormac

Early evening, 4th November, Oxford University

(Medical School).

"Do you think he'll take the bait, Sir?" asks Sheridan (Looks suspicious)

"We'll deliver it to him on a plate, Paddy" replies MacCormac

"What if it goes wrong ... remember he's a killer?" adds Sheridan

"It won't ... I'll be wired up ... you'll be recording everything" explains MacCormac (Looks serious)

"What are you hoping for, Sir?" asks Sheridan

"A confession of guilt, naturally" adds MacCormac

"Do you think they had an accomplice?" replies Sheridan

"It's possible ... but I think they are working alone" explains MacCormac

"Why has it all happened?" asks Sheridan

"A grudge, who knows, Paddy" replies MacCormac

The Chief Superintendent is wired up by his Police colleagues.

MacCormac has been given strict instructions by the Chief Constable to detain those responsible ... even though he is putting his own life on the line!

"Are you sure about this, Sir?" asks a cautious Sheridan

"As sure as I'll ever be, Paddy" replies MacCormac (Nods)

"We need to nail this murderer" adds MacCormac

Sheridan and MacCormac arrive at Oxford University campus.
The first thing that draws their attention is that the Gate Lodge is unmanned!

"Damn peculiar" advises MacCormac (Sounds serious)

"What is, Sir?" asks Sheridan

"No Gate Keeper" adds MacCormac (Looks around)

Suddenly, another voice greets MacCormac and Sheridan ...

"Sorry, were you looking for me?" asks the voice

"Hardly" replies MacCormac

"Chief Superintendent MacCormac ... and Inspector Paddy Sheridan" advises MacCormac

"... and you are?" asks MacCormac (Looks serious)

"Clive Donaldson" replies the Gate Keeper

"Where's Soames?" adds MacCormac (Looks concerned)

"Is it his night off?" asks Sheridan

"No, he's around here somewhere" replies Donaldson (Looks outside)

MacCormac nods to Sheridan ...

"Any idea where, Sir?" asks MacCormac

"I think he's doing the rounds ... inspecting the University" advises Donaldson

"Contact Control, Paddy" advises MacCormac (Looks

official)

"Sir?" replies Sheridan

"Alert status" explains MacCormac (Sounds official)

"Will do, Sir" replies Sheridan
The Chief Superintendent starts to walk away from the Gate Keeper's Lodge and wanders into the University grounds.
"Where are you going, Sir?" asks Sheridan (Looks anxious)
"I'm going to look for Soames" replies MacCormac
"Mr Donaldson, you wait here" asks MacCormac

"Be careful, Sir" advises Sheridan (Sounds concerned)

"Don't worry, Paddy, I will" adds MacCormac
"How do I know?" advises MacCormac

"I've got you watching out for me" explains MacCormac (Smiles)

The Chief Constable is updated about the proceedings, and that the Chief Superintendent has gone in as bait, to flush out the murderer!
"Stupid ... stupid man" growls the Chief Constable (Looks mad)
"Why didn't he wait?" asks the Chief Constable (Looks annoyed)
"You know the Chief Superintendent, Sir ... he always puts his life on the line" explains Sheridan

(Sounds concerned)
"Well, maybe he has gone too far, this time, Paddy" adds the Chief Constable
"Is he wired?" asks the Chief Constable
"Yes, Sir" replies Sheridan

"You know him well, don't you Paddy?" asks the Chief Constable

"Yes, I suppose I do, Sir" adds Sheridan
"OK, follow him ... shadow him ... draw out the killer" explains the Chief Constable
"Will do, Sir" replies Sheridan

The Chief Superintendent continues to tread carefully in the grounds of the University. Suddenly another voice comes out of the shadows ...

"Are you looking for me, Chief Superintendent?" asks the voice

"Soames" replies MacCormac
"Why did you do it?" asks MacCormac (Sounds serious)
"Do what?" replies Soames
"You know what ... why did you do it?" asks MacCormac a second time
"We've got evidence, and your DNA is all over the victims" adds MacCormac
"Everything is well documented" explains MacCormac
Soames ponders the Chief Superintendent's Question, then answers ...
"I'd forgotten about DNA" replies Soames

(Looks stunned)
"Why man, why?" asks MacCormac
"They both got too close" advises Soames
"Too close to what?" adds MacCormac (Looks serious)

Paddy Sheridan is now in the University grounds, and he gets closer to the Chief Superintendent and Soames ...

"That would be telling" replies Soames

"What about Parasympathetic Rebound?" asks MacCormac

"What about it?" adds Soames (Looks puzzled)
"They all died of asphyxia" explains MacCormac (Sounds serious)
" ... as if they'd seen a ghost" adds MacCormac
"You covered up the actual evidence" advises MacCormac (Sounds serious)
"Why?" asks MacCormac
"... did they get too close?" adds MacCormac

"Why did you murder them?" asks MacCormac (Sounds serious)

"Maeve Quinn and Doctor Quinn ... you knew they were related" explains MacCormac
"I'm afraid they found out" replies Soames (Looks suspicious)
"Found out what, Soames?" asks

MacCormac

"That I was indeed, related" adds Soames

"Related?" replies MacCormac (Looks stunned)

"Now I understand ... it was all about money and greed" advises MacCormac

"Not exactly, MacCormac" replies Soames (Looks pompous)

The Chief Constable and armed Police officers arrive on the scene. Soames notices their arrival in the University grounds and issues orders to MacCormac.

"Call off your colleagues" orders Soames

The Chief Superintendent calls out to the waiting armed units.

"Hold back" advises MacCormac (Sounds serious)

The Chief Constable instructs the armed officers to hold their position.

"Well, Soames ... why?" asks MacCormac

"They both found out that I was the real heir to the family fortune" advises Soames (Sounds serious)

"They had to be dealt with"

adds Soames

"Dealt with?" asks MacCormac

(Looks stunned)

"Eliminated" replies Soames

"... by fright?" adds MacCormac (Looks suspicious)

"What better way, Chief Superintendent?" asks Soames (Looks pleased)

"It's clean and virtually undetectable" adds Soames

Soames edges up the winding staircase, on to the roof of the College. The Chief Superintendent follows, with Paddy Sheridan as back up.

"Don't come any further, or I'll jump" advises Soames

Paddy Sheridan suddenly comes into view ...

"I knew you weren't alone, MacCormac" adds Soames

"It's quite alright, Soames" replies MacCormac

"So what happens next, MacCormac?" asks Soames (Sounds afraid)

"Well, that's up to you, Soames" adds MacCormac

"Your not really the Gate Keeper of the College, are you?" asks MacCormac

"Merely a diversion, Chief Superintendent ... to get near to my, so called, relatives" explains Soames (Looks fraught)

"You see they were trying to keep me out of family matters ... they had to die" adds Soames

"... but that makes you a murderer and a serial killer" explains MacCormac

"I had no other choice, Chief Superintendent" replies Soames

Suddenly, a change in tactics ... the Chief Constable uses a loud haler ...

"Come down and you won't be harmed"

advises the Chief Constable
"For Pete's sake, Paddy … that's all we need" replies MacCormac
"Call your men off, MacCormac" barks Soames (Sounds anxious)
The Chief Superintendent shouts down to the waiting officers …
"Now, Soames, take my hand" asks MacCormac
"Don't come any further or I'll jump" replies Soames (Looks serious)
"Take my hand, don't be a fool, man" adds MacCormac
Soames leans forward and almost drags the Chief Superintendent with him …
Luckily, Paddy Sheridan holds on to MacCormac …
Suddenly a big thud can be heard on the ground. Soames is dead!
Paddy Sheridan pulls the Chief Superintendent to safety …
"This way, Sir" points Sheridan
"Thank you, Paddy" replies MacCormac

"You know, I don't say that enough to you … thanks for everything" adds MacCormac
"Sir" replies Sheridan
"Come on, Paddy … we'll have to fill in the Chief Constable" advises MacCormac
"At least that's the end of the case, Sir" adds Sheridan
"I wonder" replies MacCormac (Looks serious)

"Perhaps Parasympathetic Rebound is in all of us?" advises MacCormac

"Perhaps" adds Sheridan (Looks stunned)
"Maybe, we'll never know the answer for sure" explains MacCormac
"Maybe not, Sir" replies Sheridan

EQUILIBRIUM

A STATE OF PHYSICAL BALANCE

Detective Chief Inspector Daniel MacCormac is now Chief Superintendent of Thames Valley Police, and he reports directly to the Chief Constable.

Sergeant Paddy Sheridan, is now an Inspector, based in Oxford, and still an endorsement of his old mentor, the Chief Super!

A state of opposing forces or influences become finely balanced in this murder mystery.

Influential businessman, Harry Masters is the toast of Oxford when his invention is nominated for the Nobel Peace Prize, and news that he is to be made a Knight in the New Year's Honours list!

When Masters suffers a type of stab wound, at an elaborate dinner in Oxford, in which Daniel MacCormac is also attending, several suspects are in the frame for murder!

Why has The Chief Superintendent been found, in a state of delirium, with a dagger in his hand?

Can Inspector Paddy Sheridan find the truth and evidence needed to free the Chief Superintendent from suspicion of murder?

Could Daniel MacCormac be in for a fall from which there is inevitably no recovery?

Is it all a state of intellectual and emotional balance

which defines equilibrium in medical terms?

INFLUENCES

Harry Masters is an influential businessman and an Oxford graduate.

When news breaks that he has won the Nobel Peace Prize for Medicine reaches Magdalen College at the University of Oxford, an elaborate ceremony and evening is planned in his honour at the Sheldon Theatre.

The Sheldon was opened in 1669 by Gilbert Sheldon, Archbishop of Canterbury and Chancellor of the University of Oxford.

Sir Christopher Wren designed the Sheldon.

The Sheldon Theatre is located in the heart of Oxford's medieval city centre.

Inside the Sheldon Theatre …

"Has our influential guest arrived?" asks Professor Simon Greenwood

Greenwood is the Chair of the Sheldon Curators and a senior member of the University.

"He's just pulled up in his Mercedes" replies Colleen Whitmore, director of Brasenose College (Sounds official)

Both gaze out of the windows …

"Look at him, you'd think he was some kind of famous celebrity" advises a voice

"Well, Harry always did like to make an entrance" replies another voice (Smiles)

Enter, Sir Malcolm Haigh, another graduate of the University ... and an old friend of Harry Masters ... Harry enters the Sheldonian Theatre ...

"I remember when Harry and I came here for our degree ceremony, what a day that was" advises Sir Malcolm (Looks serious)

"... that was over forty years ago" replies another voice (Smiles)

Harry Masters shakes Sir Malcolm's hand ...
"Harry ... how are you?" asks Sir Malcolm (Looks pleased)

Harry Masters is a distinguished upright man of old fashioned values ...

Suddenly, another voice enters ...
"Harry Masters" asks the voice

"Why it's ..." replies Harry
(Shakes hands)

"Daniel MacCormac" adds
Harry (Smiles)

"The very same" replies
MacCormac (Laughs)

"What happened, Daniel ... after you graduated from Oxford?" asks Harry

"Life, Harry ... life happened" replies MacCormac (Laughs)

"Why did you drop out?" asks Harry
(Looks concerned)

"While studying ... I joined the army"
adds MacCormac

"What happened ... why didn't you ever marry?" asks Simon Greenwood

"A failed romance, Simon ... set me back, but I did marry ... I'm a widower" replies MacCormac (Looks sad)

"There were always plenty more fish in the sea" explains Harry (Laughs)

"That may be so, Harry ... but I decided to enter into criminal investigations" explains MacCormac (Looks serious)

"A Policeman?" asks Harry (Looks serious)

"Not just any Policeman" advises Simon (Looks surprised)

"Chief Superintendent MacCormac, now" adds Simon

"My, my ... Daniel MacCormac, a high ranking Police officer" replies Harry

"Hardly that, Harry" replies MacCormac (Laughs)

"Are you here for the award ceremony, Daniel?" asks Harry

"Naturally" adds MacCormac (Sounds official)

"OK, I'll see you later" adds MacCormac (Nods)

"Where?" asks Harry (Looks concerned)

"In the bar of course, if anyone wants me you'll find me looking at the bottom of a beer glass" adds MacCormac (Laughs)

"Still as funny, as ever" replies Harry (Laughing)

"It wasn't meant to be funny, Harry" advises MacCormac

The exterior of the Sheldonian Theatre is quite amazing, and the interior is stunning.
An announcement is suddenly broadcast over the speaker system.

"Will all guests please make their way to their places in the restaurant" asks the voice
"Dinner is about to be served"
concludes the voice
Daniel MacCormac takes up his
place ...
Harry Mortimer and Simon Greenwood are both on the head table.

The Civil dignitaries begin to talk prior to the dinner, and welcome everyone to the event in Harry's honour.
Daniel MacCormac leaves his seat after a sudden call from Oxford Police Station
"MacCormac" replies the Chief Superintendent
(Sounds serious)
"I told no one to disturb me tonight"
advises MacCormac
"Paddy, is that you?" asks MacCormac
(Sounds surprised)
"Sorry to contact you tonight, Sir"
replies Sheridan
"Go on Paddy, what's the problem?" asks MacCormac

"It's something to do with opposing forces, Sir" adds Sheridan

"Opposing forces?" asks an intrigued MacCormac

"Very well, Paddy ... I'll see you in thirty minutes" replies MacCormac

The opening speech begins after the dinner, but Harry Mortimer is no where in sight ...
Suddenly a loud scream can be heard ...
A lady finds Harry face down with several stab wounds.
Simon Greenwood asks for help.
"Daniel ... where's Daniel MacCormac?" asks Greenwood (Looks around)
No one can find the Chief Superintendent ... but a sharp eyed Professor stumbles across MacCormac in a side room.
Simon Greenwood and several other well to do patrons follow the Professor into the room ...
They find Daniel MacCormac in a bewildered state of delusion, holding a blood stained dagger ...
"Daniel?" asks Greenwood (Looks concerned)

"What have you done?" adds Greenwood (Sounds serious)

"Why Daniel ... why?" asks Greenwood (Looks stunned)

"Someone call the Police" advises the Professor
Daniel MacCormac mumbles ...

"I am the Police" replies MacCormac (Sounds fraught)

Delusion is a state of mind and physical balance or imbalance.

In the case of Chief Superintendent Daniel MacCormac, he is far from his normal self.

What's happened to the Chief Superintendent?

The Police arrive at the scene in the Sheldonian Theatre.

Paddy Sheridan and Chief Pathologist, Mike Mortimer have just arrived.

Doctor Mortimer checks over the body of Harry Masters ...

"What have we got, Mike?" asks Sheridan (Sounds serious)
"Multiple stab wounds, made by a blunt instrument" advises Doctor Mortimer
" A knife?" adds Sheridan
"I can't be sure at this stage, Paddy ... I need to do further tests" adds Doctor Mortimer
"What about the Chief Superintendent?" asks Sheridan (Looks stunned)
"He's in a side room ... and asking for you, Paddy" replies Doctor Mortimer
"For me?" asks Sheridan
"His state of mind is questionable" adds Doctor Mortimer (Sounds concerned)
"Well, come on, lets get it over with" adds Sheridan
Doctor Mortimer enters the side room with Paddy Sheridan ...
"Are you alright, Sir?" asks Sheridan (Looks stunned)

"Do I look alright, Paddy?" replies MacCormac (Sounds groggy)
"What happened?" adds Sheridan
"If I knew that, I'd tell you" advises MacCormac (Looks shocked)
"Can you remember anything, Sir?" asks Sheridan
"Only coming round and finding that dagger in my hand" explains MacCormac
"Nothing else?" adds Sheridan
"Absolutely nothing else" replies MacCormac (Looks serious)
"What do you think?" asks Sheridan
"A frame up, Paddy ... someone has gone to a lot of trouble to make it look that I'm the murderer" explains MacCormac (Sounds serious)
"Oh, no" adds MacCormac
"No, Sir?" asks Sheridan
"The Chief Constable is here ... that's all I need" advises MacCormac
"Do you want me to talk to him, Sir?" asks Sheridan
"No, Paddy ... better if I do" adds MacCormac (Sounds anxious)
"How are you feeling?" asks Doctor Mortimer
"As if I've been hit by a bolt out of the blue, Mike" explains MacCormac
Sheridan passes over the dagger to Doctor Mortimer

...

"I'll get it analysed along with the autopsy ... don't worry I'll be in touch later" advises Doctor Mortimer (Nods)

"Don't make it too long, Mike ... my life could depend on it" replies MacCormac

"Don't worry, Daniel ... I'll be back soon" adds Doctor Mortimer (Nods)

The Chief Constable now enters the sealed off room ... "Good evening, Sir" greets Sheridan

"Sheridan" replies the Chief Constable

Paddy Sheridan leaves the Chief Superintendent with the Chief Constable ...

"What a mess, Daniel" advises the Chief Constable (Looks concerned)

"I know, Sir ... but I'm not the murderer" explains MacCormac (Looks serious)

"Of course, your not" replies the Chief Constable

"Sir?" asks MacCormac (Looks stunned)

"But we've got to prove that, Daniel" advises the Chief Constable (Looks concerned)

"Doctor Mortimer has taken away the evidence and will let us know later today the outcome concerning the knife and autopsy, Sir" explains MacCormac

"OK, but for now your suspended" advises the Chief Constable

"I understand, Sir" replies MacCormac (Looks glum)

"Await further developments" explains the Chief

Constable

The Chief Constable calls Paddy Sheridan back into the side room ...

"This is a real bloody mess, Paddy" advises the Chief Constable (Looks serious)

"Yes, Sir ... it is" replies Sheridan
"You'll have to assume command until Doctor Mortimer advises otherwise" adds the Chief Constable (Looks stern)
"... and keep an eye on the Chief Superintendent" adds the Chief Constable

"But I'm alright, Sir" replies MacCormac (Looks reassuring)

"Far from it, Daniel ... at this moment in time your our chief suspect in this murder case" explains the Chief Constable (Looks serious)

"... but I didn't do it, Sir" explains MacCormac (Looks equally serious)

"Paddy Sheridan and Doctor Mortimer will have to prove that" replies the Chief Constable

"Someone has a vendetta against me" advises MacCormac (Looks concerned)

"Don't you remember anything, Daniel?" asks the Chief Constable

"I remember ordering a pint at the bar, then walking away" replies MacCormac

"Think man, think" adds the Chief Constable

"Did you keep hold of your glass or did you put it down, Sir?" asks Sheridan

The Chief Superintendent tries to remember ...

"Come to think of it I did put my glass down on the bar for a couple of minutes" replies MacCormac (Sounds serious)

"A couple of minutes ... that's all it takes" advises Sheridan (Looks concerned)

"Someone could have slipped something into your drink" adds the Chief Constable

"I agree, they could" replies MacCormac (Looks baffled)

"I've arranged for you to have a blood sample taken" advises the Chief Constable (Looks

serious)

"It will be checked to see if there was any foul play" adds the Chief Constable

"Your drink may have been spiked, Sir" advises Sheridan (Looks concerned)

"Anything could have happened" adds Sheridan

The Chief Constable asks Paddy Sheridan to arrange for the Chief Superintendent to be seen by the Medical Team back at Oxford Police Station.

"We have to be sure, Daniel" explains the Chief Constable (Looks serious)

"Then we'll know for sure" adds Sheridan

"I agree, Sir ... something happened to me, that's for sure" replies MacCormac

PATHOLOGY REPORT

Chief Pathologist, Doctor Mike Mortimer completes his report into Harry Master's death, and startling new evidence comes to light.

The Police Medical Team complete their report into the Chief Superintendent's state of mind. Paddy Sheridan finds fresh evidence!

Oxford Police Station, Chief Superintendent Daniel MacCormac's office …

Chief Pathologist, Mike Mortimer and Paddy Sheridan in attendance.

MacCormac is awaiting the results of his blood test …

"I've carried out the postmortem on Harry Masters" advises Doctor Mortimer

"What did you find, Mike?" asks Sheridan (Looks serious)

"The blunt instrument used to kill Harry Masters was not the knife Daniel MacCormac was holding at the scene of the crime" explains Doctor Mortimer

"Can you confirm that, Mike?" adds Sheridan (Looks concerned)

"Yes … it was more likely a screw driver" adds Doctor Mortimer (Nods)

"A screw driver?" replies Sheridan (Looks puzzled)

"What about DNA, Mike?" asks Sheridan

"I've checked, and we also took Daniel's DNA too" advises Doctor Mortimer

"What were the results?" adds Sheridan (Looks serious)

"There was no match" explains Doctor Mortimer

"So, the Chief Superintendent is off the hook?" asks Sheridan (Looks relieved)

"Well, as long as the Police report indicates the same … yes" advises Doctor Mortimer (Nods in agreement)

"Does the Chief Constable know?" replies Sheridan

"I've already advised him, Paddy" adds Doctor Mortimer (Looks serious)

"What did he say?" asks Sheridan

"He was relieved … and the Chief Superintendent" adds Mike

"I think that was putting it mildly, Mike" advises Sheridan

A Police Medical Officer enters the Chief Superintendent's office and hands a file to Doctor Mortimer …

"Thank you" replies Doctor Mortimer (Smiles)

Mike reads the file …

"Well?" asks Sheridan (Looks puzzled)

"Conclusive evidence … Daniel MacCormac was given a lethal dose of something" explains Doctor Mortimer (Looks concerned)

"A lethal dose of what, Mike?" adds Sheridan

"Hydroxyzine ... it causes hallucinations and delusion" replies Doctor Mortimer

"So, he was drugged?" asks Sheridan (Looks serious) Enter Daniel MacCormac ...

"Yes, I was, Paddy" replies MacCormac (Looks cautious)

"Sir, are you alright ... should you be here?" adds Sheridan (Looks concerned)

"Well, Mike ... answer Paddy's question?" asks MacCormac

"Your cleared by the Police Doctor's I presume?" replies Doctor Mortimer

"Yes, Mike ... and the Chief Constable" explains MacCormac (Nods)

"Business as usual then" adds Doctor Mortimer (Smiles)

"Exactly, Mike" replies MacCormac

"Do you remember anything, Sir?" asks Sheridan (Sounds concerned)

"I was set up, Paddy" advises MacCormac (Sounds serious)

"Set up?" adds Sheridan

"Set up by whom, Sir?" replies Sheridan

"That's what we need to find out, Paddy" replies MacCormac

"Someone has a grievance against me ... and they could strike again" explains MacCormac (Looks serious)

"It's too late for Harry Masters"

replies MacCormac
"What was the motive behind it all, Sir?" asks Sheridan
"Something is staring us in the face, Paddy" adds MacCormac

"Well, Daniel, I must go … no doubt our paths will cross again soon" advises Doctor Mortimer (Nods)
"Mike" replies MacCormac (Nods)
"Oh, Mike … just before you go" asks MacCormac
"Daniel?" replies Doctor Mortimer (Looks surprised)
"Did you find anything at all?" adds MacCormac
"In your pathology report?" questions MacCormac (Looks concerned)
"As I told Paddy, a blunt instrument killed Harry Masters" advises Doctor Mortimer (Looks serious)
"Blunt in what way, Mike?" asks MacCormac
"A screw driver" adds Doctor Mortimer
"The knife you held was a plant … none of your DNA on anything at all" explains Doctor Mortimer (Looks serious)
"Hence my reinstatement to the case" replies MacCormac (Sounds relieved)
"Exactly" replies Doctor Mortimer
The Chief Pathologist leaves the Chief Superintendent's office.
"Where to now, Sir?" asks Sheridan (Sounds serious)

"I think we need to go back to the Sheldonian Theatre, then look into Harry Masters background" replies MacCormac (Looks serious)

"It could have been someone close or a business associate" advises MacCormac

"… or just someone who hated Harry Masters?" asks Sheridan

"Hated is a strong word, Paddy … but you could be right" adds MacCormac

"Dig and delve" replies MacCormac (Sounds authoritative)

"Where will you be, Sir?" asks Sheridan

"If you need me, I'll be on the trail of Harry Masters" advises MacCormac

Several hours later, Paddy Sheridan updates the Chief Superintendent …

"Well, what have you found, Paddy?" asks MacCormac (Looks intrigued)

"Harry Masters had enemies, Sir" replies Sheridan
"Enemies … business enemies?" adds MacCormac (Sounds official)
"Well on all sides … relatives" advises Sheridan
"So everyone is under suspicion?" asks MacCormac (Looks stunned)

"More or less … I've never come across anyone quite like him" replies Sheridan

"Here's what I found" adds Sheridan
Paddy hands the Chief Superintendent a file …

"Startling, quite startling, Paddy" advises MacCormac (Looks serious)

"I'd better discuss this with the Chief Constable" adds MacCormac

"Sir?" replies Sheridan
"This is quite damning information, and it looks as though it could implicate those at the very top, Paddy" explains MacCormac (Looks concerned)
"Do you mean in Government, Sir?" asks Sheridan

"Something like that, Paddy ... I'll talk this over with the Chief Constable, and we'll meet later" replies MacCormac (Nods)
"Keep digging and delving" adds MacCormac
"Good work, Paddy" advises MacCormac (Smiles)
"Thank you, Sir ... I'll see what else we can unearth in the murky world of Harry Masters" replies Sheridan
Paddy Sheridan leaves the Police Station in Oxford, while the Chief Superintendent contacts the Chief Constable ...
MacCormac is asked to meet with the Chief Constable as soon as possible.
"Where, Sir?" asks MacCormac
"Here, at Thames Valley" replies the Chief Constable
"Why, Sir?" adds MacCormac
"This is your new location" advises the Chief Constable (Sounds serious)

"Very well, Sir" replies MacCormac
The Chief Superintendent leaves Oxford and jumps into his white Audi, then makes his way to Kidlington ...
Daniel MacCormac arrives at Thames Valley Police HQ, knocks and enters the Chief Constable's office.
James Mannering was Assistant Chief Constable and has now assumed the role following the retirement of the previous Chief Constable. He is responsible for justice and for Counter Terrorism Policing in the South East and Regional Crime unit ...
MacCormac knocks and enters the Chief Constable's office ...
"Come in, Daniel" replies the Chief Constable (Smiles)
"You said new evidence has come to light, concerning Harry Masters?" adds the Chief Constable (Sounds official)
"Indeed it has, Sir" advises MacCormac

"Inspector Paddy Sheridan has stumbled upon the most startling evidence" explains MacCormac (Looks serious)
The Chief Superintendent hands over the file to the Chief Constable.

"My God, Daniel ... if the press get hold of this they would have a field day" replies the Chief Constable (Sounds concerned)
"Yes, I believe they would, Sir" replies MacCormac (Nods)

"Who would have thought that Harry Masters, an

upright pillar of Society would have links with the Royal Family?" asks the Chief Constable (Looks surprised) "Exactly, Sir ... that's why I thought it appropriate for me to bring you the file" explains MacCormac (Sounds official)

"You did the right thing, Chief Superintendent ... we need to keep a lid on this" advises the Chief Constable (Looks serious)

"... and the murder of Harry Masters, Sir?" adds MacCormac (Looks concerned)

"Continue your investigation ... but ask Inspector Sheridan to use discretion" explains the Chief Constable (Sounds authoritative)

"Any further issues, Daniel?" asks the Chief Constable

"No, Sir" replies MacCormac

"Are you alright after your recent brush with mortality?" adds the Chief Constable (Sounds concerned)

"Yes, Sir ... I've been cleared, and given the green light" adds MacCormac

"Well, Daniel ... you know my door is always open, and now I'm here we can both have a close relationship" explains the Chief Constable (Sounds reassuring)

"Yes, Sir ... thank you, Sir" replies MacCormac (Smiles)

The Chief Superintendent leaves the Chief Constable's office.

Two hours later, both he and Paddy Sheridan

reunite at Oxford Police Station ...

On entry to the Police station Paddy Sheridan bumps into an old friend ...

"Paddy?" asks the voice (Smiling)
"Maxine ... long time no see" replies Sheridan (Looks stunned)
"Fancy meeting you here" adds Sheridan
"You too" adds Maxine (Looks equally stunned)
"Do you live in Oxford?" asks Maxine
"Yes, I do" replies Sheridan (Smiling)
" ... and work here" adds Sheridan (Sounds official)

"I didn't know you were a Policeman" explains Maxine

"Yes, I'm afraid I am" advises Sheridan (Looks serious)

"Are you in Oxford long, Maxine?" asks Sheridan

"A few days ... I'm publicising my new book" adds Maxine (Smiles)

"We must meet up before you leave" replies Sheridan

"Yes, we must, Paddy" advises Maxine (Looks serious)

"Sorry, I have to go ... my boss is waiting for me" explains Sheridan

"It's alright Paddy, I understand" adds

Maxine

"OK, here's my phone number ... I'm staying locally" advises Maxine
"OK, I'll be in touch" replies Sheridan (Smiles)
"Bye" replies Maxine

"Bye Maxine" adds Sheridan (Smiling)

Paddy Sheridan enters the Chief Superintendent's office with a couple of coffees, straight out of a machine in the station ...
"Where have you been, Paddy?" asks MacCormac (Sounds serious)
"Oh, I bumped into an old girlfriend, on the way in, Sir" replies Sheridan
"Yes, I saw you" replies MacCormac (Sounds pompous)
"She told me she was working on a new book about the Nobel Peace Awards" explains Sheridan
"Maybe she can throw some light on Harry Masters murder?" asks MacCormac
"Yes, may be ... Maxine was a one time wife of Harry Masters" replies Sheridan
"Now that's a coincidence, Paddy" ponders MacCormac (Looks stunned)
"Just turning up out of the blue like that" adds MacCormac

"Do you think she may be hiding something, Paddy?" asks MacCormac
"Sir?" replies Sheridan (Looks puzzled)

"Now why would the ex-wife of a highly regarded man like, Harry Masters, suddenly turn up in

Oxford, at precisely the time of the murder?" asks MacCormac (Looks confused)

"Now, you've got me thinking, Sir" replies Sheridan (Looks puzzled)

STATE OF ILLUSION

Paddy Sheridan finds out more information concerning his old flame, Maxine. Chief Superintendent Daniel MacCormac has to make a journey to Wolvercote, and answers begin to emerge concerning Harry Masters …

Paddy Sheridan arranges to meet Maxine, under orders from Chief Superintendent Daniel MacCormac.

Both meet at the bar inside the Randolph Hotel in central Oxford. The Hotel is well known and stands in a prominent position on Beaumont Street …

"Paddy" greets a voice

"Evening, Maxine" replies Sheridan (Smiles)

Maxine is in her early fifties, five foot 8, has blonde hair, blue eyes and elegantly dressed …

Paddy and Maxine find a suitably quiet table away from the bar and prying eyes …

"I didn't have you down for staying in a place like this" adds Sheridan (Looks curious)

"Oh, the books pay for it … and I have an image to preserve, Paddy" replies Maxine (Smiling)

"So, why are you writing a book about the Nobel Peace Prize?" asks Sheridan

"You could say I have an invested interest in it" explains Maxine (Looks serious)

"Harry Masters?" asks Sheridan (Sounds curious)

"Ah, my secret is out" replies Maxine (Looks stunned)

"Secret?" inquires Sheridan (Looks surprised)

"Well, it's no secret really, Paddy … I was married to Harry for over twenty years" adds Maxine (Sounds sincere)

"Why all the questions?" asks Maxine (Looks puzzled)

"Harry is in my past" adds Maxine

"You do know that I'm investigating his murder don't you?" asks Sheridan

"Yes … and I suppose your Boss put you up to this" replies Maxine (Looks serious)

"Up to what?" asks Sheridan (Looks puzzled)

"Asking me a lot of questions" adds Maxine (Looks concerned)

"It's all part of the job, Maxine" replies Sheridan

"And I suppose you think I've done it too?" adds Maxine (Looks stunned)

Paddy Sheridan looks anxious …

"You do, don't you … and I really thought you knew me, Paddy" explains Maxine (Gets up from the table and walks away)

Back at Oxford Police Station, Chief Superintendent Daniel MacCormac receives a phone call, in his office …

The phone starts to ring continuously …

"MacCormac" greets the Chief Superintendent

"Listen very carefully to my instructions" advises the voice (Sounds serious)

"Who is this?" asks MacCormac (Sounds cautious)

The Chief Superintendent asks a young Constable to trace the call …

"Well, what do you want?" adds MacCormac (Sounds serious)

"If you want to know more about Harry Masters killer, meet me in the grounds of St Peter's Church, Wolvercote in an hour … and, MacCormac" advises the voice

"Yes" replies MacCormac (Sounds serious)

"Come alone" adds the voice

"You can tell your man to call off that trace now" advises the voice

"St Peter's in an hour" ends the voice

The line suddenly goes dead …

The young Policeman re-enters the Chief Superintendent's office …

"Did we get a trace on that call?" asks MacCormac (Looks concerned)

"Sorry, not enough time, Sir" replies the young officer

"OK … has Inspector Sheridan returned?" adds MacCormac

"He's just arrived back in the station, Sir"

adds the young officer

Paddy Sheridan enters the Chief Superintendent's office ...

"Have I missed something?" asks Sheridan (Looks puzzled)

"That was a call from someone about Harry Masters" advises MacCormac

"I've agreed to meet them in the grounds of St Peter's Church, Wolvercote, in an hour, Paddy" adds MacCormac (Looks serious)

"Wolvercote?" questions Sheridan (Looks concerned)

"That what I thought, Paddy ... why Wolvercote?" asks MacCormac

"What does the Chief Constable say, Sir?" asks Sheridan (Looks stunned)

"We need this information, Paddy" replies MacCormac (Sounds serious)

The Chief Superintendent suddenly gets up from his chair, and rushes out of his office ...

"I've got to be discreet ... go alone" adds MacCormac (Looks serious)

"I'll tag along in the background, Sir" advises Sheridan

"OK, but be discreet, Paddy" explains MacCormac

The Chief Superintendent walks out of Oxford Police Station and jumps into his waiting white Audi. He takes the road out of Oxford to Wolvercote.

MacCormac arrives at the Parish Church as arranged ...

Bell ringers are practising in the Bell Tower ...

The Chief Superintendent walks in to the Church grounds ... Paddy Sheridan is not far behind.

Suddenly, a voice gets MacCormac's attention ...

"That's far enough" advises the voice

"Well, I came, as instructed" replies MacCormac (Looks around)

"Yes, you did, Chief Superintendent ... but your not alone" adds the voice

"I'm quite alone" assures MacCormac

"You can call your man off now" advises the voice

"OK, Paddy" shouts MacCormac (Beckons forward)

Suddenly, a man out of the shadows steps forward ...

"Sir Montague Lynch" advises MacCormac (Looks stunned)

"I've got privileged information" replies Sir Montague (Looks serious)

Paddy Sheridan comes forward ...

"What kind of privileged information would that be, Sir?" asks MacCormac

"The type that would rock the government" explains Sir Montague

"Was Harry Masters working on something confidential?" asks MacCormac

"Something, highly confidential, I'd say" adds Sir Montague

"Why was he murdered?" asks MacCormac (Looks serious)

"Sorry, I don't know the answer to that, only that he and I were privy to some extremely confidential material" explains Sir Montague (Looks anxious)

"... and Harry paid for it with his life?" asks MacCormac (Looks serious)

"Yes, Chief Superintendent, exactly that" adds Sir Montague (Sounds cautious)

"Why all the cloak and dagger stuff, Sir Montague?" advises MacCormac

"Everyone is implicated, from the very top to the bottom" replies Sir Montague

"The very top?" asks Sheridan (Looks puzzled)

"The highest in the land" adds Sir Montague (Sounds serious)

"Do you mean ..." adds Sheridan

"Yes, Paddy ... he does" advises MacCormac (Sounds serious)

"So, what exactly was Harry working on, Sir Montague?" asks MacCormac

"It was a top secret weapon" replies Sir Montague (Sounds serious)

"What, here in Oxford?" adds MacCormac (Looks concerned)

"Yes, out of town ... at a secret location" explains Sir Montague

"What type of weapon?" asks MacCormac (Looks suspicious)

"High tech warfare, futuristic weapons" advises Sir Montague (Looks serious)

"Laser devices?" replies MacCormac (Looks stunned)

"Yes, but much more powerful" adds Sir Montague (Looks anxious)

"Have you heard of the Power Star System, Chief Superintendent?" asks Sir Montague

"No, what is it, Sir Montague?" asks MacCormac (Looks serious)

"For Pete's sake man, call me Monty" replies Sir Montague

"Well, Monty?" adds MacCormac (Nods)

"I think we should discuss this somewhere else, Chief Superintendent" replies Sir Montague (Looks concerned)

"It's not really appropriate, a church cemetery, is it?" adds Sir Montague

"What about the Jacobs Inn, just outside of Wolvercote?" advises Sir Montague

"Excellent choice … I'll follow you, Monty" adds MacCormac

Sir Montague, Paddy Sheridan, and Chief Superintendent, Daniel MacCormac leave the church yard, and make their way in separate cars to the Jacobs Inn car park.

Sir Montague steps out of his Daimler …

A speeding van takes the corner and

runs into him.

MacCormac and Paddy Sheridan run over to Sir Montague ...

"Is he dead, Sir?" asks Sheridan (Looks concerned)

"No, he's still breathing, Paddy" replies MacCormac (Looks serious)

"I'll phone for an emergency ambulance straight away" adds Sheridan

"Damn it, Paddy" replies MacCormac (Sounds dramatic)

"Someone's lying on the ground ... and all you can say is damn it?" questions Sheridan (Looks puzzled)

"Now, were looking at another possible murder, and a hit and run" explains MacCormac

"Not to mention, high tech weaponry" adds MacCormac (Sounds serious)

"A responder and emergency ambulance are on the way, Sir" advises Sheridan

"No wonder the government doesn't want to get involved" replies MacCormac

"What now, Sir?" asks Sheridan (Looks concerned)

"I'll phone the Chief Constable" adds MacCormac

"Don't worry, Paddy ... it'll be my neck on the chopping board, not yours" assures MacCormac

The Chief Superintendent takes out his mobile and phones the Chief Constable.

"Plod are on their way, Sir" advises Sheridan

The ambulance responder arrives at the scene of the accident, followed by an emergency ambulance, not

far behind ...
The Police cordon off
the area ...
"What next, Sir?" asks
Sheridan
"The Chief Constable agrees that we are on the right path, Paddy" replies MacCormac
"... but it may reflect as a state of illusion" adds MacCormac (Sounds serious)
"A state of illusion ... I don't understand, Sir?" replies Sheridan (Looks puzzled)
"What does the Chief Constable mean?" adds Sheridan
"I was just about to get to that" replies MacCormac

"An hallucination, a mirage, something that is believed to be true or real, but is actually false or unreal" explains MacCormac
"Now, you've really lost me, Sir" advises Sheridan (Looks puzzled)

"Don't you see ... Harry Masters, Monty ... they staged the whole thing" explains MacCormac (Sounds serious)
"Why?" asks Sheridan (Looks puzzled)

"They were working on something so important that it was wanted by almost everyone" adds MacCormac (Looks concerned)
"So, what did they do?"
asks MacCormac
"I don't know, Sir" replies
Sheridan

"Sell it to the highest bidder" advises MacCormac (Sounds serious)

"Yes ... as in a foreign power?" adds MacCormac

"Then, what?" asks Sheridan

"Something went wrong ... and both men had to be eliminated" explains MacCormac (Looks serious)

"But who?" adds Sheridan

"That, we may never find out, Paddy" replies MacCormac

"It's all hush hush, too" adds MacCormac (Sounds anxious)

"Why?" asks Sheridan

"The Chief Constable is on the warpath ... no doubt it's to do with government interference" replies MacCormac (Sighs)

The emergency ambulance rushes Sir Montague to hospital in Oxford ...

"What are his chances of survival?" asks MacCormac

"Fifty, fifty" replies the Responder (Sounds serious)

The emergency responder also leaves the scene of the suspected accident.

"Those people, Paddy" advises MacCormac (Looks concerned)

"What did he say, Sir" asks Sheridan

"They never commit themselves to anything" adds MacCormac

Paddy Sheridan and the Chief Superintendent head

back into Oxford and await details of Sir Montague from the Radcliffe.

INTELLECTUAL AND EMOTIONAL BALANCE

In the finale, MacCormac and Sheridan try to solve the puzzle concerning the cover up by the government with regards to Harry Masters and Sir Montague. Has Chief Superintendent Daniel MacCormac been warned off?

In the complex investigation, MacCormac and Sheridan look for fatal flaws, and several leads begin to emerge!

Oxford Police Station, Chief Superintendent Daniel MacCormac's office ...

Paddy Sheridan enters the office ...

"Well, what have you found out, Paddy?" asks MacCormac (Looks serious)

"I've spoken to Harry Mortimer's wife, Maxine" replies Sheridan

"Don't you mean, widow, Paddy?" replies MacCormac (Looks concerned)

"Yes, sorry, I mean widow" adds Sheridan (Stands corrected)

"Well, what did she tell you?" asks MacCormac

Paddy Sheridan begins to read from his black notebook ...

"She confirmed that he and Monty were working on a complex matter" advises Sheridan

"That, we already know ... anything else?" asks

MacCormac (Looks agitated)
"Yes, Sir ... something that may well rattle the powers of government" explains Sheridan (Looks serious)
"Go on, I'm all ears, Paddy" replies MacCormac

"Well, it seems that Oxford University was in on the act too, Sir" adds Sheridan

"In what way?" asks MacCormac (Sounds curious)
"Remember, when we first began the investigation, and that you were at the Sheldonian Theatre?" replies Sheridan
"How can I forget ... after being framed for murder" explains MacCormac
"Well, according to Maxine, several high ranking officials from London and New York were there too" advises Sheridan (Sounds serious)
"I can't believe they came all this way just to see an Opera" replies MacCormac (Looks stunned)
"Right again, Sir" adds Sheridan
"It would appear that a very hush hush meeting was also taking place" explains Sheridan (Looks serious)
"How?" asks MacCormac (Sounds puzzled)

"They were all connected by an ear piece" replies Sheridan

"An ear piece?" adds MacCormac (Looks serious)
"Yes, a very elaborate piece of technology" explains Sheridan
"Good work, Paddy" replies MacCormac

(Smiles)

"Now, I really think we're on to something" adds MacCormac

"Anything else, Paddy?" asks MacCormac

"Because they were political allies, the whole thing was put undercover" explains Sheridan (Looks concerned)

"Everyone's implicated" replies MacCormac (Sounds serious)

"But why kill Harry Masters ... and why did they try to frame me?" adds MacCormac (Looks bewildered)

"Apparently, Maxine says Henry Jessop was part of it" replies Sheridan

"The Dean of Oxford University ... surely not, Paddy?" asks MacCormac

"Evidence to the contrary, says it is, Sir" adds Sheridan (Looks serious)

"How do you know?" asks MacCormac (Sounds concerned)

"CCTV footage at the Sheldonian, and at Wolvercote, shows Harry Masters and Henry Jessop together" explains Sheridan

"Hardly enough for a conviction" replies MacCormac

"No, I agree ... but maybe this is" adds Sheridan

Paddy Sheridan produces a black notebook in code, and hands it to the Chief Superintendent ...

"What does it all mean?" asks Sheridan

"A type of code, Paddy" replies MacCormac (Looks anxious)

"Break the code, and we'll nail them" explains MacCormac

"What about the Chief Constable, Sir?" asks Sheridan

"Leave him to me, Paddy" replies MacCormac (Sounds serious)

"Anyway he did allow us to continue to investigate" adds MacCormac

"Come on, Paddy … let's see what we can decipher from this book" asks MacCormac (Both look serious)
After several hours of intense work, Paddy Sheridan and the Chief Superintendent seem to draw a blank …
"Have you got anything, Paddy?" asks MacCormac

"Not really, Sir … you?" replies Sheridan

"Something to do with a listing of classified locations" advises MacCormac

"Well, that could be it" adds Sheridan (Sounds sceptical)

"I've seen something relating to a description of procedures for the Emergency Alert System" explains Sheridan (Looks concerned)

"That's it, Paddy" advises MacCormac (Looks serious)

"Your right, put them together and what have we got?" adds MacCormac

"A highly explosive, volatile situation" explains MacCormac (Sounds anxious)

"I've also found this, Sir" replies Sheridan
"What is it?" asks MacCormac (Looks puzzled)
"Something rather complex" advises Sheridan

"In what way, Paddy?" adds MacCormac (Looks concerned)

"A card with codes" replies Sheridan (passes it to MacCormac)

"Authentication codes ... that's it" replies MacCormac (Sounds serious)

"Nuclear weapon devices?" asks Sheridan

"Yes ... topics in nuclear weapons law" advises MacCormac (Looks serious)

The Chief Superintendent shows Paddy Sheridan his findings ...

"By addressing in logical sequence the law regarding Sovereignty, the threat or use of force" explains MacCormac

"We've come across a highly secret formula" adds MacCormac (Sounds serious)

"There's also this, Sir" replies Sheridan
"Go on, Paddy" advises MacCormac

"Retaliatory options" explains Sheridan (Passes to MacCormac)

"No wonder, His Majesty's government didn't want us to pursue Harry Masters murder" explains MacCormac (Looks serious)

"They want to sweep it under the carpet" asks Sheridan

"To the government, we are just servants of the crown ... they would like to think they are above everyone" replies MacCormac

"... and everything" adds MacCormac (Sounds serious) "Well, we've got the evidence, Sir" replies Sheridan

"Yes, but no nearer finding the murderer" advises MacCormac

"We have one option, Paddy" adds MacCormac (Looks serious)

"Sir?" replies Sheridan

"Henry Jessop" replies MacCormac (Looks concerned)

"Come on, Paddy ... Oxford University, next stop" adds MacCormac

Paddy Sheridan and the Chief Superintendent rush out of Oxford Police Station and jump into the waiting white Audi in the car park. They make the short journey to Oxford University.

"What are we going to do, Sir?" asks Sheridan (Looks puzzled)

"Do we have sufficient evidence to charge him?" adds Sheridan

"No, not yet, Paddy ... but we do have him at the scene, and a motive" explains MacCormac (Sounds serious)

"A possible accessory to murder?" replies Sheridan (Looks serious)

"Maybe, or he too could have an emotional imbalance" advises MacCormac

Suddenly, a call from the Chief Constable to the Chief Superintendent, asking him to drop the investigation ...

"That's an order, Daniel ... and it comes straight from Number 10" advises the Chief Constable (Sounds serious)

"The Prime Minister?" asks MacCormac (Looks stunned)

"Yes, Daniel ... Harry Masters was highly intellectual and regarded by the Ministry as paramount to all their secrets" explains the Chief Constable

"Secrets?" replies MacCormac (Looks surprised)

"... concerning nuclear weapons?" adds MacCormac

"Yes ... you and Paddy Sheridan have been reassigned" advises the Chief Constable (Sounds serious)

"Where, Sir?" asks MacCormac

"Wolvercote" replies the Chief Constable (Looks concerned)

"Wolvercote, Sir?" adds MacCormac (Sounds baffled)

"But, I thought you wanted us to drop the case?" asks a baffled MacCormac

"Officially, I don't like this as much just as you do" replies the Chief Constable

"But protocol dictates otherwise" adds the Chief

Constable

"We have another lead, Sir" advises MacCormac (Sounds serious)

"It appears Harry Masters wife, Maxine, was having an affair with Henry Jessop" adds MacCormac

"Lovers?" asks the Chief Constable (Looks baffled)

"... and friends" replies MacCormac

"Or, that's what they want us to think" replies the Chief Constable

The Chief Superintendent and Paddy Sheridan obey the Chief Constable's orders. They take the road out of Oxford University towards Wolvercote and head into Harry Masters home.

MacCormac and Sheridan encounter Harry's widow, Maxine and Jessop ...

"Come in, Chief Superintendent" advises a voice

"Daniel" replies the voice

"Professor Henry Jessop" replies MacCormac (Looks official)

"I take it, you know, why we're here, Sir?" adds MacCormac

"Has the Chief Constable briefed you, Daniel?" asks Jessop

"Yes, naturally, Henry" replies MacCormac (Looks concerned)

"... but he knows me, only too well" adds MacCormac

"More evidence has come to light" explains MacCormac (Looks serious)

"Sir?" asks Sheridan

"Just what, were you working on, Henry?" asks MacCormac (Sounds cautious)

"It was something so explosive" advises Jessop (Looks agitated)

"Highly explosive" adds Jessop

"We know about you, Harry Masters, you too, Maxine … and the pact with the British government" explains MacCormac (Sounds complicated)

"Why the cover up?" asks MacCormac

"You don't understand, Daniel" replies Jessop (Sounds pompous)

"I'm arresting you, Mrs Mortimer, for the murder of your husband" explains MacCormac (Sounds official)

"Why?" asks Maxine (Looks stunned)

"You had the motive, and the inclination" advises MacCormac

Suddenly, Henry Jessop intervenes …

"Wrong" replies Jessop (Sounds coy)

"I'm the one you want" adds Jessop (Looks serious)

"Yes, I believe you are, Sir" replies MacCormac

"Sir?" asks Sheridan (Looks puzzled)

"It was the only way, Paddy ... to draw out the real murderer" explains MacCormac (Sounds serious)

"I knew it had to be you, Professor Jessop" advises MacCormac (Looks cautious)

"How did you know, Daniel?" asks Jessop (Looks bewildered)

"MacCormac's law, Sir?" asks Sheridan

"Your affair with Mrs Masters was a cover up" replies MacCormac

"A cover up?" asks a baffled Sheridan

"The Professor is a high ranking MI6 Director ... and a government Minister" explains MacCormac (All look surprised)

Professor Jessop claps ...

"Bravo, Daniel ... bravo" replies Jessop (Sounds smug)

"Very well put, but I am, as you know, protected" adds Jessop (Looks serious)

"Are you?" replies MacCormac

The Chief Superintendent motions to Paddy Sheridan ...

"OK, Paddy ... play back the tape" asks MacCormac (Looks serious)

Paddy Sheridan replays the recording on his mobile phone ... in which Professor Henry Jessop confesses to Harry Masters murder ...

"Technology today, isn't it wonderful?" adds MacCormac (Looks smug)

"Of course you do know that it won't stand up in a

Court of Law?" asks Jessop

"Oh, I'm afraid it will, Professor" replies MacCormac (Sounds serious)

"… and the scandal that goes with it" adds MacCormac (Looks serious)

Paddy Sheridan cuffs the Professor …

"Take him away, Paddy" instructs MacCormac

DCS MACCORMAC, OXFORD

SANCTUM SANCTORUM

COPYRIGHT @2024

GERRY CULLEN

THE VATICAN MONSIGNOR

THE SAVIOUR'S COMING

***** *5 STAR RATING ON AMAZON*

I thoroughly enjoyed The Vatican Monsignor by Gerry Cullen.

The character of Monsignor

Kevin O'Flaherty is unique and intriguing, and I found myself rooting for him throughout his investigations.

The mix of mystical phenomena and religious undertones added depth to the storyline and kept me engaged from beginning to end.

The collaboration between Monsignor O'Flaherty and Professor Brookstein added an interesting dynamic to the plot, and I was hooked on the suspense and mystery that unfolded as they worked together to solve unknown phenomena.

Gerry Cullen's writing style is captivating and kept me on the edge of my seat, making it difficult to put the book down.

Overall, I highly recommend The Vatican Monsignor to fans of mystery and intrigue, as it is a well-written and an engaging read.

LAURA (THE BOOKISH HERMIT)

***** 5 STAR RATING ON AMAZON

SKY HIGH:

COTE D'AZUR

"Sky High" by Gerry Cullen is an engaging thriller set against the breathtaking backdrop of the French Riviera. The story follows a Specialist Task Force composed of three 'ghost' operatives—Simon King, Steve McBride, and newcomer Bethany Williams—recruited to investigate the *mysterious disappearance of a British MI6 agent. With Countess Suzanna Minori at the helm, the group navigates both glamorous locales and complex crimes, blending action with a touch of intrigue.*

Gerry's vivid descriptions of iconic destinations like Monaco, Monte Carlo, Nice and Cannes amplify the narrative's allure.

Overall, it's a captivating read that combines espionage with the charm of the Mediterranean coast.

- 4 STAR RATING ON AMAZON

LAURA (THE BOOKISH HERMIT)

BOOKS BY THIS AUTHOR

BETWEEN WORLDS: MY TRUE COMA STORY

This true-life story includes an account of what happened to Gerry Cullen before and after waking up, having had major open-heart surgery at Leeds General Infirmary in March 2018, and the "gift" received from being in an induced coma.

Gerry explains his new found gift within the book. But

where it had come from and why he received it, remains a mystery to this day.

A spiritual awakening with messages received in dreams and other unworldly encounters, makes this story a fascinating read, leaving us wondering about life itself and beyond.

SKY HIGH! COTE D'AZUR

Nice, sun kissed jewel of the French Riviera. A popular tourist destination for the rich and famous.

When a British MI6 agent goes missing after being on attachment to the Commissariat de Police in Nice, a Specialist Task Force is set up on the Cote D'Azur to assist the Police in cracking crime on the Continent.

Three "Ghost Operatives" are drafted in by British Intelligence under an alias. Countess Suzanna Minori is placed in charge of unit in liaison with Mark Taylor in London.

In a series of assignments on the Cote D'Azur and in London suave Simon King, rough diamond Steve McBride and new recruit Bethany Williams are the "ghost" agents working under the code name: SKY HIGH!

Amazing picturesque locations on the French

Riviera taking in Monte Carlo, Monaco, Cannes and Nice add to the charm, character and atmosphere of the series of stories.

Stylish, chic, gripping with just the right amount of panache!

Action adventure guaranteed!

C'est la vie!

ANGEL'S EYES/CHRISTMAS ANGELS ANGEL'S EYES

The Angel private eyes, with a difference, undertake anything with a twist, they are all real angels!

Angel's: Rebecca, Mary,

John Paul and Nicola have been sent by Michael the Archangel to LEEDS, West Yorkshire, and the ancient city of YORK to investigate all types of problems, from all levels of society.

The Angel's are aiming to find, and guide, lost souls, to protect those in distress, and to help those without a cause.

They have been charged to give sight to those who cannot see, whatever the problem, and to heal the sick and incurable.

All the Angel's will have to undertake their assignments while also being human on Earth at the same time!

They do not want to

get their wings, they already have them!

While under the protection of Heaven, they will also be able to cloak themselves in disguise!

The Angel's are ready to assist anyone who needs their help in this stylish set of stories.

The Angel's will encounter the Grey Lady, the ghostly Centurion and a cohort of Roman soldiers, Dick Turpin and Guy Fawkes along the way.

The Angel's will also experience Speed Dating and various other problems in a very modern day World!

CHRISTMAS ANGELS -

This seasonal set of stories reunites Rebecca, Mary, John Paul and Nicola.

The Angel's have been reassigned by Michael the Archangel and assume the roles of Proprietors of the famous CHRISTMAS ANGELS shop in YORK, on a short term lease, with a view to being permanent!

However, they are shop keepers with a difference!

The Angel's become engaged in various angelic and human situations, all with a magical Christmas feeling!

The stories take place at various settings in YORK.

Will the Angel's be found out,

or will their true identities remain an angelic secret?

IT'S A KIND OF LOVE

It's back to 1987 for this Singled Out themed comedy/drama series of stories set in Leeds.

This book is based on an original, and true story, up to the end of 1991.

What happens after that continues into 1992 with the ITV Telethon.

Everything is based on real people, real parties and real events.

The locations and venues of IT'S A KIND OF LOVE tell one man's story, and the challenges he faces, after joining a national Singles Organisation!

We commence in Leeds city centre, where various characters are introduced at Zodiac, and then again at Mirage.

Zodiac and Mirage are Social/Single Organisations which have been set up UK wide. Both are run privately, by the members.

This is a time when there were no mobile phones, laptops or the Internet! When we spoke of a tablet it was usually to take away pain, and not an electrical device connected to the Internet!

Everyone used ordinary house telephones, and call boxes to get in touch, with each other.

We used A to Z map books to find addresses and locations.

Satellite for cars had not yet been invented!

Pop music and fashions were top of the list.

Gez moves in to an apartment on the outskirts of Leeds, and decides to join Zodiac.

IT'S A KIND OF LOVE tells his real story!

From joining to attending parties, and events ... to meeting lots of ladies ... getting sound advice ... to running his own event disco's on a grand scale!

This all eventually leads to events for ITV TELETHON 1990 and 1992, and a main arena event in the grounds of HAREWOOD HOUSE on the outskirts of Leeds.

But Gez is hiding something ...

Who is he, and where did he come from?

Why is he hiding a secret?

New adventures lie before him, but will he find love or won't he?

Why does he have so many female admirers at Zodiac?

Will all eventually be revealed?

MY NEXT PRESENTATION

EVERLASTING LOVE

DANCE HALL DAYS

DISCOTHEQUE NIGHTS

They say if you can remember the Sixties, you weren't there!

Well, I can categorically say that I do remember the Sixties and the Seventies, and I was there!

That is what this book is all about ... do you remember?

We were all young, innocent, and inexperienced back then!

All you needed was a place to go, sensational music,

way out

fashions, fabulous memorable days ... and luck to just maybe fall for a girl and vice versa ... we were all young teenagers in those days.

This book is a journey down memory lane, back to a time when everything was different in so many ways.

I hope you enjoy all the stories featured in this nostalgic comedy/drama back to a time when we were all growing up together in the Swinging Sixties and the sensational Seventies!

PUBLICATION DATE - NOVEMBER 2024

DCS MACCORMAC SANCTUM SANCTORUM

*CODED MESSAGES ...
DIVIDED LOYALTIES*

SANCTUM SANCTORUM

DEADLY NIGHTSHADE

*THE PLETHRON
CONNECTION*

SUBTERFUGE

PARASYMPATHETIC REBOUND

EQUILIBRIUM

COPYRIGHT -

GERRY CULLEN 2024

BETWEEN WORLDS:

MY TRUE COMA STORY

Gerry Cullen

GERRY CULLEN has written a unique and mesmerising book.

Gerry's true-life story includes an account of when he woke up after having major open-heart surgery in a Leeds hospital in March 2018. He received an unexpected gift from his induced coma.

Where had this gift of writing come from?
Why had he received it?

On reflection, Gerry now feels that he is incredibly lucky to have received this Heaven-Sent gift.
This life changing event and its aftermath have become a blessing in his life.

Gerry began to write profusely since that time; an astonishing development, as he had never authored any books or scripts before the coma.

Four years prior to his heart surgery, Gerry experienced a spiritual awakening, and regular messages were coming to him in his dreams.
They were a major source of comfort to him.

Gerry believes that people in comas are living 'between worlds' and that their friends and family members are also living between worlds with them.

The messages from above have continued ever since and today his writing is flourishing. He has a fascinating tale to tell; it is a story of our times with many lessons for those with eyes to see and ears to hear!

The plot is a true-life account based around a fascinating subject of otherworldly connections.

Gerry's life story is full of encounters with another realm, the spiritual one.
The pacing is good throughout.
The book is well thought out as each chapter flows logically.

Author's Voice - The author's voice broadly means the written style of the book, covering tone, syntax, and grammar, amongst other things. It can be thought of as how the book is written.

Gerry is a good writer; I liked his style and voice. I was interested as the book progressed to discover more and it intrigued me.

This book could be a powerful memoir of Gerry's life and times, and the Heaven-Sent gift of writing that he received after open heart surgery.
I liked reading about his visions and encounters with the spirit world and the supernatural realm of life; it's quite fascinating.
I liked the examination of current events and times at the end of the book. too.

All in all, a great read for any person interested in life beyond our earth plane.

Many books have been adapted to film from this genre, for example, 90 Minutes in Heaven, an extremely popular movie, with over 1,800 reviews on Amazon Prime.

 I feel that Gerry's book would make a great movie too.

It's a heart-warming and touching story of a man's journey and how he goes through a life changing operation that leaves him with a wonderful gift.

I loved the insights beyond our normal senses' range into another realm that will guide us if only we would allow it to do so.
In these times that we find ourselves in, I feel Gerry's testimony in the book, and his many anecdotes

and stories, will demonstrate that there are more dimensions to behold than what we know in a three-dimensional world.

Report provided by Janet Lee Chapman, in September 2021, on behalf of Susan Mears Film and Literary Agency and Merlin Agency

ABOUT THE AUTHOR

Gerry Cullen

My first book, BETWEEN WORLDS: MY TRUE COMA STORY, is a true adaptation of what happened to me, before and after, having major open heart surgery at Leeds General Infirmary in March 2018.

It is a very real and true account of the "gift" I received after being in an induced coma.

All of my books, SKY HIGH! COTE D'AZUR, ANGEL'S EYES/CHRISTMAS ANGELS, THE VATICAN MONSIGNOR, IT'S A KIND OF LOVE are adapted from my series of stories, written for television.

I had never written books or for television prior to being in a coma.

My very real and true story continues today!

FOLLOW   MY   STORY   ON   TWITTER   -

@GerryCullen15

PRAISE FOR AUTHOR

Praise For Author Reviewed in the United Kingdom on 16 May 2022
An excellent book showing that there is far more to life then we realise and that there is a continuation of our soul after the death of our body.

Reviewed in the United Kingdom on 21 April 2022
Verified Purchase
With truly moving frankness the author narrates a life-threatening experience and how it brought him closer to his spiritual life.

Reviewed in the United Kingdom on 20 May 2022
A great read and one that really makes you think

Reviewed in the United Kingdom on 12 August 2022
This book was of particular interest to me because of my line of work. I love hearing about people's experiences with things that are on a different vibration to us earthly beings. The spiritual awakenings that people go through have been documented and discussed since the

beginning of time and each person's story is unique in its own way, there are always some similarities on the surface but I encourage you to look a little deeper - you can start with this book.......

The author begins by telling us a little about himself and his life growing up. He then goes into detail about the 'messages' he has received in dreams, these are set out in a sort of diary entry format. He also speaks of visions.

All of the incidents described seem quite insignificant on their own, but when you put them all together they give a much bigger and clearer picture.

There is a lot I could say about this book but seriously, we would be here all day! It's a great read that is sure to inspire and provoke discussion. It really doesn't matter what walk of life you are from, whether you are religious or a non believer. I feel the story should be taken for what it is and that is one gentleman's extraordinary, unique and beautiful experiences which he has chosen to share with the world.

The book, its content and the author himself are a true gift to the world.

5 stars

☐☐☐☐☐ - BETWEEN WORLDS: MY TRUE COMA STORY A 3 star rating on Amazon to date with no comments -

SKY HIGH: COTE D'AZUR Reviewed in the United Kingdom on 13 December 2023
"Angels Eyes" by Gerry Cullen is a heartwarming and enchanting collection of seasonal stories that follows the adventures of Rebecca, Mary, John Paul, and Nicola, who have been reassigned by Michael the Archangel to become proprietors of the CHRISTMAS ANGELS shop in York. As they assume their roles as shopkeepers with a difference, the Angels become involved in a series of angelic and human situations that are filled with the magic of Christmas.

Set in various locations in York, the stories are imbued with a magical Christmas feeling that is sure to warm the hearts of readers. The characters' true identities as Angels are kept secret throughout the stories, adding an element of mystery and intrigue.

"Angels Eyes" is a delightful and uplifting read that captures the spirit of Christmas and the joy of the holiday season. Gerry Cullen's writing is engaging and filled with charm, making this book a perfect choice for anyone looking for a heartwarming holiday read. - ANGEL'S EYES: CHRISTMAS ANGELS No comments have yet been left for this book. - THE VATICAN MONSIGNOR - THE SAVIOUR'S COMING

Printed in Great Britain
by Amazon